ONE

"When the paramedics arrived, at around three am, they found Susan Hunter unconscious at the bottom of the stairs, with injuries that were later shown as consistent with being pushed *down* those stairs..." DI Steven Karim paused here, adding a little dramatic effect to his presentation.

"In addition, we have a statement from her neighbours who heard raised voices inside the Hunters' flat the evening before, indicative of an argument. They believe the male voice was that of Paul Hunter, Susan Hunter's husband. And then there's the fact that Paul Hunter bought a life insurance policy against his wife just a few months before the incident." Karim paused again, this time glancing around the room to ensure everyone was following where he was leading. He'd begun a little hesitantly, as if not entirely comfortable summarising his case in front of the assembled senior investigators and the superintendent, but now he'd grown more assured. He even seemed to be enjoying himself.

"As a result we're looking to send the case to the CPS, hopefully this week, and asking them for an attempted murder charge against Paul Hunter. I believe that not only was he the cause of his wife's fall, but that it was a deliberate, premeditated act." He stopped again, but this time to scratch his nose. DCI Erica Sands glanced up, not expecting this hesitation, then she returned her attention to her notepad, where she was sketching out a doodle. She hadn't heard of the unfortunate Susan Hunter, nor her possibly murderous husband, before Karim had started speaking, but already she'd assessed the case from the notes he'd provided.

"And what's he saying happened? Paul Hunter I mean?" Superintendent Yorke was wearing his steel-rimmed glasses, which he needed these days for close work. He peered over the top at Karim. "What does he say the argument was about?"

Karim shook his head. "He says there was no argument, sir. They were..." – he frowned, then continued as if quoting the accused – "*watching a series on Netflix.*" Karim shrugged lightly, illustrating the weakness of the excuse.

"Hmm," Yorke nodded, and made a note.

"And the fall? Does he have an explanation there?"

"He claims his wife was a sleep-walker, sir. He says they'd gone to bed as usual, after the series, but that he was woken by the noise of her falling down the stairs. He says she often left the bed in the night, sometimes even going downstairs and making herself sandwiches, and that never remembering doing so the next day." Karim shrugged helplessly, again acknowledging the poor explanation, and perhaps sorry he didn't have anything stronger to report. But Yorke ignored it.

"If she often did it," he pressed, 'why did she fall on this occasion?"

"Ah!' Karim brightened. "Actually he does have an answer for that. They'd had a stairgate installed. The type you put in when you have a toddler, with a metal bar that runs along the ground. He claims she must have tripped on it."

THE HUNT

GREGG DUNNETT

Storm
PUBLISHING

Ebook ISBN: 978-1-80508-555-3
Paperback ISBN: 978-1-80508-557-7

Cover design: Tash Webber
Cover images: Alamy

Published by Storm Publishing.
For further information, visit:
www.stormpublishing.co

ALSO BY GREGG DUNNETT

PART ONE

Yorke's brow furrowed and he glanced quickly through the papers. "They'd had a child?"

"No, sir. But they'd recently bought a puppy."

Sands' head flashed up again, this time there was a questioning look on her face. Yorke saw it and shifted his attention from Karim. "What are you thinking Erica? Is there anything you can add?"

Her eyes weren't focussed on Yorke, but behind him, on a window and the view beyond it. She stayed like that a while, before lightly shaking her head.

"No. Nothing." She went back to her doodle, shading something with a crosshatch pattern.

Yorke frowned again slightly, then took off his glasses to see her better.

"Do you agree with DI Karim's assessment? That we should pursue a case against Paul Hunter?"

On the desk in front of Sands was the dossier of papers provided by Karim, one copy for each of them. There were photographs of the injuries sustained by Susan Hunter, of the stairway where she was found. There were copies of the insurance certificate, showing that Paul Hunter would receive over two hundred thousand pounds in the event of his wife's death. And there were witness statements from the neighbours. Her eyes scanned it quickly, not looking at what was there, but what was missing.

"*Is* a sleep-walker, sir."

There was a confused silence in the room.

"Excuse me?" Yorke's frown deepened again.

"DI Karim noted that Susan Hunter *was* a sleep-walker; she's not dead, therefore we should say she *is* a sleep-walker."

"She might not be dead, but she is in a coma." Karim sounded combative suddenly.

"Which is not the same as dead."

"She could very well end up dead."

"We all end up dead. But in Susan Hunter's case, there's a good chance she'll wake up first. And then she can tell us if her husband pushed her down the stairs. Or if he didn't."

Sands gave what looked very much like a sarcastic smile – except she was generally too professional to do so. Then she went back to drawing her doodle. It was clearer now what it was, a sketch of a desert island with a coconut tree, and a man sat on the beach staring out to sea as if waiting for rescue. She turned the pad to see the perspective of the sketch better, doing nothing to hide it from the other officers in the room. Yorke took a deep breath before replying. It was obvious it took an effort to keep his voice civil.

"Erica, given that we're generally unable to progress a case by asking the victim what happened, would you be willing to give us your assessment of the *evidence* presented in this case? Do you agree with DI Karim that we have a strong-enough case to recommend charges with the CPS?"

Somewhat reluctantly Sands stopped the drawing – she was adding coconuts to the tree – and looked at her boss. But it was hard. The problem was she couldn't quite bring herself to care.

"How am I supposed to answer that, sir, when he hasn't even got the basics right?"

There were several seconds of silence.

"I'm sorry, what exactly does that mean?" Karim obviously decided he should be the one to break it, but Yorke cut in angrily over the top of him.

"DCI Sands, the purpose of these meetings is to share the experience of senior investigators with those who are more junior but are nonetheless pursuing live cases. You have in front of you a detailed summary of the evidence collected by Karim and his team. If you have an issue with that evidence, now is the time to share it." Yorke's tone was strict, angry, but still in control. Sands responded by sighing audibly. But then she turned to another page in the notepad and tore it out.

"I made a list." She held it out across the table to Karim.

"A list?" Karim said, staring at it. "What of?"

"Of what," Sands corrected him quietly, waggling the paper encouragingly so that Karim took it. Then she immediately went on. "Questions you haven't answered yet. Or at all." Having torn out the page, her drawing was in front of her again. She looked at it a little wistfully, but refrained from picking up her pen again.

There was another pause before Yorke spoke again, his voice now unnaturally calm. "OK, so what's on the list?"

For an awkward moment it seemed that Karim was being asked to read it out loud, which he clearly didn't want to do, but then Sands began to do it herself, despite no longer being able to see it.

"Number one. Somnambulism – that's the medical term for sleep-walking – is rare but it affects around three to four per cent of adults, so not *that* rare. However, we appear to only have Paul Hunter's word that his wife has it, so where's the corroborating evidence? There's no medical history for Susan Hunter. Nothing from previous partners. Almost all adults who sleep-walk did so much more frequently when they were children, so what do the parents say? I think it would be helpful to know.

"Two." Sands looked up now. "The life insurance policy could be suspicious, but it's not unheard of for people to take them out without intending to murder the beneficiaries. We'd have a clearer view if we knew the Hunters' financial situation. Are they in debt? Is he a gambler? Or are they doing OK? It seems like a relevant point.

Three," she went on without pausing, 'if Paul Hunter did push his wife down the stairs and has been lying about it ever since, it suggests an elevated capacity for violent and devious behaviour. If so I'd expect to see a similar pattern of behaviour in his background. Does it exist?" She shrugged to illustrate its absence. "At the very least I'd expect to see a psychological assessment of Mr Hunter to help us establish if attempted murder is a plausible scenario." Sands quickly separated the papers in front of her, as if searching through them. "Perhaps Detective Inspector Karim forgot to bring it along, but I can't see it here."

Sands stopped, her eyes on Karim. "Four. What were they watching? On Netflix? Did you even ask?"

Karim stared back at her, his nostrils flaring as he drew in deep, angry breaths. "As it happens, ma'am, I did. He claims it was a series about Pablo Escobar. It's called *Narcos*."

He stared back, clearly sending her the message that he'd won this point, at least. But she simply touched her upper lip with her tongue as she gave a tiny smile.

"Excellent. Which episode? Does it feature raised voices that could be mistaken for an argument? Have you confirmed on the Netflix account that the episode was in fact played? Does the timestamp correlate with when the neighbours say they heard raised voices? Oh, and did you ask whether they were often able to hear next door's TV? Have you tested sound transmission between the two houses?"

Karim didn't answer, but Yorke did.

"I think we should all keep in mind that everyone is doing the best they can under very severe restrictions on manpower and resources, and that we're all working together—"

"Oh, I don't doubt we're short of decent officers." Sands might have put enough stress on the word 'decent' to send a message, but it was subtle. She turned to Karim. "But I thought we could normally count on people watching enough Netflix." She shook her head, then turned away. Probably that was going a bit too far, but she wasn't ready to admit it to herself.

"OK. I think that's enough." Yorke was speaking, but it was somewhere far away from where Erica's mind was now. "Detective Karim, it's clear there's a little more work required before you submit the case, and you have a..." – he paused – "a list to go on, but let's take a break here." He looked around the room. "Next meeting is the first Monday of next month. Same time and place." He gave a tight smile. "And Erica, before you go back to work, could I have a word?"

TWO

"Are you OK?" Yorke asked her, after the other officers had filed out. On the superintendent's instructions the last of them had closed the door as they left. Sands didn't respond.

"Because I'm not the only one who's noticed how you've been unusually stressed recently," Yorke went on.

She turned slowly to face him, noting the lines on his face, that his hair had almost none of its original colour left. One day he would retire – perhaps relatively soon – and whoever replaced him would be unlikely to share his indulgent view of her. How old was he? Sixty? Sixty-five?

"Erica?"

She shook the thoughts from her head.

"All I did was point out the flaws in the case. Isn't that why I'm here? I hardly see how it makes me stressed..." She fixed him a look, then decided she had more to say.

"If I stay quiet there's a real chance Karim sends an innocent man to prison, a man who's already suffered the terrible misfortune of his wife nearly dying in a tragic accident. Is that what we want? And then there's the cost of the trial, finding a space for Paul Hunter while he's on remand—"

"No one's asking you to stay quiet, Erica," Yorke interrupted. "The whole point of these meetings is to make use of the experience of our more senior investigators, in order to catch mistakes before they go too far. But there's a way to do it."

Sands didn't reply.

"And you're not doing it the right way."

"Maybe I'm not cut out for the mentor role?"

There was a silence, and the sharp look on Yorke's face dissolved. He reached out for her notepad, hesitating as he did so, as if asking for permission. She half-shrugged and let him pull it towards him. He examined the doodle she'd drawn. Her latest addition was several shark fins, circling the tiny island.

"This may be a rather simplistic interpretation, but are you perhaps thinking of taking a holiday somewhere hot?" He offered her a smile, but Sands didn't respond. The smile faded.

"How's it looking?" he asked. "The case against Sterling?" The question changed the atmosphere in the meeting room. Charles Sterling was one of the most high-profile mass murderers ever caught in the UK; he had escaped from prison the year before, killing again within twenty-four hours. More pertinently, he was also Sands' father.

"The case against him is rock solid," Sands replied after a while. "The problem is, no one has any idea where he is."

Yorke nodded, picking his way carefully into the conversation.

"It's ironic in a way," he said. "I used to give you updates on Sterling and the bullshit he was pulling in prison." He smiled. "Now you're the one giving me updates."

"There's depressingly little to update on, sir," Sands replied, thin-lipped, but when Yorke simply waited for her to go on, she did so, sighing again.

"Interpol has the case. It's being handled by an officer named Jonathan Briggs – do you know him?"

Yorke waved a hand to show he didn't.

"He's... it's not that he's a poor officer. He was assigned by the Interpol General Secretariat as part of a specialised task force on international fugitives."

"And what's he doing?"

Sands looked like she was considering her response. "I think *fuck all* sums it up best," she said in the end, her voice dripping with bitterness. Yorke's eyebrows rose a little and Sands waved a hand in apology.

"I'm sorry sir, it's just frustrating. It took Briggs almost a month to issue a Red Notice, and even then—"

"Hold on..." – Yorke held up a hand – "I've had a few suspects run off to the Costa del Crime, but my career hasn't included that many international fugitives. Can you explain what a Red Notice is?"

Sands nodded. "It's a request to law enforcement worldwide to locate and arrest a person of interest. It's something Interpol issues if they're satisfied there's a valid national arrest warrant – which we have. But the problem is it's just a request, it doesn't *compel* anyone to do anything, so there's no active investigation into where he is."

"So it's literally just a list?"

"Right. If he happens to get arrested and his fingerprints or DNA are checked, he'd show up as having an open arrest warrant, and then the arresting country *might* agree to begin extradition proceedings. But he's far too smart to get his prints checked, and there's a good chance he's holed up somewhere that doesn't have an extradition treaty, in which case the red list gets ignored anyway."

"And what could an investigation do, if there were one?"

Sands took a breath to reset. "We know that Sterling was being assisted while he was in prison by a guard named Barney Atkinson. He helped plan and execute Sterling's escape, in return for a generous share of the money Sterling had acquired from his early involvement in cryptocurrencies..."

"And when you say generous, you're rather understating it, as I recall?"

"We identified a transfer of Bitcoin that was valued at nine million dollars at the time of Sterling's escape. The market's since retracted quite significantly, but it's still worth around five million."

"Five million? That was Atkinson's cut? I understand Sterling himself kept a lot more?"

Again Sands paused.

"Yes sir. He had access to almost nine *hundred million*. However, the cryptocurrency disappeared shortly after Sterling did. We don't know if he moved it, or he was lucky enough to convert it into cash before the market crashed..."

"Perhaps he was lucky; perhaps that's just another example of his astuteness." Yorke shook his head, partly in wonder. "Nine hundred million dollars. I wonder if that's actually larger than Interpol's operating budget?" A wan smile appeared on his lips at the idea of this.

"Annually it's over six times larger, sir. Interpol has a budget of 142.7 million."

The smile faded. "Well, is there any way he can be tracked by this money? There must be some sort of digital footprint?"

Sands shook her head. "It's cryptocurrency. It's built upon the concept of it being anonymous and it's both theoretically and practically impossible to break that anonymity. It would all fall apart if that wasn't the case."

"Well maybe that wouldn't be such a bad thing," Yorke mused. "The way it's being used by criminals."

"Unfortunately the global financial system would collapse along with it. And that would bring down every national government and likely spark a mass human-extinction event."

"Hmmm." Yorke had to glance to see if she was exaggerating for effect here, but her face betrayed no emotion.

"Still, his great wealth could be one way to locate him. I

assume this Briggs character is monitoring any large investments that might indicate his location?"

"He says he is."

"But you don't believe him?"

"Let's just say I'm visiting him regularly to keep him
honest."

Yorke smiled again and thought for a moment.

"And you're quite sure there's no evidence that he's actually
still here? I'm sure you haven't forgotten what happened to John
Lindham?" It didn't need to be said; they were both aware that
Sterling had played a significant role in the death of Erica's
former deputy, Detective Inspector John Lindham, along with
his wife and two children.

She shook her head. "There's been nothing. I think Lindham's death meant so little to him, he's moved on." Her voice
was quiet, and Yorke was silent a moment out of respect.

"Well, stay vigilant. Keep me informed if anything
changes." Yorke gathered together his notes from earlier,
preparing to leave.

"Oh, and go easy on DI Karim. He's doing his best."

THREE

Sands drummed her fingers on the leather steering wheel of the Alfa. She put the heavy car into first gear, moved a few metres further up the M3 motorway before lifting off the accelerator and coasting to a halt again behind the rear bumper of the Mercedes in front of her. She had weighed up whether to take the train or drive into London, with all the hassles of the traffic and the Low Emissions Zone. It had been a fairly easy decision to take the car. With Sterling out of prison and his whereabouts unknown, the truth was she felt a little unsettled in public places. It was ridiculous – if he wanted to hurt her he would have already done so, and being locked in her car would certainly not protect her. But even so, she felt better watching the world from within its comforting interior. She stared at the back of the head of the Mercedes driver, suddenly aware she had memorised the car's number plate for no good reason. She glanced at the clock on the dash, calculating. Maybe she was lying to herself. Maybe she just didn't like trains, and being exposed to other people.

Whatever was causing the hold-up ahead seemed to ease and as the cars around her began to move forward, the relief and hope was somehow palpable in the atmosphere on the motor-way. The speed breached sixty miles per hour, and she flashed her lights to tell the Mercedes driver to get out of her way.

She arrived, half an hour later than she'd planned, outside the strangely anonymous glass-and-steel building of the Interpol UK Bureau, set just back from the river. Had it been located anywhere else it might have stood out, with its mirrored glass windows and odd steel fairings running up the side, but here these details seemed designed to make it blend in. Don't look at me, it said, look at the big city skyscrapers instead. She waited until the revolving door offered an entrance, and then had to wait again to exit the other side, into a spacious lobby with the agency's logo set into the marble floor. She had to pass through an airport-style security check manned by an unsmiling man in blue uniform before she arrived at the discreet reception desk, where a young woman was at least smiling politely. Her name was printed on a badge on her blouse: Suzanne Johnson.

"I'm here to see Agent Jonathan Briggs."

"Certainly. Is he expecting you?"

"Yeah, he said I should go right up. I know the way."

The woman started to protest, but Sands waved her away and was already walking to the lifts. where she pressed the button. She turned to see the receptionist already on the phone. The security guard was looking interested too, but the lift came and Sands stepped inside, selecting the seventh floor.

"Detective Sands!' Agent Briggs was on the phone at his desk, which was near to, but not quite in front of the window in a wide, open-plan working space that hummed quietly as fingers tapped on keyboards and low voices spoke on telephones.

"Thank you, Suzie, she's with me now." He put down the receiver, stood and held out his hand. He was in his early thir-ties, with dark hair brushed back into a ponytail, revealing an open, symmetrical face. He wore a well-cut suit, and an amused smile on his face.

"Don't tell me, you were just passing?"

"No. I have very few reasons to come into London. I'm here specifically to see how the case is going. I'm not satisfied with the progress you're making, and I'm not convinced it's getting the attention it merits." Briggs' hand was still there, so Sands shook it.

Briggs threw a glance around at his colleagues, but his smile barely faltered.

"I'll grab us a meeting room."

"If you like."

She waited while he worked on his computer, apparently securing them a meeting space.

"I do have a telephone, you know," he said as he worked, and as if feeling the need to prove this was true, pointed at an iPhone on his desk. "You could telephone me. For an update, I mean."

Sands frowned in response, but instead of looking at his phones, her eye settled on a green folder open on his desk. It was a little hard to read upside-down, but she was just about managing, until he spotted her looking.

"That's nothing to do with your..." Abruptly he closed the file and set it to one side. "Just a couple of armed robbers; we think they're in the Czech Republic." He clicked his tongue. "None of the meeting rooms are available at short notice... Tell you what, how about we go out into the real world? I'll shout you a coffee?"

Sands looked around, as if asking what was wrong with sitting where they were, and she caught the eye of some of the other agents stationed near Briggs' desk. She shrugged again as he picked up an iPad and slipped it into a protective neoprene case. He stood, looking happy to do so, then led the way back towards the lifts.

"Actually, you won't believe me," he said as they descended, 'but I was actually going to contact you. I have news."

"What news?"

He didn't reply as the lift slowed and he led the way across the lobby and into a Starbucks opposite. He asked what she wanted and Sands waited at a table while he ordered. Just as in the car, she felt slightly uncomfortable being out in the open. Surrounded by people. She put it down to paranoia.

"What's the news? You haven't located Sterling or you'd have already told me," Sands said, as Briggs slipped into the booth opposite her. She kept her voice low, even though no one was near enough to hear. Just a few suits elsewhere in the café, sitting in pairs or staring at laptops.

"No, there's still been no response to the red listing, but as I told you before, these things can take a long time. Even if we had the capacity to actively investigate Sterling's whereabouts, we have almost nothing to go on. Before his escape he was in prison for over twenty years, which makes it unlikely he'll still be contact with the people he knew before his arrest. Although he was a prolific letter writer – thank you for arranging to have copies of all his mail sent to me by the way, I've had it put on file, or quite a few files, actually – we also know he was sending other correspondence through the prison officer who helped him escape. So if he was arranging how he'd leave the country and where he'd go afterwards, we likely don't have access to that information." He opened his hands into a gesture of helplessness, but there was something about the smile that stayed on his face that made Sands let him continue speaking. After all, she'd spent two hours sat on the motorway to get here.

"Obviously, should he make the mistake of applying for a bank account using the name Charles Sterling, or crossing an international border, we'll know all about it, but from what we know about him he's not going to be that stupid." Briggs sat back.

"So what's the news?"

Briggs paused, still leaning back in his chair, before he moved closer again, picking up the iPad and unlocking it with his thumbprint.

"I don't know if this is going to be any use to you but..." His finger swiped a few times on the screen before he turned it round to face Erica

"Recognise this dude?"

On the screen was a poor-quality still from a CCTV camera, monitoring what looked like an office in an air-conditioned showroom. Two men were visible; Sands couldn't see the face of who was presumably the salesman, but the customer was a large man in a short-sleeved Hawaiian shirt and shorts. It took her a few seconds to connect him in her brain.

"Barney Atkinson."

"According to our facial recognition system, yes, though I didn't see it myself. I figured you weren't going to stop hassling me, so I had the idea to monitor high-value transactions in cities near to where we lost track of him. We know he flew to São Paulo after Sterling's escape, and then we suspect he took an internal flight north to Natal. Beyond that he disappears. Until..." He held out his hand for the iPad, and fell silent when Sands handed it back to him.

"Where is this?"

He didn't answer her directly. "Like I said, I focussed on Natal, and a few cities that are less than a five-hour bus ride away – coastal cities: it's hot out there, and your man has five million in the bank, more than enough to get some real estate within reach of the sea breezes. So I pulled a *lot* of favours with my counterparts in the Brazilian bureau, and had them pulling images from every high-value purchase we could think of – sports cars, property, yachts – and then ran it through our facial recognition system. We must have missed the property purchase, but not this."

"Where is it?" Sands asked again. "It looks like a car showroom."

"It's in a Brazilian city called Fortaleza, and assuming you and the system aren't wrong, that's Barney Atkinson purchasing a state-of-the-art security system."

FOUR

"So you have an address?"

Briggs opened the maps app on the iPad, where he'd previously dropped a pin. It was set to view satellite images, and when he handed it back, Sands found herself looking at a house from above. All she could see was the orange-brown of the tiled roof, the dark green of shrubs in the garden, and a large extent of brighter green, with a kidney-shaped swimming pool cut into it and glowing turquoise-blue. She zoomed out a little, revealing more garden, grounds really, with a large driveway – empty. If there was a car it would presumably be in the garage. There were neighbours, with equally large houses, and when she zoomed out a little more there was a strip of faded yellow beach, and then the azure blue of the southern Atlantic Ocean.

"Can you get him? These contacts you have, can they arrest him? How do we get him back here?"

Briggs pulled a face, and Sands went on at once.

"Come on, the guy assisted in the escape of a multiple murderer. They have to arrest him?"

"It's tricky. Had he done what he did in Brazil, they'd be all over him, and pretty heavy-handed too. But Brazil's legal system works in a very particular way."

"What way?"

"Well, in a way that doesn't actually work, if you really want to know. Before the local law enforcement would even pick up the phone we'd need to get their Supreme Federal Court to issue an arrest warrant, which won't be valid until it's personally approved by the President himself. Now I don't know how much you follow Brazilian politics, but the current President is a prize asshole, and even if he wasn't, the simple reality is that no president ever has the time, except for the most high-profile cases. The court knows this, so they don't issue the warrants, which all means..." – he shot her a smile – "we can't touch him. There's a reason that criminals like to run off to Brazil." He smiled ironically. "*A burocracia é um pesadelo.*"

"What?"

"*Um pesadelo,*" Briggs repeated. "It's Portuguese. It means the bureaucracy there is a nightmare."

"You speak Portuguese?"

"Yeah, that's one of mine. Everyone over there speaks at least two languages." He jerked a thumb towards the Interpol building opposite. "Other than English, I mean."

She stared at him, storing away this piece of information. Then she sighed.

"There must be something we can do?"

"There is. There's a lot we can do. Now we've identified where Atkinson is, we also know the name he's living under – Sean Jones – and we can watch him. We can monitor him online, and should Sterling make contact with him, it'll give us an excellent chance to locate him too. Hey, it's even possible they're living close to each other, him and Sterling. He's pretty much the only guy that Sterling knows."

"No." Sands shook her head.

Briggs opened his hands. "Yeah, probably not. But you

never know. And let's say we do locate Sterling there. With the crimes he's committed, we actually would stand a chance at getting an arrest warrant issued."

"No," Sands repeated. "Sterling won't be anywhere near Atkinson." She fell quiet, thinking, while Briggs went on.

"But they did work closely together," he insisted. "Preparing for the escape? So it's likely that Atkinson played a part in helping Sterling get a new identity, assuming he has one. And we still don't know how Sterling got out of the UK, again assuming that he did, but the most likely explanation is that Atkinson helped. So, he might have some idea where Sterling is now, or what name he's using—"

Sands cut him off, not letting him finish the thought.

"What are the legal implications for me to go out there and question him?"

Briggs hesitated. He pulled a face. "Difficult. Very difficult. As a UK detective, you obviously wouldn't have jurisdiction, so any kind of investigation would have to be coordinated with the Brazilian authorities. Interpol could assist with that, but..." – he seemed to run through several options in his head – "it's more of a diplomatic issue. Brazil gets sensitive about other nations infringing upon its sovereignty – I told you the President was an asshole. We'd need to get the British Embassy to put in a request, and that would mean we've got to get the Foreign and Commonwealth Office on board. I have a contact there but..."

He stopped, apparently becoming aware of how Sands was staring at him.

"I misspoke. I meant to ask, is there any legal..." – she hesitated, raised her eyebrows a touch – "or *diplomatic* problem with me travelling out there to speak to him? As a friend, I mean?" She gave a sarcastic smile.

Briggs looked confused for a moment, but then he understood. He took his time replying.

"In theory you can go and visit old friends in almost any

country you want. Give or take. I don't fancy your chances in North Korea." He paused, suddenly serious. "But you need to be clear, if he doesn't want to speak with you, there's nothing you can do. You'd have to walk away. And there won't be any help from the local authorities – the opposite come to think of it. And then obviously you won't be authorised to make the trip in the first place, so you'll have to fund it yourself, and I don't know what you'll say to your bosses about why you're going out there..."

"Don't worry about my bosses. Can you come too? Atkinson will know I have no jurisdiction, but if there's someone from Interpol it might frighten him enough to trade what he knows for you leaving him alone. Plus I don't speak Portuguese."

Briggs blinked in surprise. "Did I just say all that in my head, I thought I spoke out loud—"

"I don't have time for jokes," she cut him off. "Can you get time off? Do you have holiday or something you can take?" She sighed, resisting the urge to check her watch.

He answered carefully. "As it happens I'm on leave next week, I'm going with my sister to Center Parcs. But even if I could go with you, without formal investigative powers I can't do anything. I won't even be able to speak with him."

Sands stared at him, her eyes narrow. She considered asking what Center Parcs was but had a fair idea and decided to look it up later.

"I'll cover the costs, obviously," she said, still thinking. "I have a few things I need to sort out tomorrow; how are you fixed for flying out Sunday?"

FIVE

"No, no and just in case that wasn't clear enough, absolutely no way." The voice of Superintendent Yorke filled the Alfa's speaker system. Sands hadn't even left the multi-storey where she'd left the car before dialling his personal mobile.

"Sir, you need to understand, Atkinson worked in secret with Sterling for months planning the escape. There's no way he didn't also help Sterling once he was outside the prison walls. He'll know something."

"And you need to understand, Erica, that you have a department to run. You can't just run off to Brazil at a moment's notice, you have a case."

"Golding can handle it. If he needs me I'll be on the phone."

"No."

The Alfa's tyres squealed as she took the corner to descend a floor towards the exit.

"I can be back in a week."

"*No*. How much is it going to cost anyway?"

"It's irrelevant. This is the best lead we're going to get to find Sterling, and Atkinson might move again at any moment."

"Can't we track him? Isn't that what Interpol do? Can't we monitor him online? And you just said he's had a security system installed; that suggests he plans to stay where he is."

Sands found herself shaking her head. She rolled down the window to insert the ticket, then frowned in momentary irritation at a handwritten sign saying the machine was out of order, but at that moment a large man began ambling towards her from his cabin, bearing a set of keys. He inserted one into the barrier. Sands left the window lowered, to snap at the man to hurry up if she needed to.

"This is our only chance to get a lead on Sterling. We can't just sit on our hands."

"I'm not suggesting you do." Yorke's voice rang out now, beyond the car and out into the concrete space around her. "But there must be an official route you can take. You'll need to liaise with the Foreign Office – I don't know, isn't that what Interpol are for?"

Sands sighed; in her mind she played out what would happen if she explained how the Brazilian President was an asshole, and that even if he wasn't, the chances of her getting permission to speak to Atkinson in any kind of official capacity were close to zero.

"Maybe you're right, sir," she said instead.

"I know I'm right, Erica. It does sometimes happen—"

"Not with this," she interrupted. "The other day I mean."

"I don't understand?" He sounded confused.

"You said I needed a holiday. I think you're right. I'm feeling very tired all of a sudden. I think a week or so somewhere hot and sunny would really sort me out." The barrier lifted, and the fat man stared as she eased the car past, buzzing the window closed as she did so.

"I'm going to Brazil."

. . .

There were no direct flights, but there were two options: flying via Amsterdam to São Paulo, almost a thousand kilometres further south than they needed to be, and then getting a connecting flight back north; or flying to Lisbon and then taking a flight the next day to Fortaleza. Both flights arrived at around the same time, so Sands found herself adding twin rooms in a hotel near Lisbon airport to what was already a very expensive week. She hadn't been sure that Briggs would agree, but simply sent him his tickets. It turned out the week with his sister had been negotiable after all.

It had been Sands' idea to spend the day in Lisbon at the hotel, looking through the information that Briggs had managed to secure on Atkinson and his location. But the place had lived up to its budget reputation, with nowhere suitable for working, and nowhere nearby appealed either. And then Briggs, who had turned up in full-tourist mode, wearing a T-shirt, shorts and flip-flops, had suggested they take the opportunity to see Lisbon, and worked out a route on his phone which took in the waterfront. She'd acquiesced, but then before they were halfway there he sat down at a table outside a café.

"I can't walk in these things." He kicked the flip-flops off as a waiter arrived.

"*Eu gostaria uma cerveja si faz favor.*" Briggs spoke fast and fluently.

Sands replayed what he'd said in her mind, and did her best to translate it. The word '*cerveja*' on a menu card in front of her gave a clue, next to the English word beer.

"We're not on holiday," Sands said.

"Technically we are though, remember?" Briggs replied with a smile.

"*E você senhora?*" The waiter turned to Sands.

For a moment she was tempted too, but she shook her head. "*Café,*" she said instead, then pulled out her laptop. It was difficult to see the screen, but she persevered while Briggs sipped his beer in the sunshine. The truth was she was beginning to worry. It was going to be difficult to approach Atkinson. The more she thought about it, the less likely it seemed he would even agree to talk to them. And once he knew they knew where he lived, he might decide to disappear again, and then they wouldn't even have the option of monitoring him, as Briggs had first suggested. Furthermore nothing in the file that Briggs had prepared gave her any comfort or ideas. Having found the house they'd also discovered the real-estate documents, setting out how much Atkinson had paid – a cool 1.4 million dollars – and the high levels of luxury he'd received for the money.

"*Obrigado.*" Briggs thanked the waiter as he brought them a plate of fried squid, breaking Sands away from her thoughts. But then the waiter went on to say something she didn't catch. At one point he gestured at the laptop, open on the table.

"What did he say?" Sands asked Briggs when the exchange was over.

Briggs waved a hand to dismiss it. "Nothing, he just said to be careful with the computer. Lots of thieves in the city these days." He squeezed lemon over the squid and popped a piece in his mouth. "This is the life, isn't it?"

The comment prompted a thought for Sands, and she turned back to the particulars of Atkinson's new house, scanning quickly through the text, which was written both in Portuguese and passable English. A moment later she'd found what had caught in her mind.

"Security," she said, frowning.

"What about it?"

"You found him because he was installing a state-of-the-art security system. But look here, the house already had security when he bought it."

Briggs leaned in to see but shrugged.

"Maybe he wants more. This calamari is spectacular, by the way. You should try it." He pushed the plate towards her.

· · ·

They checked in for the overnight flight just as the city was coming to life for the evening. Sands' generosity had extended only to budget tickets and she squeezed in beside Briggs, happy to have at least selected the window seat so she could rest her head. She expected him to talk most of the way across the Atlantic, as he'd spent the day recounting irrelevant details about Lisbon and its architecture, but it seemed he was an experienced long-distance traveller, and as soon as the meal was finished, he inflated a travel pillow and pulled out a pair of eye shades.

"I'll see you on the other side."

SIX

With the time difference they landed disconcertingly the same evening they had taken off, the aircraft rolling down bumpily towards a city of bright yellow lights that cut off abruptly where it met the still-dark ocean. The moment they stepped out of the plane and across the tarmac they were hit with a wall of hot air, and underneath the reek of aviation fuel there were notes of something else, the freshness of tropical vegetation. Even before she arrived in the terminal Sands felt the trickle of sweat down her neck. But Briggs seemed entirely relaxed. He drew in heavy lungfuls of air and stretched his arms contentedly.

They picked up a rental car and took it to a hotel where, although it was only just eleven o'clock, it felt like the middle of the night to Sands.

The next day – early on account of how the jetlag had woken Sands at five am, and despite her having to hammer on Briggs' door to wake him – they drove out to take a look at Barney Atkinson's new house, in a small town about an hour north from Fortaleza. From the ground it didn't look quite as impressive as it had on Briggs' iPad. Not the house itself, of which the ground floor was almost impossible to see behind a high wall, with iron gates giving only a glimpse inside, but the rest of the environs. While Fortaleza had been chaotic and in some places run-down, it was modern and busy, but out here it felt sleepy and unloved. The streets were unfinished, poorly laid concrete slabs giving way to sand, and roads where clearly expensive houses stood side-by-side with basic shacks. Three enormous radio aerials dominated the little town. And the beach, though it was lined with coconut palms, had a scruffiness that Sands hadn't expected. A line of rubbish marked the high-tide line, and the sea, rather than being turquoise as it had looked from the air, was the same grey-blue as the sea at home.

"What are you thinking then?" Briggs called her out of her thoughts. He'd driven them from the hotel as Sands wanted to observe the city, and had parked in the street outside Atkinson's new property, careful to avoid any CCTV cameras.

"Not quite what I expected."

Briggs shrugged. "Brazil has a bigger gap between the rich and poor than we're used to. But then again, you see the same thing in London." He pressed the button to wind down the window, and a wave of hot air blasted in. He closed it again, and the car's air-conditioning found it harder to cope.

"You got any plans then, or are we gonna sit here and cook for a while?"

Sands looked around again. There was no one about, but it didn't look like the kind of street that ever got busy. On the plus side that meant they'd be unlikely to draw attention to themselves.

"Let's watch for a bit. See what happens."

From where they were parked they could see through the iron gates at the front of Atkinson's house. At first Briggs left the engine on for the air conditioning, but after a while Sands told him to kill it, concerned the noise might announce their pres-ence. But that left them in a metal box that quickly grew hot as the sun beat down. Sands opened the windows and tried to ignore the heat, concentrating instead on the house. The gardens were well cared for – luxurious vegetation, palm trees and colourful bushes with pink and orange flowers. The upper part of the house was visible too, well-maintained, pristine white paintwork and the orange roof tiles she'd seen on Google. But nothing happened. Nothing moved inside Atkinson's house or in the gardens. No one even walked past them on the street. The car became hotter and hotter.

"You sure you don't want to ring the bell?" Briggs asked.

Sands shook her head. "Atkinson knows me. The moment he sees me he'll know his attempt at disappearing has failed. I don't want to lose the advantage of surprise."

"I should have gone to Center Parcs," Briggs muttered, almost too quiet for her to hear, but when she did, he gave a sarcastic smile.

Another hour passed before something finally happened. The front door of the house opened and a man came out. He was large, with heavily muscled and tattooed arms, shown off by a black vest. He whistled as he strode towards the garage, zapping open the up-and-over door as he went.

"That him?" Briggs asked, squinting against the light.

The man was still too far away for Sands to see clearly; if it was Atkinson he looked very different from when she'd seen him in his prison uniform. But there was little doubt.

"That's him."

They watched as he backed a black Mercedes jeep, with the top down, out of the garage. Then he paused while the door closed again on its electric motor. Another click from his remote and the front gate began to open.

"Close the windows and get out of sight." Sands spoke quietly. Briggs gave her a look, but did as she asked as the Mercedes drove towards the gates, but then stopped with its nose pointing out into the street. The road was so quiet that it clearly wasn't traffic that Atkinson was being careful about, but still he looked first one way then the other, like a fox sniffing before it leaves its hole. Finally he committed to giving up the protection that the house and the walls afforded. Sands kept her head just high enough to watch, and saw how Atkinson spent a few seconds staring at their car, as if registering that he hadn't noticed it before. But she'd deliberately picked a common model, and eventually Atkinson pulled the Merc clear of the gates; when they'd closed fully, loud music began playing from the Mercedes, and he set off down the street, passing their car. They waited a few more seconds, then sat up again.

"Are we following?" Briggs asked.

"We are."

It was a relief to get the engine back on and the air conditioning flowing, and not difficult to keep the Mercedes in view while not drifting too close. For someone who was trying to be inconspicuous, Atkinson had made a poor choice of vehicle. Driving with one hand on the wheel and the other draped casually on the door, he led them towards the main part of the town, but then pulled over abruptly by a large café where tables were interspersed around large plants in pots. He pulled his feet up onto the seat and jumped out of the car, not bothering to open the door first, and then looked around, as if hoping someone had noticed his athleticism. But he failed to spot Sands and Briggs, who had already pulled over on the other side of the road. Thinking he was unobserved, Atkinson now stretched out one arm – as if he'd tweaked it slightly – before shaking himself loose and sauntering inside. Briggs moved the car again, parking it closer so they could see some way into the café.

"Go inside, see what he does," Sands said. Briggs nodded, pushed open the door and crossed the road towards the café. Sands slid across into the driver's seat in case she needed to give chase quickly, but otherwise she just watched and waited.

Briggs reappeared about five minutes later and walked up to the open window.

"What's he doing?"

"Having breakfast. Looks nice too, if you're hungry. Which I am."

Sands thought for a full minute, running through the different possible approaches they could make, but in the end everything came to whether Atkinson would agree to talk with them, and the only way they could find that out was to ask him.

"Damn it. Let's do it," she said. But before she got out, she started the engine and pulled the car forward so that the bumper was touching the Mercedes. Then she pulled the keys from the ignition and felt a wave of heat hit her as she left the car, the edge taken off it by a gentle breeze from the ocean.

"*Alright*," Briggs said.

The café, which was nearly empty, had a relaxed vibe. It had no external walls, and the concrete posts holding up the roof were disguised by huge vibrant ferns and palms which seemed to cool the air. A TV screen showed a football match, the volume up loud enough to hear the commentators' excited voices. Atkinson was sitting alone at a table facing the TV, a gigantic plate of fresh tropical fruit in front of him. He was working his way through a huge slice of papaya, one eye on the TV, another on a phone he'd placed on the table.

When a waitress spotted them, Briggs quickly spoke to her in Portuguese, presumably asking for a table. Sands noticed how Atkinson turned around quickly and looked closely at Briggs. She stepped casually sideways towards a table where a large palm blocked his view of her; she sat down. The waitress left Briggs with a smile and he took the seat opposite Sands.

"I told her we'd have what he's having," Briggs told her. But Sands wasn't listening. She pulled a notepad from her bag and then wrote something down.

"Go walk past his table, and make a show of dropping this." She folded the piece of paper in half and handed it to him.

"Make sure he sees you."

"What's it say?"

"That someone wants to speak to him. Go to the toilet; with luck he'll follow you back here." Briggs took it, opened it to read what she'd written, and nodded.

"OK. Sure."

Sands watched as he rose to his feet and casually walked across the café to where Atkinson was seated. As he passed the big man's table he let the paper slip from his hands, and it landed at Atkinson's foot. Sands watched through the foliage of the palm as Atkinson paused, as if confused, and then reached down to pick it up. By then Briggs was already some way past, and rather than call out to him, Atkinson opened the paper. And then he froze.

A few seconds later his demeanour changed; he glanced around, looking first over one shoulder and then the other, but the other few diners ignored him, and Sands was still hidden behind the fern. A few minutes passed, Atkinson seemingly unable to decide what to do, before the waitress brought a tray to Sands' table, laden with fruit so fresh she could smell its perfume, cakes and a Thermos flask of coffee. Then Briggs reappeared from the toilets, shaking his hands dry. This time he avoided walking directly past Atkinson's table, but made eye contact with the big man, who rose uncertainly to his feet. Casually Briggs inclined his head towards Sands' table, as if inviting Atkinson to join him. A moment later, still holding the note, Atkinson walked stiffly over towards them. He stopped when he saw Sands sitting there, sipping her coffee.

For a moment he just stared at her, but then – fast for such a big man – he ran.

SEVEN

Atkinson knocked into a chair as he sprinted for the exit, Sands and Briggs close behind him. But when he got outside he saw at once how Sands had pulled her car right up to the rear bumper of the Mercedes, so that it was impossible to move it.

"I only want to talk to you." Sands spoke rapidly to his broad back. "There's no point running, we'll find you again, and it's too damn hot."

Atkinson turned to her now and glared, furious. "What the fuck are you doing here?"

"I could ask you the same question." Sands put up her hands to calm him. "But come sit down and I'll tell you."

It took him a while to decide, but slowly Atkinson did what she'd asked. As they walked back to Sands' table she picked up the chair he'd knocked over. The few other diners and the waitress looked at them warily, but Briggs made some cheery comment in Portuguese that seemed to reassure them that everything was fine. Atkinson sat down, taking Briggs' seat, who seemed quite happy to pull over another chair.

"Hello, Barney," Sands began.

Atkinson glared, his heavy tanned arms folded across his chest.

"This is Agent Jonathan Briggs." Sands held out her hand to introduce him. "He's from Interpol. A specialist in the extradition of international fugitives."

"Hi, Barney, lovely to finally meet you." Briggs offered a welcoming smile, and reached across to help himself from the plate of fruit. Atkinson watched but said nothing. His hands clenched into fists.

"This is a great place you've found here. The fruit's *amazing*," Briggs said.

Atkinson's nostrils flared. "It don't matter, him being here. You can't do nothing to me, there's no extradition from Brazil to England." He sounded defiant.

"Is that what he told you?" Sands enquired. "If so, he's wrong."

"Who's wrong?"

"You know who."

Atkinson grunted dismissively, glanced again at the exit as if thinking about running again. But he stayed seated. He turned back to Sands, almost smiling now.

"Bullshit."

Sands smiled too. "OK, you know what? International law isn't my area of expertise, so how about we let Johnny here explain how the system *actually* works, because we very much can bring you back, whatever Sterling told you."

Briggs looked up from his fruit at Sands, then at Atkinson's twisted sneer. Then he picked up his napkin and began to wipe his mouth.

"Sure. No problem." He paused, took a noisy sip of coffee and put down the napkin.

"It's a little complex, but it makes sense after you've done it a few times." He offered a smile to Atkinson and carefully replaced the coffee cup.

"Basically there *is* an extradition agreement between Brazil and the United Kingdom, but the legal system here offers a very high level of protection to its citizens or anyone who becomes naturalised here, so extradition doesn't really work in practice. But your problem, Barney – can I call you Barney? – is that it takes eighteen months' residence before those protections start to kick in. Before that?" – he shrugged – "*Nada*. So if we wanted to, we could get you arrested today, and we'd have you on the ground at Heathrow by..." He glanced at his watch, fell silent.

"Middle of next week?" Sands suggested.

"End of, I'd say. It might take a day or two to find a flight," Briggs corrected her. "Shall we say Thursday latest?"

Atkinson seemed to have calmed himself down a little. The sneer changed to a genuinely amused smile as he turned back to Sands. "You think I'm gonna fall for that? You think I didn't do my own research before coming out here?" He glanced again at Briggs. "You're such an expert, you tell me how many successful extraditions there's been from Brazil in the last ten years?"

For a few seconds Briggs seemed to be counting in his head, then he shot a look at Sands, signalling that their bluff wasn't going to work.

"They got Ronnie Biggs, the great train robber," he said eventually.

"They didn't *get* him," Atkinson replied. "He got fucking bored waiting, and went home of his own accord."

Briggs shrugged as if this was a fair analysis, and then went back to his fruit. Atkinson turned back to Sands.

"The answer is none. You think I'm some kind of meathead but I spoke to lawyers. This all took planning. *I* chose where to go. I know it's theoretically possible I get extradited, but in practice it needs the authority of the President of Brazil. And good fucking luck getting that."

Sands opened her hands as if acknowledging they'd failed.

"How long did you have?" Sands asked, keeping her voice casual, as if they were just chatting. "You said you chose where to go. How long did you have to choose? How did it all happen? You and Sterling, working this out?"

Atkinson shook his head. "No way. I ain't saying nothing. You're probably recording this."

"Barney, you're living under an assumed name in Brazil. You left a note in your flat admitting to what you did, and the prison has CCTV footage of you helping Sterling escape. You think we'd need to record you to prove your guilt?"

"I don't know. I don't know what the fuck you're doing here, but I ain't telling you nothing, I ain't admitting to nothing. That way you got nothing."

Sands glanced at her coffee cup, still empty, while Briggs noisily slurped his way through his slice of papaya. She tried another tack.

"OK, I understand. I don't know exactly what arrangement you had with Sterling. But I can guess the basics. He gave you his spiel about free will, and how none of us really have it, and then he oiled the wheels with nine million dollars in Bitcoin. That's a powerful combination. But I also noticed that you didn't like the man. And I looked into you. A long and distinguished career locking up people like Sterling."

Sands leaned in. "I saw in your eyes how much you hated him. So I'm asking for your help. He had you working on his escape plan, so he also had you working on what *he* did after he got out of prison. You must have helped him, or he wouldn't have been able to disappear so completely. So help us catch the bastard, put him back where he belongs. And we'll leave you alone. We might not be able to get you back to the UK, but we can tie you in knots, we can drag you though the Brazilian courts, make your life here not worth living. And none of us wants to do that." She sat back.

Atkinson didn't reply, but he glanced at the Thermos of

coffee. He'd seen that Briggs had filled his cup but Sands still hadn't, and he took the second mug and emptied the coffee pot into it. Then he carefully took a sip.

"I got nothing to tell you."

Sands bit her lip and tried again. "Did he tell you he'd changed? That he wasn't a killer anymore? That's what he told me. He said it wasn't right that he was locked up with no chance of parole, when he wasn't a threat to anyone. Did he tell you that?"

Sands waited, but Atkinson didn't reply. She went on.

"But then, the first thing he did when he escaped was to track down his old colleague, a mathematics professor named Jeremiah Robbins. And he stabbed him the stomach. I was with Robbins when he died. It's a very painful way to go. Sterling will kill again if you don't talk to us."

"Maybe he will, maybe he won't," Atkinson finally replied. Sands lifted a hand, as if not understanding what he meant.

"Sterling told me about that guy, the professor. He said how he stole from him, his life's work or something – I didn't understand it, but it was like this old debt he had to settle. But he isn't gonna go crazy like he did before, killing innocent people. He promised me that. He was doing his meditation every day, hours he did it for. It did change him."

"And you believed that?"

Atkinson shrugged, and Sands shook her head, genuinely frustrated.

"He hasn't changed. It's an act, Barney; he conned you. He played you. He's made you an accessory to murder, when you're not a killer. So help us. Tell us what you know."

Atkinson said nothing but firmly shook his head. He took a sip of his coffee, which Sands took to mean that when that was gone, so was he, even if he had to smash his car out of the parking space. After all, he could certainly afford a new one. Sands glanced briefly at Briggs to see if he had any ideas, but he returned a tiny shake of his head. Sands had just the one approach left.

"You know how we found you?" she asked suddenly. As she spoke she used her spoon and fork to lift a slice of the papaya onto her own plate, and she focussed on it, as if it were more interesting to her than whether Atkinson replied or not.

"No." But he sounded interested. Sands glanced at him.

"You upgraded your security. Briggs was monitoring high-value purchases in cities near Natal, where we knew you flew to under a fake ID. It was a good piece of detective work."

Atkinson shrugged as if he didn't care.

"So? I'll be more careful in future."

"So, it got me wondering." Sands ignored the sarcasm in Atkinson's voice. "Your new house, or should I say, your new mansion, it already had a security system installed when you bought it. A good one, we saw it listed in the property particulars. Which raises the question, why would you need another one?" Atkinson narrowed his eyes, as if he wasn't sure where Sands was going with this.

"And then, the answer's so clear, I don't know why I didn't see it right away." For a split second her lips curled into a smile.

"You're not scared of extradition, because you saw some lawyer somewhere and they advised you, correctly as it turns out, that we couldn't bring you back. But your lawyer couldn't ease your other fears, could they?"

"What fears?"

"Your fears about Sterling."

Atkinson put the coffee down suddenly, as if he didn't like the taste.

"That's why you wanted extra security. That's why your beautiful house has a perimeter wall almost as high as the damn prison you spent your life working in. And that's why you looked so nervous this morning when we followed you here. You're looking over your shoulder the whole time because you're shit-scared Sterling's going to come looking for you."

"Uh huh." Atkinson shook his head.

"Oh come on, admit it. It's kind of funny, when you think about it. A guy the size of you, scared of a sixty-year-old man."

"He doesn't know where I am."

"Oh *come on*. We found you, you think he won't be able to?" Sands stabbed a piece of papaya with her fork.

Again he shook his head, but his voice betrayed his doubts. "You found me because you had Interpol on your side, and because I made a dumb mistake. But I won't make it again, thanks to you."

Sands put the piece of papaya into her mouth and enjoyed the tender sweetness. It was remarkably good. She waited.

"Even if he does know where I am, he ain't got no reason to do nothing. Sure, I helped him out, I can say that because you already know it. But if I helped him, then there's no reason for him to come looking for me."

Sands smiled. She knew she had him now.

"Unless I give him a reason."

EIGHT

"What?" Barney looked concerned.

"There's lots of ways to do it." Sands' mind was working fast now, the full extent of the idea opening like a beautiful flower. "I'll release a press statement, saying that we've located you – I won't give your address, but maybe the name of the town, just to help him on his way – and I'll thank you for your cooperation. I'll say we've agreed to drop all charges against you because of how helpful you've been. I'll give Sterling every reason to believe you've double-crossed him, and then *you* become an old score he needs to settle." She smiled, actually considering it now. "All I have to do then is sit back, and wait until he comes to get you." She smiled at the thought. Maybe she could even stay out here in Brazil while she waited. From what she'd seen so far, it seemed like an interesting country. In front of her Barney's face was contorting itself into several different expressions. It finally settled on fear.

"You can't do that. You wouldn't do that." He turned to Briggs, shaking his giant head. "She can't do that, can she?"

Briggs looked thoughtful. "I don't see what's stopping her. And it doesn't bother me. I've got over thirty cases on my files. If she wants to take one off my hands, I'm a happy guy." He shrugged, and started on the cake.

Atkinson responded by dropping his head into his hands, his huge chest filling and emptying as he drew in deep breaths. For a moment Sands thought he might actually be crying, but when he lifted his head his eyes were dry.

"OK. I'll tell you what I know. But it ain't much, and I'll need your word you won't send that fucking freak after me."

Sands met his gaze and nodded slowly, the fantasy disappearing as quickly as it had arrived. "I just want to catch Sterling, before he does any more harm. Including to you."

"What is it you want to know?"

Sands told Briggs to go and order more coffee, then leaned forward, inspecting Atkinson.

"How did it begin? You helping him, the whole escape thing, how did it start, how did that happen?"

Atkinson looked thoughtful for a while, then he shrugged. "You know what? Most of the people down there, in those fucking dungeons, they're little better than animals. They're so messed up by what they done and what got done to them, they don't even talk, they're barely human." He stopped. "But not Sterling." He shook his head. "I watched him down there, day after day. He kept his dignity, somehow. So yeah, we got talking."

"What about?"

Atkinson paused, thoughtful. "He used to do this meditation, for hours and hours at a time. I was curious what he got out of it. And when he told me, he made it sound like this amazing thing..."

"What did he say?"

"He told me it was like freedom. Freedom of the mind he called it. I didn't believe it, but he kept on, about how it had helped him, and how it could help me." Atkinson slid a glance at Sands. "I don't know if you know, but my partner and I – we broke up. We fought, physically fought I mean. And Sterling – he explained how it wasn't really me that did that." Atkinson stopped, frowning deeply. He looked down at his lap. When he next looked up he was shaking his head. "Fuck this. This ain't no therapy session. You don't need to hear this."

"He told you about there being no free will? How every action we take isn't the choice that it appears to be?"

Atkinson nodded.

"He gave me the same spiel." She offered him a thin smile.

Briggs returned with a fresh flask of coffee and a fresh mug. Sands poured it out.

"So you became friends?"

Atkinson seemed to recoil physically from this idea, but then sighed. "Not friends, but... he told me he'd changed, and I guess I believed him. Then he told me about the money."

"Go on."

"Years ago, when he was first brought to the jail, he was allowed to use the prison computers – same as the other prisoners. Only they didn't know he was some kind of genius. He told me how he had some Bitcoin, and other cryptocurrencies too – I didn't even know what they were. But he made me look it up, see what it was worth. It was the kind of money you can't even imagine. Millions. Hundreds of millions."

"So you agreed to help him?"

"Only because he promised me he'd changed. I wasn't gonna let some monster back out into the world."

"Who planned it? The escape?"

"He did. I had some ideas, but he didn't like them. He made me explain how the whole prison worked, everything from the laundry to what happened in a major emergency, like a fire or a riot. In the end he decided the best way was to pretend he was someone else and I'd just walk him out. But there was no way of doing it without making it obvious I'd helped him, so I knew I'd have to disappear too."

"And that was all set up before the escape? You had a flight booked, you knew where you were going?"

Atkinson nodded.

"Who set that up? How did it happen?"

"He told me how you could search directories on the dark web, how you could buy fake identities. He gave me some of the money to do it, some of the cryptocurrency I mean."

"So you set yourself up with a fake ID? Did you get one for him too?"

Again he nodded.

"What was the name?"

Atkinson hesitated, then gave it up.

"David Smith. I don't think it'll help you much, because he'll have changed it again since. But I got him a passport in that name, and I booked him a load of flights. He was real specific about where he wanted to go, and how."

"OK..." Sands waited.

"The first one was from Bristol airport – that's the closest airport to the jail – to Amsterdam. Then from there to Madrid. After that he went to Qatar, then to Bangkok, in Thailand. Then the last flight I booked for him went to Laos. I didn't even know where that was."

"And after that?"

Atkinson shrugged. "Nothing. I dunno. That was all he made me do."

"You can prove this? You can give me the evidence?"

"I dunno. You can check it, can't you? See if a David Smith took those flights? How else would I know?"

Sands considered.

"He wore a disguise too. He figured you'd be checking the airports, so – before we did the escape – I smuggled a wig and a false beard down to his cell, and we took new passport photos there." Atkinson chuckled, apparently at the memory of it.

"I left him a car, outside the prison. He had a disguise, his new passport, ticket, all inside. After that I assumed he'd drive to the airport. I didn't know he was gonna visit the professor before he went. That wasn't part of the plan."

Sands thought back to that night. How Robbins had died in her arms, and her last view of her father, climbing the cliff path up from the pool and shining a torch up into his own face, so they'd see who had done it.

"Is there anything more you can tell us? Any way you can know if he's still using that name? Has he been in contact with you since the escape? Is there anything you can give us that might actually tell us where he is?"

Atkinson seemed to think for a moment, but in the end he just shrugged.

NINE

As they flew back, both Sands and Briggs were already working on following the new leads. It didn't take long to confirm that flights had indeed been booked in the name of David Smith, to the destinations that Atkinson had told them about. However, they also discovered that in each case the seats had remained empty. Smith – or Sterling – hadn't checked in to any of them.

However, by the time they landed in Lisbon, this time for a two-hour stopover, an Interpol colleague of Briggs messaged to say she had uncovered another flight in the name of David Smith. And in this case the passenger *had* flown. Also significant was that the flight, from London Heathrow to Bangkok – the penultimate destination of the flights booked by Atkinson. It felt like something, and Sands paced anxiously up and down the Lisbon layover lounge until the Interpol agent messaged through images of "David Smith' from the airport's CCTV records.

"Is that him?" Briggs held his mobile phone up to Sands. The screen showed a poor-quality image of a line of passengers queueing to board a flight. Sands snatched the phone from him and stared closely. She tried to zoom into the image, but it pixelated.

"Is that the clearest we can get?" She offered the phone back to him, irritated.

"It's been months. We're lucky to have anything."

Sands took the phone again. David Smith was slightly overweight, balding, but wore a large dark beard. But it wasn't possible to see his face clearly enough to confirm whether he was or wasn't Sterling in disguise.

"The height's right. This guy looks heavier, but it could be padding." She shook her head. "I don't know. It could be him." Sands turned to the window and frowned, looking out over the runway where a large jet was taxiing to its berth.

They discovered that two CCTV systems were in use at Heathrow. The most up-to-date recorded high-resolution images of every passenger as their passport was checked, but with almost a quarter of a million passengers flying every day, the storage cost meant the data was only kept for sixty days before being overwritten. But David Smith had been spotted on a second, older and lower-resolution system where the records were kept indefinitely. And despite all efforts to improve the rendering, they weren't able to get an image clear enough to run facial recognition algorithms and confirm either way.

Over the next few days they did what they could to chase David Smith down in Bangkok, or establish his onward destination. But it quickly became apparent that few of the small hotels and guesthouses, which catered to thousands of tourists each day, bothered to accurately record their names or passport numbers. Furthermore, David Smith wasn't booked on any onward flights, nor did the bus companies have any records of a man of that name travelling overland from the Thai capital. And by then Briggs had explained how the city's Khao San

Road was infamous for the free availability of fake IDs. The quality wasn't great, but would have easily been good enough for him to disappear for a month or so, plenty long enough to source more convincing documents from the dark web.

All of this became irrelevant, however, when Sands was able to clarify from the UK end that the David Smith they were chasing was in fact a real person who lived in Cardiff, where he worked as a dentist. His reasons for travelling to Thailand looked suspiciously unsavoury, but once it had been established that his appearance matched the CCTV footage, there was no need to dig further into precisely why a late-middle-aged man might travel alone to a city famous for its lax attitude to sex tourism.

However, soon after, Sands began to turn up other men by the name of David Smith, who had also flown out of London in the days immediately following Sterling's escape. And the more she widened the net of airports he could have flown from, and the number of days after the escape, the more David Smiths she found. Eventually she calculated that an average of ten people by the name of David Smith took a flight from somewhere in the world every single day, the number doubling if you included international travel by ferry or rail.

Perhaps for Sands the gargantuan task of identifying and verifying each and every one of these David Smiths, and eliminating the possibility that they might actually be Charles Sterling in disguise, might have been worth the effort. But it wasn't just a case of working through the backlog. With every day that passed, more David Smiths travelled from one country to another, and the nature of crossing international boundaries meant that authorities in both countries had to be involved in tracking them.

For the next few months she spent her days working her day job, overseeing a number of minor cases where the cause and culprit was generally obvious, but which still required a well-

constructed body of evidence to pass the file onwards for prose-
cution. And then in the evenings she attempted to assist Briggs
in using Interpol's reach to track the world's population of
David Smiths as they went about their business. But if it hadn't
seemed obviously hopeless at first, it soon became exactly that.
Sterling had picked the name David Smith precisely because it
was one of the most common for English-speaking men of his
age, and he'd known Atkinson would likely give it up to the
police. If he planned to actually use this false identity, he would
be almost impossible to track. But it was becoming increasingly
likely that he never intended to use it at all, meaning all their
efforts were for nothing.

Finally, when Briggs phoned to say he was shelving the case
– not closing it, but simply unable to justify actively investigating it any more, Sands wasn't even able to feel outraged.
There was simply nothing to explore. Charles Sterling, who
might or might not also have been known as David Smith, had
simply vanished.

But then something extraordinary happened.

TEN

Sands didn't often run, but when she did she tended to run a very long way. She managed to maintain a relatively high level of fitness through being careful about what she ate and working extreme hours. But every now and then she felt the need to top that up by pulling on her running shoes and giving her legs and heart a beasting. Her normal route was down towards the seafront at Poole and then along to the end of Hengistbury Head, some twenty kilometres, and then the same route back. Normally it caused her little trouble, but this time, as she fought her way back against a strengthening headwind, she was feeling it in her legs. She wasn't as young as she used to be, and she hadn't taken that much care of herself professionally, getting shot twice being perhaps the most careless of her oversights. She mulled this over as she finally drew close to her apartment building on the harbour waterfront, looking forward to getting inside, resting and refuelling. As a result she missed the man in the dark suit waiting in a dark saloon car. She got to the front door, with its keypad entry system, before he approached her.

"Excuse me, Erica Sands? Ms Erica Angela Sands?"

She froze, as much as her tired legs would allow, and slowly spun around. He was a wolfish man, short and wiry, but with an intelligent and sharp-featured face that seemed be examining her with keen interest. He wasn't physically threatening, but she still felt a sense of menace.

"Who are you?"

"My name is Damien Reynolds, I'm a lawyer, with a firm of attorneys based in Singapore. I wonder if we could have a short conversation?" He paused, then showed a flash of yellowed canines as he noted the sweat running down her face. "Of course I can wait for you to shower, if you'd prefer?" He backed off a step, but continued to watch her carefully.

"What's this about?" Sands ignored the offer, and tried to absorb the details of his appearance.

"I apologise, Ms Sands." He held up a hand. "I've travelled a very long way to speak with you, and I'm a little tired, but our conversation can certainly wait for fifteen minutes. I'll be in my car."

She said nothing, her brain slowly beginning to fire. His suit jacket had fallen slightly open, and she noted the label inside the breast pocket: Tom Ford. Her eyes went to his wrist, taking in the Patek Philippe watch. For all she knew they could be fake, but she guessed otherwise.

"How long do you need to shower?" the man went on, as if his suggestion had been agreed to.

"What do you want to talk about?" Sands asked again, but he'd already turned around, lifting a hand above his head in a strangely carefree gesture. She stood, fixed to the spot, as he opened the door to the car – a rental, but an expensive one – and climbed in. Suddenly the effects of her run came back to hit her. She keyed in the number to the lobby and felt only slightly better when she closed the door behind her.

Normally she took the stairs to her third-floor apartment, but this time she waited for the lift, wondering whether she ought to call for assistance. There was something about the man that brought Charles Sterling to mind – perhaps it was simply the reference to Singapore: not exactly where her father had last been seen, but on the same continent. But that was crazy. Singapore was hundreds of miles from Bangkok, and this man might need to speak to her about anything. Yeah, right, she told herself, as she wolfed down a peanut butter sandwich while setting the shower running.

When she was done she wrapped a towel around herself and looked out the window. He was still there, standing outside his car now, leaning against the bonnet and looking up at her apartment. He lifted a hand again when he saw her looking down at him. She didn't move.

Angela. He'd called her Erica Angela Sands. Nobody called her that. She dressed quickly, then returned to the window. This time when he waved at her she pointed to the building's front door and then headed down to buzz it open. She arranged a couple of chairs by her dining table, and then glanced around for something she could use as a weapon should the need arise. There wasn't much. She considered fetching a knife from the kitchen, but dismissed the idea. Still she didn't quite understand what was making her so jumpy. The doorbell to her apartment rang.

"Thank you so much for agreeing to see me," Reynolds said. He offered her a card which she took and studied.

Damien Reynolds, Attorney at Law, Giles, Patterson and Daniels, based in Collyer Quay, Singapore.

Sands had never heard of them.

"What's this about?" she asked for a third time, not letting him inside.

Reynolds hesitated. "May I actually come in?" He looked

past her into the apartment, into the kitchen with its views of the harbour. "And actually, a glass of water would be most welcome."

She led him to the dining table and told him to sit, then fetched two glasses of water and sat opposite him, arms folded. He looked around.

"This is a very lovely apartment you have." He offered another smile.

"For the fourth, and please believe me – final time – what is this about?"

The lawyer nodded, the smile disappearing. He drew in a deeper breath and then picked up his glass of water. He drank from it slowly, then placed it down carefully to his left.

"Ms Sands. Seven days ago I was instructed to travel to the city of Hoi An in Vietnam, to meet with a man named Jeremy Collins. I was told it was extremely urgent, that he was a VIP client of the firm, and that I should follow his every instruction to the letter." Reynolds gave a short cough.

"I met with Mr Collins in a private hospital, and he informed me that he had arranged for an aircraft to bring me here to you, to have this conversation." Reynolds hesitated. "A private aircraft, I believe it was what they call a Learjet, my first time in one." He gave a somewhat rueful grin.

"I don't know anybody by the name of Collins," Sands took the opportunity to interrupt, but Reynolds carried on, dismissing her objection.

"I spent nearly twenty hours with Mr Collins in total, in which he told me something of his story – and yours – as well as handing me several documents that he asked me to pass on to you. Personally." This time the pause came with a smile.

"I don't know a Mr Collins, or anybody in Vietnam."

"It was immediately clear that the name this gentleman was using was not the name he was given at birth, and he was very honest regarding the reasons why. He was also, I might add, extremely regretful for the reasons why he was unable to use his birth name." Again the rueful smile. "I'm sure you've already guessed it, but the man's birth name was Charles Robert Sterling."

He was right, she'd already known it, but still the room was spinning as he said her father's name. And then the spinning accelerated.

"It is my unfortunate duty to inform you that Mr Collins, alias Mr Charles Sterling, passed away two days ago."

ELEVEN

"Passed away?"

"That's correct. He was extremely frail in appearance when I first met him, and he explained that he was suffering from the final stages of an aggressive and sadly untreatable form of bowel cancer. He was in some pain, and taking only the minimum amount of pain medication, such was his desire to ensure I received his instructions in full."

Sands was barely listening now. Every synapse in her brain seemed to be screaming at her that this was some sort of trick, a joke perhaps, something arranged by her father to con her, to scheme, to gain some advantage.

"This is not a trick, Ms Sands." Reynolds seemed to read her mind. "Mr Sterling – shall we use that name? He asked me many times to be quite clear about this. You will shortly receive official notification of your father's death. This will include fingerprint confirmation, dental records and a DNA analysis. For reasons you will be familiar with he is not in possession of a full set of medical records, but you will receive those that he does possess. They will show that he was first diagnosed with cancer six months ago, shortly after he arrived in Vietnam, and after suffering symptoms for a number of weeks before that."

"Sterling escaped from prison six months ago," Sands said, immediately feeling stupid for saying so; clearly the lawyer knew this.

"Seven, actually," Reynolds smiled. "Yes. He explained this to me, along with the reasons he was in prison." He gave her a look, as if acknowledging the part Sands herself played in that drama. "A tragic story."

"I don't believe you," she blurted out, and her arm jerked across the table, knocking over her glass of water. She just stared at it as the liquid flooded over the dark wood, spilling onto the floor.

"Mr Sterling advised me that you would find this difficult to accept." He glanced at the water, unsure what to do about it. "He asked me to take a photograph of him, which might help you process this." He placed his leather briefcase on the table, but paused before opening it. "Would you like me to get a cloth?" When Sands didn't answer he took the initiative, heading to the kitchen. He opened cupboards at random, and then returned with several sheets of kitchen roll. He used them to absorb the water and wipe down the table before returning to the kitchen, where Sands heard him washing his hands in the sink. All the while she stared at the briefcase on the table.

Reynolds sat back down, adjusting the case so that it was square in front of him before tumbling the twin combination locks and clicking them both open. He lifted the lid, took out a tablet computer and waited a few moments while it booted up. Finally he handed it over to her. Sands took it with both hands and stared at the screen.

Looking back at her was, unmistakably, her father. He was lying in a hospital bed, blue bedcovers and white-painted walls; next to him was what looked like a dialysis machine. His face was white, almost yellow, and far thinner than the last time she'd seen him. He appeared to be trying to smile, though the effort of doing so was apparently so great it was more of an exhausted stare.

"Why?" Sands asked. "Why did he want you to come here, and show me this?" She handed the tablet back, not wanting to look at that face; the pain it showed was something she'd long desired, but now it was here she wasn't so sure.

"That will become clear in time. But before we get to that, Mr Sterling thought you would need some time to check with your own sources, for external verification?"

She wasn't thinking straight, she couldn't think straight.

"You are working with a gentleman named Briggs, I understand, at Interpol?"

How did he know that? How could he know that?

"Yes."

"I've been informed that he will soon receive news of Mr Sterling's unfortunate demise. No doubt when he does so, you will be the first person he contacts. I would like to speak to you again once he has independently confirmed what I've just told you. Until then I shall find myself a hotel – would you happen to know one you can recommend?" His eyebrows went up questioningly, but he dismissed his own question. "Never mind. I shall make my own arrangements. Could I perhaps have a telephone number that I could contact you on?"

Without really being aware of what she was doing, Sands pulled a card from her bag and handed it over to him. Reynolds hadn't turned off his tablet, simply laid it face-up on the table, and she couldn't stop herself staring at the image of her father, lying there on his actual deathbed, gaunt and frail. Or perhaps not, perhaps this was a trick? She screwed her eyes shut, physically tired from the run, overwhelmed mentally, as if she'd been driving and her car had been sideswiped by a train.

"I'll leave you in peace for now," Reynolds said. "But before I do, there's one last task I have been instructed to perform at this meeting." He reached into the briefcase again, this time riffling quickly through some paperwork. He pulled out a high-quality cream envelope.

"This is a letter written by Mr Sterling, addressed to you." He stood up, closing the lid of the case and snapping the locks shut before he held it out to her.

"I'll see myself out. And we'll speak again. In a week or so?"

Reynolds gave her his rueful smile, nodded smartly and walked to the door. He opened it and disappeared.

TWELVE

Sands sat for a long while, just staring at the envelope. Her name was written on the outside, Erica Angela Sands, and the handwriting was clear – definitely her father's, but unlike the confident calligraphic style she knew, this seemed weaker, as if his hand was unable to grip the pen. After a while she turned the envelope, noting it was sealed with a tamper-proof sticker across the flap bearing the letters GPD, presumably the logo for Giles, Patterson and Daniels, Lawyers Practice. She picked it up and tore open the seal.

My dear Erica,

By the time you read these words, I shall be no more. I apologise for leaving you alone in this world not once but twice. I had hoped that our recent meetings might have led to some form of reconciliation, but it was not to be. And now – the sands of time have slipped so far, that barely dust remains. Alas, but none of us can escape the final curtain call.

You will see, in the days that follow, that I have taken pains to plan my departure with some care. I have done so not only to ease my own passing – though I freely confess to that – but also to do what I can to help you, my dear Angel, in the years that you have left.

What do I mean by such words? Put simply, that I understand how difficult this news will be for you. Not perhaps emotionally, it really did seem as though no vestige of our mutual affection remained. And perhaps I had no right to hope that it might. No, I speak of the tenacious nature that was born within you, and which I recognised and sought to encourage in your tutelage. Along with, of course, that peculiar fault of mine, a habit of not being entirely truthful, or even good. I mean to say that I understand you will have doubts. That you will suspect my death is nothing of the kind, but some form of trickery, some sleight-of-hand designed to evade the long arm of the law which you now – so ably – represent. I assure you it is nothing of the kind. To prove this you will receive, over the coming days, and through the official channels, evidence that I speak the truth this time. You will receive samples of my fingerprints, my dental records, my medical history – such as I have access to, my very DNA. This latter you may, should you wish, test against your own. It will be hard to accept, but I urge you, I beg you, I implore you. For your own good, do not gnaw upon this bone and waste your life. Accept this truth and move on.

Get out from under my dark shadow, my Angel. Go and become who you were born to be.

I ask one final favour – and in the certain knowledge that you would refuse such a request, were I to leave it as such – here I have taken matters into my own hands. I do not wish to allow the police, nor the courts, nor the newspapers, or anyone at all, access

*to my body once I have left it. For this reason I have given
instructions that I be cremated as soon as possible after my death,
and that my ashes be scattered in the river that runs below my
window. I hope you will forgive this one, final indulgence, and I
will now explain the reason why this is important to me.*

*I am not, nor have I ever been, a religious man. But events have
conspired so that I have spent a great deal of time in quiet
contemplation. I believe this has taught me certain truths about
the nature of the things – the universe, if you will, of which we
are all a part, however infinitesimally small. I have also done
some very wicked things – wicked that is, as viewed by the
narrow and arbitrary rules of humans (meaningless furless
monkeys that we are). But also wicked in that they were at odds
with a wider, deeper power. It is my belief that only when I am
dust, floating in the sacred waters, will I be absolved of the guilt
I carry for these acts. I have carried this guilt for a long time, and
I ask that you do not begrudge my impatience for this
absolution.*

*I do not expect you to understand this sentiment, but I promise
you it is honestly felt.*

*I hope, Erica, that you will be wise when you receive this news.
But I fear that you will not. For that reason I have held back one
final surprise, which my lawyer will visit upon you in due
course. I hope that with this parting gift you can finally find
acceptance. Perhaps even a little happiness.*

*Farewell now, my Angel. My hand is weak and I have said what
needs to be said. Perhaps now that I am gone from this world you
will feel freer to accept that it is now yours. Dance, Erica. Sing
freely. Rise with the larks and run. Love whomever you desire,
madly, wildly. Be whatever you wish to be.*

Until we meet again,

Your father,

Charles Sterling.

THIRTEEN

Sands' hands were shaking violently as she pulled out her mobile phone and called Briggs. He picked up on the third ring.

"Have you heard?" She could hardly speak through the swirl of emotions, some she couldn't even recognise, but she fought through it. "We need to stop them burning the body."

"Body? What body? It's Sunday morning, Erica," Briggs replied, then he noticed the tone of her voice. "What the hell's happened?"

Sands looked around her apartment. What *had* happened? Nothing in her life had changed. Except that he was dead. Or claiming to be.

"A lawyer just doorstepped me. Sterling's lawyer apparently. He told me that Sterling died two days ago. He was living in Vietnam, by the name of..." – for a second her mind betrayed her – "Jeremy Collins. He died in a private hospital, in a city called..." Again she paused, closing her eyes this time. "Hoi An. He's told them he wants to be cremated. You need to get onto it. *Right now.* You need to stop them burning the body. We need to see if it's really him."

The room span around her head. When she tuned back in Briggs was still speaking.

"Erica? Are you still there? *I need the line*. I'll call you back. Just stay where you..."

She hung up.

After a long while she got up, unsteady on her feet, and went through to the kitchen where she made a coffee, but then sat looking at it, and the world beyond the window, until the cup went cold. When she noticed she put it in the microwave, overheating it until it frothed over and made a mess everywhere. She burned her fingers getting it out, and repeated the process. Setting it on the table and staring past it. Trying to make sense of what was happening. Her phone rang.

"Briggs?"

"It's Sunday night in Vietnam, nearly ten pm."

"Just tell me you've stopped it. Please, tell me?"

"OK. OK." Briggs was quiet a moment, apparently settling himself. "I have got confirmation that a man in his sixties, using the name Jeremy Collins, died at nine pm on Wednesday in the Hoi An Private Medical Clinic. He was suffering from an advanced form of bowel cancer, and he'd been resident in the facility for six weeks."

"Can you stop it? Can you stop them cremating the body until we get there?"

"I need to tell you about the centre."

"*Tell me you've stopped it.*"

"*Erica!* Give me a chance."

She fell silent.

"The Hoi An Clinic claims to have the best medical care in all of South East Asia. English-speaking doctors, luxurious surroundings and marvellous views of the Thu Bồn River, and yes I am quoting fro its website. But I've also spoken to my counterpart in Hanoi, and he knows of it. All the expats out there do apparently, the wealthy ones at least."

"So what? Why are you telling me this?"

"Because its relevant, damnit. It's also known for putting a very high degree of emphasis on the privacy of its clients. And on following their requests to the letter."

"What do you mean?" Erica sensed the truth now, but needed to hear it. "What are you saying? *Surely* this can be stopped. Charles Sterling is a multiple murderer and an escaped convict. He's wanted in over a hundred countries, there's no way his wishes should be—"

"I'm telling you it's already happened, Erica. If Collins really is Sterling, then his ashes were spread on the river about four hours ago. I suspect your lawyer was told not to contact you until it was done."

FOURTEEN

At first confusion reigned. With the time difference, distance and language barrier, and the disputes over which organisation had the authority to act, along with the reputation for privacy that the clinic was eager to protect, it was probably inevitable. Indeed it was doubtlessly planned that way.

And then there was the situation itself. At first the clinic insisted the man who died really was an Englishman named Jeremy Collins, a former engineer from Birmingham, and they provided a wide range of documentation that appeared to prove this, including a well-worn passport, a driving licence and credit cards from three major banks. But then, on the insistence of the Vietnamese authorities, themselves pushed by Interpol and ultimately Sands, they accepted the possibility that the documents could actually be false, in which case it very well might have been Charles Sterling who had passed away. Except that the message then came through – again on Sands' insistence – that it wasn't Sterling after all. Or at least, if someone there really *had* died, then it wasn't Sterling, and it wasn't his body which had been cremated. That somehow, within the layers of confusion, Sterling had pulled some form of confidence trick.

But *somebody* had died. At least Briggs was certain of this, arguing that it was impossible that so many professional people – doctors, nurses, administrative staff, funeral directors and the operators of the crematorium – were all risking their reputations by lying, and all telling the same lie.

And then the information started to change. The patient known as Jeremy Collins had, on his arrival, made several highly unusual requests, the very existence of which he'd issued strict instructions to remain secret until after his death. He'd paid to see a dentist, and arranged for x-rays and other imaging records to be taken of his teeth. He'd ordered a DNA sample to be taken, with the senior doctor signing a legally binding affidavit that the man he took the sample from was indeed known as Jeremy Collins, and following a carefully controlled chain of custody to ensure the integrity of the evidence. He'd done the same with his fingerprints. Finally he'd left a letter with another lawyer – a local Vietnamese firm this time – with instructions that it should be delivered to the director of the clinic seventy-two hours after the cremation. In this letter the man known as Jeremy Collins finally shed any pretence about his alias, and identified himself as Charles Sterling. He then instructed the clinic to release everything they had on his file to prove his identity to the local police, to Interpol and to anyone else who cared to ask.

When this evidence made its way halfway around the world to the Interpol building in London, it wasn't quite enough to convince Agent Johnny Briggs. And Sands' badgering quickly resulted in them both being granted the authority to fly out to Vietnam and meet with the local police, and the medical staff who'd attended to Sterling, to try and sort things out. But everyone out there told the same story. The man who had died had given his name as Jeremy Collins, but every sample he'd provided, every record he'd given matched those of Charles Sterling. And that same man had most certainly died.

And there was no question he had been ill. Sands and Briggs were shown imaging scans of the cancer, a dark mass among lighter masses, that meant little to Sands but caused the doctor who showed it to them to shake his head sadly, as if he were caught up in some family tragedy and not a search for a missing international fugitive. Sands was shown the death certificate and spoke with the doctor who'd signed it. She even insisted on speaking with the porters who'd moved the body, showing them several photographs of Sterling and asking them if this was indeed the man they'd wheeled down to the morgue. They'd nodded, eagerly, as if hoping this would finally satisfy this angry and crazy Englishwoman who was causing so much disruption in their previously tranquil clinic.

After three days on the ground in hot, sticky and vibrant Vietnam – attributes that Sands had barely even noticed – she realised that she was losing Briggs. She saw it in his silences, and the way he looked at her when she insisted over and over again that somehow this was a trick. That either Sterling had been fooling them about his illness and had sneaked out of the hospice. Or that he'd switched the body, or that he'd never been Sterling at all. Matters came to a head as they met for dinner in the hotel dining room.

"Everything checks out, Erica," Briggs told her, biting his lip as if readying himself for a row.

She shook her head. "How can you say that? Nothing checks out."

"The dental records are a match. The DNA is a match. The fingerprints match. It all matches, and he had different people record them each time. It's just not credible that he could have fooled all of them. Nor that they could all be lying for him."

"So that's not how he did it. But he still did it."

"Have you considered the other possibility?"

She frowned at him.

"Maybe he just wanted to give you peace of mind? You said

he was talking about reconciliation, how he said he'd changed. Maybe he had?"

"He murdered a man within hours of escaping from prison."

"Yeah, but you said he had a reason, the guy stole something from him, some mathematics paper."

"He also ordered a paranoid and delusional young man to shoot a police officer and his young family. Just before he broke out of prison, and while he was telling me how much he'd changed."

Briggs nodded. "OK. Yes, so he did that. But maybe he wanted to give *you* peace of mind? Have you considered that?"

"I've considered it, and I've rejected it. Tell me this," – she leaned forward – "if that was the case, why didn't he do the one thing that would prove his death beyond all doubt? Why didn't he leave us his body?"

Briggs made a face. "Didn't he say something about that? Didn't he give some reason to do with his spirituality? How he could only find peace when he was dust, and that he didn't want the police messing with him?"

Sands raised her eyebrows theatrically. "Give me a break. You believe that?"

But Briggs stayed quiet for a while, thinking. Then he gave a sad shake of his head. "If you want to know what I really believe, I reckon it's maybe the opposite of what I just said. I think he maybe wanted to screw you over one last time. He's given enough proof for anyone –anyone reasonable at least – to conclude that he died here last week. But he's left just a tiny chink of doubt. And he knew that would mess with your head, probably for the rest of your life, because he knows you're never gonna be reasonable about this."

The same thought had occurred to Sands. "So that's it? You're what... you're done here? You're the reasonable one and you're convinced?"

"I'm..." He looked around the restaurant; it could have been anywhere. Briggs had mentioned on the flight over that they should take the opportunity to see a bit of Vietnam, eat out in a few street markets. She hadn't replied and it hadn't happened. They'd lived on whatever they could grab from the clinic cafeteria and vending machines. He scratched at his head.

"I'm ninety-nine per cent convinced. And maybe that's all I can ever be. Normally you'd have a body, and you'd get that ID'd, but you wouldn't have everything around it, the DNA check, the teeth. This time it happens to be the other way around, but maybe we're only *ever* ninety-nine per cent convinced." He paused, about to drop the hammer. "Either way, I've been ordered back. And I'm told you have too."

Sands wouldn't meet his eye.

"What else are you gonna do? What more can you do here? Everyone dies sometime, somehow. What if this is just how he died? If that's the case, he's not gonna come back, no matter how long you stay here." He glanced up as Sands' phone vibrated to announce the arrival of a message. She picked it up, read it, and her eyes widened.

"Shit."

His eyebrows went up questioningly.

"That was the lawyer who first told me about all this. He's asking if I'm ready to see him yet. I'd forgotten about that bastard."

FIFTEEN

The bastard in question was waiting in the bar beside the swimming pool of the Oceanside Hotel in Poole. He stood when he saw her, showing off his navy pleated shorts and stick-thin hairy white legs. Then he raised an eyebrow at the fact that Sands hadn't come alone.

"This is Interpol agent Johnny Briggs. He works for a unit specialising in tracking down international fugitives," she said, taking a seat opposite the lawyer. "Damien Reynolds of Giles, Patterson and Daniels. Apparently he works in international fugitives too."

"Touché," Reynolds smiled, offering his hand to Briggs, then turning back to Sands. "You didn't mention company?"

"Briggs is handling the Sterling missing-person case. It's easier for him to hear whatever you have to say directly, rather than me waste time reporting it."

"As you wish. Though..." – the eyebrow went up again – "one presumes it's no longer a missing-person case?" There was a real question there as if he were fishing for information, but neither Briggs nor Sands reacted. Reynolds held up his hands.

"No matter. It's no concern of mine. I'm just pleased you're back, so that I may conclude my business. Or rather the business that Mr Sterling asked me to perform." He looked around, catching a waiter's eye and beckoning him over. "The hospitality is very good," – he spoke as if he were recommending it to them – "but I do find it stifling to stay too long in a hotel, don't you?"

The waiter arrived wearing a starched white shirt and an apron printed with the hotel's logo. He nodded respectfully to the new arrivals. "Good morning, madam, sir? Can I get you anything to drink?"

"It's on Sterling by the way," the lawyer cut in. "My whole stay here was paid for in advance by Mr Sterling, so have whatever you like."

"I'll take a herbal tea," Briggs said, and Sands just shook her head. The waiter left.

"So what's this about?" Sands asked.

Reynolds sat forward in his chair. His briefcase was by the side of the table; he glanced at it but didn't reach for it.

"This is rather exciting," he grinned, but glanced again at Briggs. "Are you quite sure you wouldn't like to hear this news in confidence? It's of a personal, as well as financial nature."

Sands' nostrils flared but she said nothing, simply shaking her head.

"Very well." Reynolds reached down for the case, again taking care to place it precisely on the table before rolling the combination locks open. He removed his tablet, followed by two envelopes, one sealed as before with the law firm's logo. He placed all three items on the table, then closed the briefcase lid and put it back down by his side. He checked that he had their attention.

"Another letter?" Sands asked.

"No," Reynolds replied. "Not exactly."

At that moment the waiter returned with a silver tray and a

white china cup for Briggs' tea. He placed it down carefully and left.

"Ms Sands. Despite the crimes which Mr Sterling committed, and for which he was convicted, his right to own assets remained identical to ours. He was able to control property, shares or currency in the same way as any other individual. The only exception to this would be if it was shown that any assets had been acquired illegally. In such a case a state, or states, could make a claim upon those assets, and if that claim was successful they might be seized. As I'm sure you're aware, no claim has ever been made against Mr Sterling."

He paused, before continuing in a quieter voice. "And given the nature of his crimes – there being no suggestion that they were carried out in the expectation of financial gain – no claims can reasonably be expected." The lawyer paused again, fixing his eye on Sands. "He asked me to be quite clear on that point."

Sands didn't reply.

"Furthermore, Mr Sterling gave me very precise and very clear instructions for what I am about to tell you, and immediately prior to doing so he had himself declared of sound mind, and certified as such by a qualified doctor of psychiatry. I have that certificate here."

Reynolds opened the larger of the envelopes and handed the contents to Sands to inspect. It was a sworn statement by a Dr Tran Quang Huy. She skim-read it and handed it on to Briggs, who was blowing the steam off his tea.

Reynolds smiled his wolfish smile again, as if he were enjoying the drama of his role. "Are you quite sure you wouldn't like something to drink, Ms Sands? You might feel you need one in a moment."

"Quite sure. Are you getting any closer to a point?"

The lawyer lifted his hands palms outwards as if apologising for not being more concise. Then he took the tablet and turned it on, holding it so that neither Sands nor Briggs could see the screen. For a few moments he tapped at the device. Then his eyebrows rose again. He sighed, whistled under his breath.

"There are of course tax implications, but I can assist you with those, should you so desire." He glanced at Sands, seemingly enjoying her look of confusion. "And one benefit of Mr Sterling's death in Vietnam is that the country recently deleted its inheritance taxes from the statute books, although there may be a challenge from UK Revenue & Customs." Reynolds seemed almost to be talking to himself. But then he sat up, this time looking her squarely in the eye.

"Erica Angela Sands. This second envelope contains the digital key to a computerised wallet, which in turn contains all of the outstanding funds held by Mr Charles Sterling at the point of his death, minus expenses due to the clinic where he was treated, and to the firm where I work, which I have duly deducted. Mr Sterling had no other assets, apart from the contents of this wallet. He instructed me to hand this wallet to you, and inform you that, as his sole surviving relative, his wishes are that these assets will pass to you in their entirety. He also asked that I perform a calculation at the exact moment of handing you this wallet, informing you of its current value in pounds sterling. That value is..." He turned the tablet so Sands could see the screen.

"Four hundred and sixty-three million, seventy-six thousand, five hundred and thirty-two United Kingdom pounds. And twelve pence." He beamed triumphantly. "Ms Sands, congratulations. As of right now, you are outstandingly rich."

PART TWO

SIXTEEN

Pierre Cloarec raised his left hand and clicked his fingers. The waiter saw him and wordlessly glided over to the table, placed a glass down and half-filled it with red wine. His actions had little flourish, just a style born of decades of repetition. Pierre nodded his thanks and turned his attention back to his daughter, on the other end of his mobile telephone.

"And the doctor? What did he say?" he asked.

"It's a she. But it could be weeks, maybe even months." Monique's voice became a little whiny as she went on to explain how she needed to rest and ice her ankle, and then there'd be the rehabilitation. She had twisted it – she said – simply running down the stairs in her apartment, but Pierre had his doubts. More likely it had happened at the damn dance school where she was throwing away her life instead of getting a serious job. Either way, his attention was taken by a woman walking two tiny dogs on the pavement in front of him. Her thin hips swayed from side to side, check trousers so tight he wondered how she could even get them on. He smiled at the thought, feeling his age. Surely he ought to care more about how to get them off?

"*Papa!*"

"*Oui, Monique.*" They were speaking French, their accents refined Parisian, the harsher vowels softened, but sometimes he spoke to her in English too. Her education had cost him enough, they might as well use it.

"What are you working on, Papa?" she asked. "Or is it still *top secret?*" The last two words were in English.

"Very much top secret."

"I hope it's not dangerous."

"Not as dangerous as you becoming a dancer."

"Papa. I told you, I didn't hurt it dancing. I was running for the post."

"OK." He wanted to wrap this up. "Give my regards to your mother."

"I will."

"Take care, I hope you feel better soon."

Pierre ended the call, then took a sip from the wine. His eyes scanned the street. Another young woman passed on the other side of the street. He watched her as he pulled a cigarette from a soft pack on the table in front of him. He lit it, filled his lungs and blew out a cloud of smoke. He checked his watch.

"*Bonjour, mon ami.*" Eric Miller's voice sounded from behind him, causing Pierre to twist his neck awkwardly. He rubbed the muscles as the newcomer pulled out a chair and sat down, indicating to the waiter for a second glass of wine. Without explanation he began to lay out a chess set on the table.

"We have to be quick," – Pierre leaned across and helped him – "I have a meeting at three. An important one."

Eric scoffed. "And it's the AGM of the Institute of International Relations this evening. But don't worry, I will beat your ass quickly and we can both be on our way." The game was set up now, and he moved, king's pawn, two squares forward. "I'll be white."

At once Pierre responded with his own pawn. The rule was

no more than thirty seconds per move. After all, they were both working men. In the background the Eiffel Tower loomed over the white stone buildings of the city.

They played in silence, Eric pushing an attack on his queen's side and threatening a knight fork on the black king and rook. But he was always one move away from being able to action it, as Pierre squeaked through a series of tight escapes, moving his king left then right. Then he offered an exchange of pieces which looked to be in white's favour, but ended up being equal because of one overlooked pawn. The endgame quickly led to a draw – only their second of the month – which prompted Eric to offer a rematch. But Pierre shook his head.

"*Non.* I told you, I must go and see the 'Breton Dragon' at three." He checked his Apple iWatch, the latest model.

"You didn't say you were seeing *her.*" Eric widened his eyes in mock fear. "What does it want, *le dragon?*"

"Nothing. She's worried about me is all. She thinks the Italian Mafia plan to track me down and slit my throat."

Eric narrowed his eyes at this. "Why would they do that? Aside from the obvious?"

Pierre offered a sarcastic smile, but shook his head. "I can't tell you. Need to know."

Eric considered this. "OK. But do they actually want you dead?" He sounded mildly concerned now.

"It will make a good story if they do."

"But you wouldn't be the one writing it."

"*Non,* but it would still be a good story."

Eric smiled, then helped himself to a cigarette, offering one to Pierre as he did so.

"Perhaps we should move on to something you can talk about. Are you still working with the lovely Clémence?"

"She's helping," Pierre grunted. "A little."

"But have you helped yourself to her yet?" Eric's eyebrows rose meaningfully.

Pierre waved the suggestion away with his cigarette. "*Non.* We have a professional journalistic relationship. That is all."

Eric scoffed again. "And you're telling me you haven't even noticed her tits?"

"I notice them on a daily basis," Pierre chuckled. "I told you, she's helping a little."

He finished his cigarette, leaning forward to stub it out.

"Talking of porking the underlings," Pierre continued, speaking languidly, 'how is our good mayor? Still at it with that researcher?"

Eric shrugged. "As far as I know, yes. But it's not exciting. She's not at all pretty, and I don't think the wife could care less." He waved a hand. "If you think there's a story there I can tell you another time, but it's... dull." Pierre nodded, satisfied that he wasn't missing anything, not that it would be his area anyway. The woman with the two dogs returned, her walk around the nearby park completed. This time both men watched, falling silent as they did so.

When she was too far away to see clearly, Pierre stood up, tossing a twenty-euro note down on the table.

"Same time on Thursday?"

Eric nodded, reaching behind to another table where a copy of *Le Monde* had been left folded in half. He shook it open and settled back in his chair. For a moment Pierre watched him enviously. Suddenly Eric laughed at his friend, still loitering by the table.

"What?" Pierre asked.

"Nothing," Eric replied. "But give my regards to *le dragon.*"

SEVENTEEN

Ever since it was established, shortly after the Liberation of Paris towards the end of World War II, *Le Monde* had always been edited by a man. Until that is, its owners – known for their progressive leanings – made the surprise appointment of Lucille Amelia Dubois as Editor in Chief. Technically it was true that Dubois had worked her way up, beginning her career at *Le Parisien* as a political reporter, going on to spend nine years as deputy editor and then editor of *L'Express* magazine. But it was still a surprise, not least to her, when she was given the most prestigious role in French journalism. To the dozen or so more senior, and exclusively male, reporters who considered themselves a better fit, it was nothing short of a scandal. What was worse, few could convincingly argue that she wasn't handling the job well, despite the difficult times that newspapers were going through worldwide.

Pierre arrived at her office, seeing her PA tapping away at her keyboard. "Summoned to see the dragon," he interrupted, not waiting to be asked.

Dubois' PA kept working on whatever it was she was writing, but in the end looked up and replied with equal sarcasm,

"She's waiting for you." She glanced at her watch. "She's been waiting for seven and a half minutes."

She hadn't been though. Dubois had used the delay to make a long-overdue call to her mother, and was still on the phone as Pierre entered the office. She switched from French to Breton as he walked in, but so smoothly he almost didn't notice, except that he couldn't follow her words as she waved him impatiently to a chair. He sat twiddling his thumbs, literally, as she finished the call. One of the walls of the high-ceilinged office was floor-to-ceiling glass, providing an impressive view out onto the 13th *arrondissement*.

"My mother," Dubois said, as she placed her iPhone down and slid it to one side of her large desk. She made a face as if the call had gone badly. Pierre smiled back like he didn't particularly care.

"How can I help?"

She ignored the offer and fixed him with a probing look. "How's it going?" she asked instead, then sat back in her oversized white leather chair while Pierre considered how to respond.

The timescale was what freaked her out the most, so he went with that. "There are over a million separate documents in my section of the cache. It's going to take as long as it takes." He shrugged. "I warned you about this."

But she surprised him by shaking her head. "I'm not concerned about the speed. At least not at the moment. I am concerned about the safety of my staff, including you, Pierre. As much as that might shock you."

He rolled his eyes, knowing it would piss her off, and then, since she was sitting far enough back from her desk to let him see, he let his eyes drop down to her legs. In good shape, considering her age.

"Have you come across anything more regarding the Mancini family?"

He shrugged. "Bits and pieces. I'm pulling it together."

"They're implicated?"

"Up to their necks."

"Tell me about it."

Before he did so Pierre considered, unsure why she was interested in this particular aspect.

"As far as I can gather, every couple of months a lawyer representing the Mancini family travels to George Town and—"

"George Town? The capital of the Cayman Islands?" she interrupted. She liked to have things completely clear.

"Yes."

"OK." She waved her hand for him to continue.

"It seems he goes with cash, literally a suitcase of cash, and always by private jet because there's less danger of customs inspectors discovering what they're carrying." He paused to check she was following. Her soft hazel eyes didn't leave his.

"Once there the money's put into a bank, and then moved to one of several new accounts, each placed within a different shell company. These don't appear to do anything except hold and funnel money. But it doesn't stay there long. It might be days later, it might be weeks, but soon the money is moved again, and then again – different routes every time – and then finally it starts to turn up in various investments overseas. Shopping malls, government infrastructure – bridges, that sort of thing."

"And how do we know this, how do we show it?"

"It's difficult. Sometimes it's a case of the amounts matching up as the money flows from one to the next. But," – he paused – "other times we find notes explaining it."

"What do you mean?"

Cloarec smiled. "The process they use is so complex that the lawyers routing the money seem to get confused, so it's like they leave themselves a map." His eyes glinted at the memory of when they'd established this, and began to crack the code the firm had used to hide their activities. "But I need more time. There are millions of individual documents to work through."

Pierre fell silent, assuming she would tell him he needed to work faster, but instead she just sat there, those elegant legs crossed, her forehead lightly crumpled in thought. Pierre thought again how strange it was that she – an ordinary girl from a fishing village miles out west – had ended up on that side of the desk while he – from a well-known family and with a distinguished career behind him – was still on this side. On the other hand, he rather liked the fact that his byline would be taking the lead when they published the story – the biggest, most important leak of confidential financial information the world had ever seen. He waited.

The story had come in completely out of the blue. A woman in her sixties, with dark skin, greying hair and a spark of defiance in her eyes had arrived at the front desk and asked to see Pierre Cloarec, the famous journalist. When he came down, a little reluctantly, she handed him a pen drive which she claimed to contain information downloaded from a secret server from a company in the Cayman Islands, where she'd worked for over twenty years vacuuming and mopping the floors. Only this time, she promised, she'd really cleaned them out. Cloarec had told her to wait while he went back upstairs and checked the file. He quickly discovering millions upon millions of emails, financial spreadsheets, photocopies of passports, company incorporation papers and other corporate records detailing movements of money, and ultimate ownership of obscure financial entities. Almost immediately names leapt out at him. Politicians – not just famous names in France but world leaders – sportsmen, celebrities, fashion icons. It was a veritable who's who of tax avoidance and, by the looks of it, tax evasion.

It was obviously far more than even Cloarec could handle,

and he'd had no option but to bring the woman upstairs to
Dubois' office. There the negotiations had begun. At first she
had demanded one million euros in payment, but that was
crazy. For some time Dubois had tried to explain to her that
journalism didn't work that way. That if they paid for the information it could leave the paper open to a law suit, accusations of
incentivising theft. But the former cleaner had stood her
ground, rather impressively Cloarec had thought. She'd told
Dubois that if they wouldn't pay for the information, she would
destroy it. She claimed she'd already risked her life to bring
them the drive, and that when the first articles were published
she would need to hide behind a new identity, and that it would
take money to do so. It was quite clear this was true.

At that point Dubois made her most controversial decision
as editor in chief. She called the heads of several other newspapers – the *New York Times*, the *Guardian* in London and *El
País* in Spain, amongst others – and explained what they had.
Together they brokered a deal. Each newspaper would
contribute a small amount to enable the cleaner to build a new
life, under a new identity, where she would be safe. Working
together the newspapers would spread their own risk against
legal action.

At the same time, the vast haul of data would be split into
smaller chunks, and each title would provide a small team of
journalists to examine one piece, sharing what they discovered
to allow each paper to publish a series of stories, each exclusive
in their respective countries. In *Le Monde*'s case the journalistic
team would be headed by Pierre himself, but aided, when available, by a junior reporter named Clémence Girard.

"How close are you?" Dubois broke her thoughtful silence at
last.

"I need another..." – Pierre pretended to think – "two

months. Three at the most. Then we'll be ready to blow this thing apart."

He knew full well he could be ready sooner, but – along with the journalists from the other papers – they had settled on giving this timescale to their editors. It was wise to build in a little float to their deadline. But it seemed that this time Dubois' concern really wasn't about the time it was taking.

"And you haven't noticed anyone? Following you perhaps? Nothing out of the ordinary in your apartment?"

Pierre frowned. "Nothing." He thought a moment, then dismissed the idea as ridiculous. "No. Relax."

"*Non.*" Dubois shook her hair, cut short and dyed blonde. "I cannot relax." She took a deep breath but said nothing more. Something about her demeanour unsettled Pierre more than he'd expected.

"I cannot relax," Dubois repeated, then fell back into her previous brooding silence.

"What is it?" he asked after a while.

Her eyes flicked up and met his. "I don't know if I should tell you this or not."

"Then you probably should."

"No, I probably should not." She rolled her chair forwards, putting her elbows on the desk, and fixed him with a stare.

"I have been informed that the firm where the data was taken from is aware that documents were copied."

Pierre felt his eyes widen in surprise. His heart rate increase.

"How do they know?"

Dubois waved a hand, dismissing the question. "Something about a computer logging the file transfer." She shook her head again. "I don't have the details."

"Well how do you know *that*?"

For a moment she wouldn't meet his gaze. "Let me just say that it has come to my attention via a source. I cannot say more."

"*What?* What kind of source? Where?"

"I cannot say." She touched a finger to her lips and lowered her voice. "A source inside the security services. Obviously I cannot reveal their identity."

"And you *told* them?" Pierre's voice rose sharply. "You confirmed we had it?"

"Of course not." She shook her head impatiently. "It was a fishing expedition. My... friend enquired whether this was something that might be of concern to us. I told them I didn't know what they were talking about. And I think they believed me."

"You think?"

She opened her mouth to reply, but stayed quiet. Pierre was silent for a moment too, thinking hard.

"So no one knows we have it? The data?"

She shook her head. "I don't know. *Our* source" – as per standard practice they didn't name the cleaning woman who'd brought them the files – "is a French speaker, so presumably it would not be difficult to work out she would come to a French newspaper, if her intention was to go to the press. From there, *Le Monde* is the most obvious choice." Her lips were thin.

Pierre didn't reply, but he parsed the logic of this and found nothing there to reassure him.

"*Merde.*"

Dubois ignored this. "Furthermore, I do not know how *much* the firm knows – whether we have nearly all of their files or if they've simply lost a few unimportant papers. And I do not know who they have told about the leak. But clearly it puts us at some considerable risk." She leaned closer, tapping a red-painted fingernail on her white desktop.

"I also fear that, should anybody be watching us, they would see you working hard on a confidential story, and thus it would be easy to put two and two together."

Pierre pushed his chair back and let his legs fall a little open, trying to project a confidence he wasn't feeling.

"I'm not concerned."

"You should be. While you've been focussing on how the Mancini family move their money, I've been looking at how they handle other aspects of business. They're known for their extreme brutality, even in the world of organised crime. They have a particular calling card. When people cross them they cut off their fingers, before garrotting them to death."

Dubois stared at Cloarec, and despite himself he felt a tingling sensation in his hands.

"What do you want me to do?" he heard himself protest. "We're not going to stop. *I'm* not going to stop." He did feel brave now. "This is what we're here for, this newspaper. You know that, or you ought to."

"I have no intention of killing the story," she snapped back. "Only in protecting it, until we are ready to publish. After that no one will dare to attack; their guilt would be too obvious." She paused. "At least that is the hope."

Pierre didn't reply.

"I think you should get out of Paris."

"Huh?" His eyes flicked up in surprise. "*What?*"

"Get out of town. You're known here. You would be easy to find if someone was looking for you. You have regular habits. Even *I* know that if you're late for a deadline on Tuesday you'll be at the café playing chess with Eric Miller. And squash on... what is it, Thursdays?"

Pierre's expression darkened. "Where do you want me to go? The Cayman Islands?" He meant it sarcastically, but she didn't rise to it.

"You'd hardly be any safer there. No, I have a better idea." The beginnings of a smile played on her lips. As if she was aware that he had no idea what she was going to say, and that's why it would work.

"My uncle died earlier this year. We haven't dealt with the house yet, so it's empty. You could live there. And it's in the middle of nowhere. In the village of Plourec. Out on the west coast." She stopped, and watched him.

"Have you gone mad?" he asked.

She didn't reply, but simply kept her eyes on his, until he heard himself speak again.

"Plourec? I've never heard of it."

"That's the idea, Pierre."

"But..." he began to protest, but failed to find the words.

Dubois changed tack.

"It's only a small place," she said. "But it's very comfortable, and it backs right onto the ria – it's really very pretty." She smiled, as if picturing it in her mind. "It even has its own jetty. But more importantly it's quiet, and there's Wi-Fi, you'll be able to work—"

"No," he interrupted. "Absolutely not. Where is this we're talking about anyway? *Brittany?*" He said the last word as if the far north-western region of France was some distant and highly inferior backwater, still home perhaps to tribes of Neanderthals.

"Yes." Her voice was cold. "Finisterre, to be precise." Her eyes flicked to a photograph on the wall. A lighthouse in a storm on a Finisterre headland.

"That's miles away." He backed off a little.

"Yes. And that's why you'll be safer there."

Suddenly Pierre got to his feet. He strode to the window, stopped but didn't look out, then turned on his heel.

"I can work here. I can change my habits. I'm completely safe in my apartment, and I can visit different cafés, change when I go—"

"I know you believe the pen is mightier than the sword, Pierre," she interrupted. "But it's not *literally* true. They operate two-man teams of professional assassins. They're completely ruthless."

"But..." – he searched for an argument to defeat this point – "this is *Paris*. They wouldn't—"

"Are you sure about that? If they learn of the hell we're about to unleash on them, they wouldn't murder to try and stop it?"

"It wouldn't work. We have the *New York Times*, the *Guardian*."

"They don't know that. Even if they did, I don't think it would stop them."

Pierre pressed a hand into his forehead.

"I need to be here, Lucille. I can't work anywhere else."

"Why not?"

For a moment Pierre considered telling her he couldn't work surrounded by uneducated farmers and their cows, but something about the look on her face – and the position she occupied – stopped him.

"I just cannot."

She looked away, dismissing the response.

He took a moment, trying to think clearly about what she was saying.

"There's really no need," he said a moment later. "The Mancini family might not even know anything. And even if they do, how would they know I'm working on the story?"

She stared at him a moment before replying. "You're the best journalist this paper has. One of the best it's *ever* had. Who else am I going to give it to?"

The answer bewildered him, catching and keeping him in a trap of flattery.

"How long do you envision me staying there for? Not the whole two months?"

"You said three a moment ago."

"Two, three whatever." He flushed, angry now.

She shrugged. "Maybe. Maybe it would be wise to stay a little longer, after we publish I mean. At least until things settle down. The point is, if neither of us tell anyone else that you're out there, it doesn't matter what the Mancini family know: they won't find you."

"But what about *my* family? I can't just leave them."

"Your daughter's studying dance in Seville. And you already left your wife, I heard you weren't speaking?" That was a low blow, and Dubois lifted a hand in apology. "I'm sorry. But you have to see the logic in what I'm saying. While you're here there's a risk, however small, that you're going to attract the attention of someone who doesn't want you working on this story. But no one's going to notice you in Plourec. And the cottage is empty; there's no rent to pay, so it won't cost the newspaper anything." His eyes met hers sharply, and she lifted her hand a second time.

"I'm sorry, but I cannot pretend such things do not matter."

Slowly and gradually, but with a depressing inevitability, the issue of money had grown with each year that Cloarec had worked in the newspaper industry, until it now impacted every decision. Yet it was still the domain of an editor, and her mentioning it now was a reminder to Pierre that she had the authority to make this decision, whatever he felt about it. He could fight it, but she could take him off the story if she'd made up her mind. Obviously she was thinking the same thing.

"This is not an option Pierre. If you say no, I'll give the story to Jérôme."

He shook his head. "It'll take him weeks just to get back to where I am now. You'll miss your deadline with the other papers."

"Clémence is better than you think, she can bring him up to speed."

He briefly considered going over her head. The newspaper's billionaire owner rarely intervened in its day-to-day running, but for a story this big... On the other hand, the same owner had already backed Dubois by giving her the editorship.

"*Merde*," he said again, shaking his head. "What's it like, this cottage?"

She smiled again, the wistful smile. "Like I said, it's nice. You could even do a little fishing." She thought for a moment, then added, "If there's time."

"I don't have a car. How would I get there?"

"This will come as a surprise to you, Pierre, but France has an extensive network of public transport known as trains. For a small fee you can even ride one as far as Brittany, would you believe." Her smile was deeper now. She knew she'd won. "When you get there, my uncle had a Peugeot, it's still there. I believe it's still running."

"And what about Clémence? You're surely not suggesting she comes with me? I cannot share with her."

"*Non.*" She shook her head. "The cottage only has one bedroom, and I don't think she would thank me." She offered Pierre an ironic smile, and he tutted as he looked away.

"The village has a small hotel. The tourist season is over for the year. I've checked and they can put her up." Dubois shrugged. "She won't be there that much anyway, a couple of days each week, at most."

Pierre turned back to her darkly. "What about the cost of that? I thought this was about saving you money?"

Dubois shook her head again. "*Non.* This is about you not winding up murdered and your body dumped in the Seine."

Pierre stared at her, angry but out of arguments. It didn't quite stop him though.

"I don't think this is remotely necessary. But I don't see that I have a choice."

EIGHTEEN

The journey began considerably better than Pierre had imagined. The TGV train took him all the way to Quimper, taking only three-and-a-half hours, and his seat in Première Classe gave him a table on which to sort through a few more documents, a glass of passable *vin rouge* and even Wi-Fi to exchange emails with his counterpart in Madrid. After that things started living satisfactorily down to his expectations. There was an hour wait, in the rain, for a regional bus that stopped at every tiny village, and in one case – inexplicably – at a telegraph pole, before it finally lurched to a halt in the little village of Plourec. The rain had reduced to drizzle when he stepped down and shouldered his sports bag in which he'd packed a few clothes. He looked around.

Dubois had provided him with a hand-drawn map, very quaint. Obviously he'd ignored it and instead typed the address into Google, but now he'd arrived his mobile had no signal. He tried waving it hopefully in the air for a few moments, but eventually was forced to dig around in his work bag – a shoulder-slung laptop-sleeve that was fashionable on the streets of Paris –

for the map. As he did so a tractor approached, thick mud stuck
to its huge wheels. Pierre stepped back in some alarm when he
realised the driver had no intention of slowing the monstrous
machine for mere pedestrians, and as it swooshed past he
caught the man scowling at Pierre as if he were somehow in the
wrong.

Pierre muttered several expletives under his breath about
the nature of the backward locals in this part of the country,
before following Dubois' map along a deserted main street and
down towards what must be the edge of the ria. There was the
hotel, small – and apparently closed – but clearly one of the
larger buildings in the village. There was a bar too, Pierre was
pleased to see, although it looked sad, a handful of tables sitting
empty in the rain. The door was open however, and he was
tempted to go in, but decided to pace himself and at least drop
off his luggage first. Finally he came to a row of what were
presumably thought by some to be delightful cottages – they
had tiny windows with brightly painted frames, some with
flowers in window boxes. But to him they just looked cramped
and damp. The first door he passed was painted blue, and the
map made it clear this wasn't the dead uncle's abode, nor the
next, with the green door, but the one at the far end, its door a
rich shade of red. Here he stopped at the gate, studying the little
cottage that was to be his home for God-knows-how-long.
Finally the still-falling rain propelled him unhappily towards
the door, where he fumbled in his pockets for the key. He
unlocked the door and stepped inside.

It smelt musty; that was his first impression, that and the
darkness. Most of the curtains were drawn, and when he
opened them he coughed at the amount of dust they launched
into the air. He opened the windows too, despite the weather, to
let some of the fresh air inside.

He looked around. The place was not just fully furnished, it looked as if the mysterious deceased uncle had just popped out for an aperitif. That thought reminded Pierre that he hadn't enquired about the man's fate. But perhaps he could piece it together? The walls were full of paintings, photographs and even newspaper clippings, and a rather beautiful wooden bureau pushed into a corner was stuffed with papers, which would doubtless tell the story of the uncle. A much younger Pierre might have been interested, but now he had plenty of work to be getting on with. He sighed at the thought.

There was a note on the table addressed to him, placed under a glass vase with a few flowers in it:

Bonjour

Welcome to Plourec! I have had a little clean-up, changed the sheets and put a few things in the fridge to get you started. Lucille tells me you might need the car so the key is on the hook on the wall. I think it has some diesel in the tank. But André thinks it might not work. Très desolee!

Enjoy your stay!

Jeanne

Pierre frowned. He guessed Jeanne must be Lucille's mother, but of André he had no idea – father perhaps? She had left a pen next to the note, and he picked it up, casually adding the correct accents to the word 'désolé' before tutting loudly and screwing the note into a little ball. Then he went to the fridge to see what the woman had left, where his continued contempt that anyone could live out their life in such a place was tested by the quality and quantity of food. There were sliced meats and sausages, cheeses, fresh-looking salads, enormous eggs – with actual feathers still stuck to their shells – a glass bottle of milk and jar of yogurt, pots of crème fraîche, and what appeared to be home-made pâté and a fine-looking quiche. There were two bottles of white wine in the fridge too, and now that he looked, three bottles of red lined up by the cooker, along with a baguette in a brown paper bag. He tutted again, but less loudly this time.

Pierre checked his watch, and since it was past three he opened one of the bottles of red and poured himself a glass, which he drank while smoking a cigarette with the back door open. It had a split halfway down so you could open just the top half and lean on the lower part while watching the rain on the water – which he did. There wasn't a breath of wind and the rain still wasn't that heavy, but it was hard to be clear where the sea stopped and the rain began. Perhaps it was all water, just different degrees of wetness, he thought. Far away, perhaps a mile on the other side, the inlet met low-lying land, and somewhere in the middle a lonely yacht motored silently by. He wondered quite how he had found himself in what appeared to be a literal backwater.

He went to see the bedroom, just big enough to fit the double bed and a single wardrobe. He braced himself when he opened this, expecting to see the dead uncle's clothes hanging from the rails, but it was empty, except for a clattering of hangers. He sniffed, detecting a whiff of mould, but no worse than his own apartment in Paris, which suffered terribly from the problem. The idea occurred to him that he should have arranged for a man to come in and fix it while he was away, but he knew it wouldn't happen. He would be too busy.

He closed the wardrobe and his eye was taken by a glowing green light from the wall – the Wi-Fi router. He pulled out his laptop – the code was printed on the device, as Dubois had promised, although the speed was predictably provincial. He would be able to work, but streaming anything interesting seemed out of the question. Not that Pierre Cloarec watched much television. He had little interest in sports, and considered most popular entertainment beneath him. But at the same time, he did occasionally like to watch a detective series – but even that pleasure would be denied him.

At least the bed seemed comfortable and clean; the woman – the name of Dubois' mother had already escaped him – had put fresh sheets on. He wondered for a moment if they'd be changed while he was staying there. But probably not. It wasn't a hotel.

The bedroom window also looked out over the water, and its still surface told him the rain had finally stopped. So he went outside to check the car, an old Peugeot 306 that had been parked alongside the cottage long enough for weeds to grow up around its wheels, which made it hard to open the door. When he finally forced it free, he discovered the springs in the driver's seat were broken when he sat down and felt so low to the ground he might have been in a racing car. That effect was lost when he tried to start the motor and found the battery quite dead. He got out again and tried to slam the door, except the weeds prevented him. He kicked them away, staining his brown brogues with smears of fresh green, and swore as he tried to rub them off.

Beside the car was a tarpaulin coving a sizeable deposit of chopped wood; he gathered as much as he could hold and took it inside to the little stove that seemed to be the property's only source of heat. He spent fifteen minutes trying to get the damn thing to light. There was a supply of tinder and old newspapers – *Le Monde* and a local paper – but he used most of it up without success. Finally he filled the metal firebox almost full with newspaper and squirted it with an entire bottle of lighter fluid refill which he happened to have bought at the station that morning. Then he struck a match and tossed it in. This time when he closed the glass door the newspaper quickly turned into a roaring inferno, and the logs he had stupidly placed underneath finally caught. Rather satisfied with his work, he poured himself a top-up of wine and quickly knocked it back, while around him the room warmed.

Perhaps it wasn't so bad. If only he wasn't a bit too drunk to do any work.

NINETEEN

Pierre's habit, when in Paris at least, was to make himself an espresso upon waking, work for a couple of hours, and then take his second coffee of the day at about eleven in one of the small bars near his apartment. Obviously that was out of the question, but the need for caffeine remained. He rooted in the cupboards, eventually finding a French press, but he despised the weak, watery coffee it produced. So he browsed painfully slowly on Amazon until he found an espresso machine, then added his new address. But he paused before submitting the order. The entire purpose of coming here was to keep a low profile. Would this simply announce where he was? A recent story he'd worked on, which incidentally had won him a nomination for one of the most prestigious journalism awards in Europe, was an exposé on how governments and multinational businesses had greatly increased the breadth and depth of their online surveillance of individuals. He had fought with Dubois over one paragraph in particular:

We think we know, from the likes of Edward Snowden, that our government is watching us. But their capacity then was nothing compared to what they can achieve today. Every single one of us should now assume our every email is being read, our webcams are always watching us, and our cell phones never stop eavesdropping as we work, sleep and fuck.

Dubois had insisted upon changing the last words to '*work, sleep and play*', destroying the sense of shock he'd been aiming to achieve, and quite possibly resulting in him not actually winning the award. He shook his head at the memory and hit 'buy' on the order. Then he filled the French press.

He turned his attention to the bureau. Someone – presumably Lucille's mother – had cleared space on it ready for Pierre to work. He set himself up there, and managed an hour before his rumbling stomach and the weakness of the coffee made him give up. He checked the fridge again, but one thing that hadn't been provided were the fresh pastries he usually ate for breakfast. He considered another round of bread and meat, but the remains of his plate from the previous night looked unappetising so he pulled on his jacket and stepped outside to see what Plourec could offer.

The rains from the day before had cleared the air, giving it a freshness that he found he could taste. It was startlingly different from the heavy, particle-filled Parisian air he was used to, and he begrudgingly found himself enjoying the inhales and exhales that filled his lungs with a champagne-like fizz. He almost – but just stopped short – put a spring in his step.

He continued down what passed as Plourec's main street. There was a little more than he'd seen the day before. A couple of art galleries had window displays. His eyes ranged over the offerings as he passed, dismissing everything that was either a seascape or a beach scene, which left nothing else. There were a couple of shops selling plastic water-shoes, plastic buckets and plastic fishing lines for children, which made him think briefly of vacations past when his daughter was young. Outside the bar he'd seen the day before, two old men were sitting at a rusty table, as if on guard. He decided he'd go in, but only if he found nowhere better. The men stared silently as Pierre passed, their faces not unfriendly, but certainly not friendly either.

At the end of the village he came to a small harbour, where three large fishing boats were tied up way below him, since the tide was out. A fourth boat was approaching, just passing the harbour entrance, protected from the ocean's waves by long, rocky arms. Pierre joined a handful of other people watching it arrive as if this were the chief entertainment of the day, a group of bored-looking locals and tourists. A small boy on a bicycle eyed him curiously, a young man in dirty jeans and T-shirt huffed plumes of smoke from his vape, one eye on the approaching boat, the other on a video game on his phone. The sun came out and Pierre noticed that the dock sparkled, as if the concrete it was built from had been laced with diamonds. For a moment he couldn't understand it, but then he saw each diamond was in fact a fish scale, glued to the dock by the oils of its former owner.

The boat approached close enough that Pierre could hear the shouts from on board, though they were speaking in Breton. Yellow-trousered fishermen did things with ropes, quickly and expertly, and the engine suddenly roared as the vessel neared its berth, apparently too fast but then somehow slowing in the last moments, sending whirlpools of oily water rolling out from the harbour wall. Moments later it was secured, but the activity didn't cease. They'd parked the thing below a hoist-like device – a small crane really – and one of the fishermen expertly scaled a ladder set in the wall of the dock and jogged towards it. He popped a cover off its controls, and moments later a hook descended to the deck of the fishing boat, and then lower, through a hatchway that had been opened in preparation.

There was more shouting, then the hook reappeared. But now it was attached to a large plastic container filled with ice and fish. The smell of diesel and salt mingled with the wet, bloody odour of the fish, while the electric whine of the winch cut into the air. Pierre felt himself drawn with the other watchers towards the boxes as they piled up on the dock.

Another man appeared and poked a foot into the crates, digging into the ice to better see the fish that were laid underneath. Pierre realised that he, along with the young man with jeans, were probably buyers, waiting to bid for the catch. Standing next to the dock was a large modern building with wide, shuttered doors. One of the fishermen disappeared inside, reappearing a moment later in a forklift truck. More diesel fumes pumped out, black and smoky this time, as he collected the fish and carried the crates back inside. Again the small crowd followed him, Pierre flowing with them.

Inside, the building was set out almost like a theatre. At one end was a row of seating, but on the other, instead of a stage the crates of fish were placed on a conveyor belt. Everyone quickly found their place, and within minutes the fish had been sold. Pierre struggled to follow exactly who had bought what: although some of the men had spoken in rough, heavily accented French, the names of the species of fish were unknown to him. But everyone appeared satisfied with the transaction. A lorry appeared, its side bearing the logo of a seafood company, and ten minutes after they'd been offloaded from the boat, the fish were loaded inside and driven away. The younger man in jeans shrugged and walked away. The fishermen returned to the boat, tidying away ropes. The small crowd on the dock melted away.

Pierre was left alone and, feeling suddenly self-conscious, he walked away. But instead of heading back to the cottage, he wanted to keep exploring his new environment. Past the harbour there were more cottages. These didn't have the ria, but they were closer to the beach – which he hadn't even known existed. He soon reached it, climbing down a few rocks before stepping onto the firm, pale sand. The tide was still out, a long way away, but the ocean sparkled like diamonds. There were a handful of people on the beach, just figures in the distance. A pair carried surfboards under their arms. Pierre felt a twinge of guilt as he sat to remove his shoes and socks – he ought to be working – but something made him keep going, a strange desire to reach the water's edge. The sand was cool under his feet, crumbly and soft like brown sugar where the sea hadn't washed it, then hard and firm where it was stripped clean and packed hard each day by the tide.

As he walked towards the sea he spotted small pools of water, apparently sculpted by mysterious forces as the sea drew back. He stumbled into one, but found it so warm and pleasant that he sought out more. Eventually he reached the water's edge, a blurred line between land and sea. He paddled in cautiously, shocked at first by how much colder it was. But there was a pleasure somehow within the pain and he forced himself to stay there, the tiny wavelets washing every now and then up his hairy calves. His soft white feet were soon shrivelled and pruned from the water.

On the way back he found his mood significantly lifted. He came to the bar, with the same two men outside, who still stared at him. But this time he nodded a polite good morning and stepped inside. He was pleasantly surprised: from the street the front room had looked dark and uninviting, but a second room beyond boasted a large glass window looking out over the ria, and framed in such a way that the view was spectacular. A barman was washing glasses next to a fair-sized coffee machine. A handful of the tables were in use; Pierre recognised some of the crowd who'd been watching down at the harbour. Another man caught his eye, around the same age as Pierre and well dressed, in a good-quality woollen jacket and shirt. He sat reading a newspaper by the window.

Pierre ordered a coffee and croissant, and greedily breathed in the smell as the machine ground the beans. When he took his first sip he was finally forced to reassess his opinion on Dubois' idea to send him here. He had arrived with pre-conceived ideas that Plourec was the arsehole of nowhere, with absolutely nothing going for it and populated only by insular, inbred morons who did nothing and understood nothing about how the world really worked. This, he was now willing to acknowledge, was an exaggeration. There *was* a sort of life here, very different and clearly inferior to the pace, power and gravitas of the city: the beating heart of the nation. But the people here did serious work nonetheless – such as harvesting the bounty of the ocean to supply the dining tables of the capital. And there was a wild beauty to the place too, he conceded, looking out of the plate-glass window at the ria that sparkled in the mid-morning sun. And it might even help him to focus on what could be the most important story he had ever worked on. Perhaps coming here would help him as he struggled to tease out from the documents the stories and narratives that would resonate not just with his fellow Parisians, but with ordinary people all across France and all around the world.

He sipped a first-rate coffee, and resisted the temptation to have another. Instead he left a generous tip and returned quickly to the cottage, where he went straight back to his laptop. This time he was able to lose himself in his work.

TWENTY

The bar – it didn't seem to have a name – quickly became a new habit for Pierre. It opened early and closed late, and though there was a steady stream of tourists who advertised themselves as such by the guide books they studied at the wooden tables, Pierre also began to recognise the faces of the locals. The same barman was there every morning, while at midday an older woman took over. The two old boys who guarded the door were also a fixture in the morning but disappeared in the afternoons – though Pierre had no idea where they went. The well-dressed man who sat by the window was a regular too. On the third or possibly fourth visit he must have noticed Pierre, as he offered a polite *bonjour* as he came over to where Pierre was sitting at the bar, folding away his newspaper to leave for other customers. Without giving it any thought Pierre asked if he might read it. The man nodded politely.

"Of course."

He replied in French, but the accent was strange. It took Pierre a moment to place it.

"You're American?"

A look of mild surprise came over the other man's face, but he nodded again.

"I'm working with some Americans at the moment, and you have a similar accent," Pierre explained, but as he finished speaking he wondered if the other man would understand. But he smiled and, when he replied, his grammar was perfect.

"It doesn't matter how long I'm here, I get found out with a single word." The humour was subtle enough that Pierre read it as an invitation – or perhaps a test – the man wanted to see if his words would go over Pierre's head, as they doubtless would with the farmers and fishermen who mostly populated this town.

"Pierre Cloarec." He held out his hand. "I'm here for a few weeks, getting out of Paris to work on a project."

"Richard Brown." The handshake was measured. Cautious still.

"What brings an American all the way out here?"

Brown held out his hands for a moment, as if that was an answer, but then smiled.

"I moved here a while ago. Got out of the rat race."

Now it was Pierre's turn to size him up.

"Government?" It was evident from his clothes, the way he held himself.

"Nearly. Diplomatic service." Brown paused, glancing at the newspaper that lay on the counter between them.

"*Pierre Cloarec?* I've read you. There was a big piece a while back. Something about how our governments are spying on us all, no?"

Inside Pierre was delighted, but he kept his face casual. It wasn't often his name was recognised, but when it was, the people who knew him were almost always the right sort of people.

"*Oui.*"

Brown paused. "And you're here working on something?

He raised his eyebrows, but kept his voice discreet. "Must be something interesting?"

Pierre gave an offhand shrug. "It might be."

"I'm sorry, I don't mean to pry."

"No, it's fine." There was a silence between the two men, before Brown nodded again.

"Well, it's very nice to meet you, but I have to go." He paused, offered the briefest of smiles. "But perhaps I might see you here again?"

"Perhaps," Pierre found himself replying.

That afternoon Clémence turned up for what would be a two-night stay in Plourec's only hotel, to help sift through the data. She arrived on the same bus that Pierre had taken just over a week before. He decided to meet her off the bus, keen for some air, and perhaps the chance to watch her descend from the steep steps. She usually wore tight jeans, which showed off her shapely legs and an admirable behind.

Pierre had given Clémence the tedious role of looking through each document as they appeared in the files, and entering it onto a database which had been set up by someone from the *Le Monde* tech department. She would give each document a unique number, against which she would list various keywords – the names of which lawyers had worked on it, for which client (if known), using which shell company, and the exact amount involved. It was then much easier to see which documents were linked, and begin the process of under-standing exactly how – which was Pierre's role. At the begin-ning of their work he'd come up with the analogy of a jigsaw puzzle, explaining that she would be finding all the green pieces and setting them aside so that he could assemble them into an image of a tree. Except that he was actually building an incriminating picture of the financial dealings of the Mancini crime family, three prominent French politicians, a Ballon d'Or-winning footballer and several of France's most well-loved celebrities. He'd thought it a helpful analogy, but Clémence gave him the same look his daughter did when she accused him of mansplaining. Even so, she'd done a decent enough job and he could have done with more of her time – thousands of names appeared in the data, thousands of wealthy clients who had used the Cayman Island firm to obscure their wealth either legally, illegally or in a complex mixture of both.

When Dubois had told him Clémence would only be part time, he hadn't even bothered arguing. Cloarec's career with *Le Monde* had spanned two very different eras: from when newspapers were well-staffed and unthreatened in their role of appointing the powerful and holding them to account; to today, where a toxic combination of social media and agile online-only websites, or individuals with Twitter accounts, could match or surpass the reach of an entire media organisation. These days, if it could be done on the cheap, it probably would be.

"How was the trip?" he asked as they walked the few hundred metres to the entrance of the small hotel.

Clémence shrugged, flicking her long blonde hair over one shoulder. "Fine. I worked. Did you get the papers on Vicenzo Mancini? I think he's implicated, no?"

Pierre made a non-committal sound, meant to suggest they would talk work later, and they went into the hotel. Pierre waited in the small lobby while she went up to her room to drop off her suitcase. He watched her buttocks while she climbed the stairs.

They worked the whole afternoon, breaking finally at eight when Clémence finally announced she was tired and hungry from the journey. He admitted he had given little thought to dinner, but she surprised him by digging around in the kitchen and making a meal with some pasta and sausages, which he had so far not touched. They ate, discussing the case in general, and worked another hour before she left for the hotel.

TWENTY-ONE

Pierre and Clémence went to the bar for coffee at eleven the next day, already with a few hours' work under their belts. He had quite forgotten about the American – Richard Brown – but there he was, sitting in his window seat and reading *Le Monde* as on the first day Pierre had noticed him. Brown raised a hand in greeting, but didn't come over to interrupt them. Nor did he the next day, when they again saw him in his regular seat. But the third day, when Clémence had returned to Paris and Pierre was again seated at the bar, Richard Brown did come over. He folded the newspaper, ready to place it in the rack for customers to read with their coffees.

"Good morning! Would you like to read it?"

"Morning." Pierre waved his hand, to indicate both his thanks for the offer but that he didn't require the paper.

"Of course. I suppose if one actually writes the newspaper, there is no requirement to read it?"

Pierre smiled. "There's nothing of mine today. But I already glanced through the online edition."

"Ah. I see." Brown considered this a moment, before offering an opinion.

"I myself prefer the feel of a real newspaper in my hands. A traditionalist, I suppose." He was about to take his leave when Pierre replied, not taking the time to consider his words before they escaped his mouth.

"Do you have time for a glass of wine?"

It was a little early, by any measure. But Pierre felt the twin pulls of a slight sense of loneliness, having that morning seen Clémence to her bus, and the ever-present temptation of procrastination.

The American seemed about to politely refuse the offer, but then changed his mind.

"If you're not too busy? I'm retired, I have all the time in the world. At least for now."

Pierre ordered a bottle, choosing a good vintage but nothing showy, and they took it to the table by the window. Pierre noted it offered the best of the views, the ria stretching out away from them, the far side of the estuary only just visible in the light mist.

"So you're here every day?" Pierre asked as he poured the wine.

"I'm afraid I'm a creature of habit."

"Where did you work? Before you retired?"

Brown took a while to reply.

"I ping-ponged. In Washington, obviously, but then Senegal, and Belgium, since I had the language. I studied French with International Relations at university," he explained. "Then Switzerland, before I was transferred to the US Embassy in Paris." He shrugged. "I was there nearly ten years."

"You know Ambassador Walker then?" Pierre asked, interested. The man was well known, a political appointee of an American administration that represented almost the opposite of *Le Monde*'s liberal politics.

"A major reason I retired," Brown replied with light

humour. They both smiled. But Pierre wasn't done asking questions.

"And what brought you out here?"

Brown spread his hands. "I used to come here in the summers. I like the calm. The peace and quiet. We don't get so many tourists here, not like in the south. And not too many Parisians either. I'm less likely to be found."

"Found?"

"I'm officially retired, but they still ask me to do bits and pieces. If I can avoid being seen, I can avoid any more work." He smiled, then paused as if considering whether to go on. "I'm also trying to write a memoir. But very slowly. I'm not a real writer, not like you."

Pierre liked this, and he smiled accordingly. Brown's next words surprised him though.

"We are near neighbours, it seems."

"We are?"

"You're in the cottage with the red door, yes? I'm just a few doors down. I saw you the other day, looking around the car. The little Peugeot, is it dead?"

"I think the battery's dead."

"I have..." For the first time Brown's French seemed to let him down. "I don't know the words. In English we call them *jump leads*. To transfer the electrical power from one vehicle to another. If you like we can try to start it?"

"Ah! *Câbles de démarrage*. We call them *start-up cables*." Pierre smiled, and contemplated. On the one hand he detested driving, and had really only inspected the car in the hope it wouldn't work. On the other hand, there was something about the American he liked. He was very different to the popular image of his countrymen – less stupid, more cultured, although Cloarec had long concluded that the best Americans were those one found outside the USA. But even beyond that, there was something about Richard Brown personally that he connected with. He perhaps had stories that could provide colour for any number of future articles. And even if not, he was clearly a potential source of interesting conversation in a town where that was a rare commodity. And if they could get the car going, there was also the possibility of getting out of here without using the damned bus.

"Yes, that would be helpful. *Merci.*"

Brown turned out to own a Peugeot of his own, a 505 estate which even Pierre, with his dislike of driving and all things motoring, nevertheless regarded as a classic. Moreover it ran a big battery, and a few minutes after Brown had manoeuvred it close to the smaller Peugeot and connected the jump leads (Pierre had added the word to his own vocabulary in English), they had it running, grey smoke and drops of dirty water running from its exhaust pipe.

"You should run it for a while to charge the battery," the American advised. "Perhaps take it for a drive to the lighthouse." He pointed up the road, but Pierre looked momentarily confused.

"You haven't been there?" Brown interpreted. "It's most dramatic, especially in a storm."

"I'm actually not sure of the way," Pierre admitted.

"I can show you, if you'd like?"

Pierre paused. Brown had already been more than helpful.

"Are you sure? You don't have work to do? Your memoir?"

Brown gave a light laugh. "It'll keep. I'm not sure it's the most interesting of stories, anyway."

"Come on, let's ride together." He disconnected the cables and slammed the bonnets shut. A few moments later they set off, Pierre's weight causing the smaller Peugeot's seat to sag uncomfortably, while Brown wound down the window and rested a tanned and lightly muscled arm on the frame.

TWENTY-TWO

For Pierre the next few weeks passed in a most amicable way. By rising early (he got up each day at six) and working until midnight, he was able to make good progress on the series of articles, and there was plenty of time in between to deepen his new friendship with Richard Brown. He had eaten his way through most of the food left by Dubois' mother. When he hadn't bothered to replace it Richard had seen it as an opportunity, as he knew of several excellent restaurants only a short drive away. And as expected (and despite Brown's self-deprecatory modesty about his memoir), the American turned out to be an excellent dining companion, with a deep well of interesting stories. However, after a while a strange gap opened up between them. Pierre had learned much of the American's work and family (divorced and no longer speaking to his wife, but on reasonable terms with his two sons, who both worked in Washington), and while he'd shared similar broad details about his own life, he'd stayed silent on what he was working on right now.

In part this was because Brown – presumably with his background in the diplomatic service – had been discreet enough not to ask. But when Pierre took the time to consider the situation, he found it slightly irked him. After all, when the articles came out they would dominate the news agenda worldwide, further cementing his position as one of France's leading journalists, but also raising his profile to being one of the most famous investigative journalists worldwide. And this was something that Pierre would rather like to talk about, even before it happened. Thus he began to drop small hints, both about what it was he was doing and that it wasn't *necessarily* a subject that should be off limits between them. But it wasn't clear whether Richard had picked up on them or not. Clearly, diplomacy was a habit that ran deep.

"Do you fish?" Brown asked one day while they were taking their morning coffee.

"I *eat* fish," Pierre replied.

"I know that, *mon ami*. But do you *catch* it? I have a boat. I only use it when the weather forecast is favourable, since the currents here can be fierce. But tomorrow looks very good. I was wondering if you would like to accompany me? I'll understand if you can't. I don't mean to take you away from your work."

He considered. Richard had mentioned Pierre's work several times in recent days. It was also possibly his last chance for a bit. Clémence would arrive again tomorrow to liaise on the stories, and no doubt also to report back to Dubois. But that was no problem: there were a few small areas where he was behind, but she would be able to catch them up.

"Why not?" he replied.

"Excellent!" Brown beamed. "We'll need to leave early to catch the tide. I can pick you up from your dock at nine?"

"I look forward to it."

. . .

Richard Brown was not quite as expert as the professional fishermen down in the harbour, bumping the little boat against the rickety wooden posts and old car tyres of the small jetty that cut out from the shore. And the boat was very different too. Much smaller, and with only a little part-cabin with bench seats and a VHF radio that crackled into life every now and then. Off the back hung two boat rods, wedged into stainless-steel holders. Bolted to the floor was a cool box, which Brown opened and pulled out two Budweisers, passing one to Pierre.

The engine, an inboard diesel, looked ancient, needing to be started with the help of a large wrench that hung from a hook in the cabin, but Brown swore it was entirely reliable, and indeed it puttered smoothly as they motored out of the ria and into the wide-open sea. Here the boat felt even smaller as it rolled from side to side as the low, lazy swells passed beneath them. Pierre, who wasn't experienced on boats, was unsettled by this at first, but he soon relaxed to match the demeanour of his new friend, who seemed quite at ease. Brown then swung the boat in close to the low cliffs, shouting to Pierre above the din of the engine that this was where the best fishing could be found. Finally he signalled he was going to drop anchor, and the chain rattled violently as it flew out from its locker. Brown waited a few minutes to check they were holding, then he killed the motor, again using the wrench. Finally it was quiet again.

Brown had purchased portions of chopped-up squid from the fishermen in the harbour – which they claimed was the best bait around – and both men threaded them carefully onto their hooks, then dropped the lines down into the clear blue water. It was too deep to see the bottom, but Pierre could see the sunlight penetrating and flashing as it cut its way below them into the blue. Brown opened a locker under the bench seat and pulled out cushions, handing the plumpest to Pierre and making himself comfortable with the other.

The fish, if they were any down there, weren't biting. But the sun was out and the wind so light that the surface of the water took on a glassy appearance. The light swells continued to wash underneath the boat, sighing softly as they expired on the rocks at the base of the cliffs a few hundred metres away. Seabirds wheeled and soared around the jagged towers of rock, which hid the boat from the land. They each drank two beers, crushing each can when they were finished and – following Brown's lead – putting them back into the cool box rather than tossing them into the ocean. Every now and then one of them wound in their line to check the bait was still there or to replace it. And then finally there was a moment of high excitement when Brown's rod tip sunk suddenly, and he fought for a few minutes to reel it in. As the hook neared the surface Pierre could see something silver down in the water snaking first one way then the other. And then, as if it had never been there at all, it escaped the hook and vanished, back into the infinite blue.

"Bad luck," Pierre said. "Did you see what it was?"

"I'm not sure of the name in French." Brown shook his head. "In English I know." He hoisted the hook aboard to add more bait. "In English we call it 'the one that got away'." He grinned.

At twelve o'clock Pierre was starting to feel hungry, and Brown surprised him. It turned out the cool box didn't just contain beer: he'd arranged for a nearby restaurant to pack them a decent lunch. There were fresh baguette sandwiches, some filled with brie and butter, others with thick-sliced ham and Dijon mustard. There were portions of quiche Lorraine, individually wrapped in silver foil, and a Tupperware container with pre-sliced charcuterie. They washed it down with a local cider, and when Pierre was already more than satisfied, Brown produced with a flourish two miniature Tarte Tatins.

"It seems we are not lucky today," Brown said, once lunch

was over and they turned their attention back to the fishing. As usual he spoke in his curious accent and the slightly odd word choice of the non-native speaker. Pierre shrugged, more than content with how the day was going.

"I'm not complaining. I needed a day away from my laptop."

"Of course. I forget, while I laze my days away pretending to write, you really are working hard." Brown smiled, and seemed to notice something with his line, perhaps a fish sniffing at the bait. He picked it up and gave it a cautious, testing tug. But there was nothing there, and he resettled it in the holder.

Pierre sensed the question coming and waited, knowing that this time he would answer.

"What is the mysterious work, if it's not inappropriate for me to ask?" Brown went on, appearing to keep his attention on the tip of his rod. Then he glanced across. "If you cannot say then I do not mean to push you. But you cannot blame a man for being curious."

Pierre felt deeply satisfied, in all sorts of ways. That the question had come, that he had anticipated it would. And that his friend had waited such a respectful length of time to ask it. He looked around a little theatrically, as someone in the empty sea surrounding them might overhear.

"I think I can trust you." He let his eyes twinkle as he spoke. Brown's eyebrows went up, equally playfully.

"It's a very big story, perhaps the biggest of my career."

"Do go on."

Pierre settled himself more comfortably in his seat. "We all suspect that the super-rich, politicians, the very famous use nefarious methods to hide their money, but we've rarely been able to catch them in the act. At least not en masse." He paused to let a smile pass over his lips. "There's a law firm out in the Cayman Islands – I doubt you'll have heard of it, but it's called

Hawthorne and Langley – and we got hold of a data leak from their files. A large leak. A very large leak." Pierre was smiling so hard he had to stop speaking.

"Actually the largest such leak in history."

Brown looked intrigued.

"And? What's in it? This leak?"

"What *isn't* in it might be the better question. We have an almost complete record of everything the firm has been up to for the last fifteen years." Pierre shook his head, still not quite able to believe this himself. "The legal mechanisms to shelter money from tax, and the illegal activities that do the real work beneath the surface. I'm talking politicians, business leaders, footballers, celebrities, even royalty. Some of the most famous names globally."

Brown's forehead was crumpled into a light frown, perhaps still not quite understanding.

"And what have they been up to exactly?"

Pierre shrugged. "You name it, it's there. From simple tax evasion and the hiding of money to full-on money-laundering, on a scale you would not believe. The main story I'm working on involves the Mancini family. They're officially into haulage, construction and waste disposal, but what they really do is operate across Europe bringing in drugs from South America. This earns them an enormous amount of cash, which is then flown into the Cayman Islands, laundered through banks and into shell companies, and invested in all sorts of legitimate projects around the world. I'm talking billions of euros every year. And we have enough proof to bring it all crashing down."

"I haven't heard of the Mancini family," Brown said, but now his face was registering concern.

"You soon will. Arturo Mancini is the head of the family. They say he only became the boss when he murdered his own brother, but of course no one can prove it wasn't an accident. They're old-school mafiosi gangsters."

"They sound dangerous."

"Yes, they are. Actually that's the real reason I've had to come out here. There's a slight risk that the Mancini family are aware of the leak. If that's true there's no limit to what they'd do to stop a story like this coming out."

Brown said nothing, but Pierre was enjoying himself now. He gave a laugh that didn't sound quite as brave as it had in his head.

"The Mancini family likes to leave a particular calling card with its victims. They're garrotted to death, but they're tortured before being killed. They have their fingers cut off."

"Oh, my Lord."

"Yes, exactly." For a moment Pierre wondered if he might have overdone it, if the American might consider it too dangerous to dine out with him, knowing what he was working on. He decided to tone it down a bit.

"But don't worry. There's only a small risk that they'd connect the leak with the work we're doing. Me staying here is simply a precaution. Stay out of Paris until the articles are published – that sort of thing." He offered a courageous smile.

"But of course," Brown replied, but he still looked concerned. "But what happens *when* they're published? Won't they come after you then?"

This was something that Pierre – and his editor – had considered. "Perhaps," he said, and for the first time he wasn't only putting on an act of bravery. "We're also working with the police, sharing some information. When the articles are published it will be coordinated with arrests. Plus it'll be too late by then. It'd be obvious it was them if they tried to retaliate."

"You are a very brave man," Brown said, his voice solemn.

Pierre made a show of waving away the suggestion, but inside he swelled. "I am doing my duty as a journalist. Just as you did yours as a public servant."

"Hardly, *mon ami*. I did not risk my life."

"The risk is very small," Pierre insisted, and then a joke occurred to him. "Unless of course I've made a terrible mistake, and you're not really a former American diplomat, but an assassin for the Mancini family!"

Brown looked shocked for a moment, but then laughed. "Good Lord," he said again, in his slightly off French. "If I were, this would be the perfect place to bump you off. But alas no. I told you my life is not that exciting."

Both men smiled at the modesty of their lies.

The tide hit low at about three, and Brown tried motoring the little boat to different spots, but still without any success. Finally he suggested they head back, though stopping at one final place before giving up.

"The locals tell me that one can sometimes find bass off the sand bar in the mouth of the ria, as the tide rises. Or do you need to get back to work?"

Pierre shrugged again, lazily. The point of the day for him was never about catching fish. But he thought about it. With the time they'd put in, it would be nice to catch something.

"Sure. Let's try one more spot."

A strange thought passed through Pierre's mind. As Brown started the motor, he asked him if he'd mind pulling up the anchor. As he did so, standing on the exposed bow of the little boat, and pulling the rope through one hand then the other, he thought that if Brown really was an assassin for the Mancinis this would be the perfect chance to get him. Brown could come up behind him and hit him over the head with the wrench. With his attention and effort focussed on the anchor, and the noise of the engine, Pierre wouldn't hear a thing. He wouldn't stand a chance. And just thinking that gave him a curious sense of anxiety, despite the ridiculousness of the notion. He was so engaged with the anchor rising towards the boat that Pierre was unable to even check behind him to ensure that Brown was where he should be, at the wheel.

Finally the rope gave way to the chain, which towards the end was covered with a kind of soapy grey clay from the ocean bottom, and then the anchor appeared. He placed it carefully into the locker and turned around. Brown was at the wheel, squinting into the lowering sun. He gave Pierre a thumbs-up and pushed the throttle handle. The little boat surged forward.

With the change of scene the water flattened off, and they worked with lures instead of dead bait. Brown was quick to change their tackle over, and soon they were casting their lines out and reeling the lures back in. And something felt different now. There were strange patterns on the calm surface of the water that suggesting something stirring below. Their conversation slowed as they focussed on the fishing. A buoy in the distance was being tugged nearly underwater by the pull of the tide, flooding quickly now back into the ria.

"Got something," Brown muttered suddenly, and the tip of his rod dipped. The muscles in his arms tightened as he wound the line in, but before he got the fish to the boat Pierre felt his own rod twitch, and then jerk violently in his hands.

"Me too," he said, his attention now focussed on the line pulling off the reel.

"Careful," Brown said, 'we don't want them tangled." He moved to the front of the boat while Pierre fought to pull his fish in. Out of the corner of his eye he saw Brown swing his rod aboard, a handsome silver fish still thrashing from the lure, and then in the water he saw the flash of his own fish.

"That's a good size." Brown's voice cut into his attention. He'd dealt with his own catch now and stood by the side of the boat, a landing net in his hand. "Bring it close and I'll scoop it in."

Pierre did so, and on the second attempt Brown got the net

under the fish and lifted it into the boat. It was a bass, at least half a metre in length and, when compared to Brown's catch, almost twice the size.

"Pierre Cloarec," Brown said, once he'd removed the hook from its mouth and killed it neatly with a knife to the head, 'always the one catching the big fish."

TWENTY-THREE

Clémence tried working as the bus wound its way along the narrow roads from Quimper to Plourec, but her laptop didn't fit on the small table that folded down from the seat in front, and eventually she gave up, watching fields of ripening corn slide by the window. She texted Pierre with her arrival time but told him not to bother coming to collect her. She knew where the hotel and his cottage were by now, and she'd rather he kept working. There was pressure from the other journalists to be ready to publish their stories in a coordinated manner, and that meant there was no possibility of slipping on their deadline. But the cache of information they hadn't even begun to look at was still enormous, and she sensed that Pierre hadn't really accepted this.

Pas de problème. His text came back. *By the way, fish for dinner tonight.*

She frowned at her phone, then slipped it back without replying. When the bus dropped her off she walked the short distance to the hotel and checked into the same room as before. It was small, but the view was nice, over the roofs of the cottages opposite onto the waters of the ria. The paper had actually paid for a cheaper room with a view facing inland, but there were so few tourists about this time of year that she'd been upgraded at no extra cost. She showered and headed over to Pierre's cottage, carrying her laptop bag.

"*Bonjour*," she said when he opened the door. As was customary she kissed his cheeks and began setting up her computer, piling beside it some of the more important papers she'd uncovered from the cache.

"How's the story?" she asked as she worked. "Did you include the piece about how they're funding the football team?"

"Uh huh."

"Good. I have more on that. It seems the funding for a player bought last summer was routed through this shell company. Literal drug money buying their new striker." She shook her hair in amazement as he took the paper she held out to him, his eyes wide in surprise, yet again, at what secrets the treasure trove contained.

"I'll have to rewrite," Pierre muttered. "This is important." He made a fist, pleased at the scandalous nature of what she'd uncovered but irritated at the additional work it created. But it was inevitable; the data had come to them only semi-organised. There were bound to be surprises like this.

Cloarec waved his hand at her. "Do you want a coffee?" he asked. "And make me one, while you're there?" He didn't wait for her to answer but frowned as he worked his way through the papers, already lost within the new chain of documents she'd pieced together.

Clémence did as he'd asked and then settled into her own work. Her relationship with Pierre was complicated. Sure, he was a bit of a shithead – a huge shithead, to be honest, who would stare at her chest if she made the mistake of letting any cleavage show – but he was an excellent journalist, and had consistently broken important stories over a long career. Clémence knew little about the source of the documents other than it involved a cleaner at the law firm, and that she had chosen to give the documents to Cloarec – which didn't surprise her. And perhaps this was key to how Clémence felt about Cloarec. She believed that if she worked hard on this story, if she did what was asked of her – and more – then eventually the day might come when a source would seek *her* out, with a scoop that would change the world.

And in the meantime, she had Dubois' promise that her byline would appear on every story published. Below Cloarec's of course. But it would be there. So if she had to do the majority of the dull spadework on the data – and make the arrogant bastard coffee at the same time – well, that was a deal she was prepared to take. For now.

Four hours later Cloarec leaned back in his chair and stretched out his arms.

"Are you ready for a break?"

Clémence's eyebrows went up, expecting to be sent to the kitchen to see what scraps of food were left. She'd forgotten his text.

"I did a bit of fishing yesterday, caught myself a nice fat sea bass." He stretched his arms again, his shirt rising up and revealing a strip of untoned stomach, lined with thick black hairs.

Clémence frowned; she hadn't noticed a fish in the kitchen, nor in the fridge when she'd fetched the milk. And the cottage was so small there was nowhere else it could be.

"It's not here. A friend's cooking it for us."

"What friend? I thought you didn't know anyone here?"

Pierre waved the comment away.

"An American friend of mine. He's retired now, but he worked for many years in the US Embassy back in Paris." From the way he said it, Clémence gained the impression that Pierre had known him for many years.

"And he's *here*?"

"Yes, he has a cottage a few doors down." Cloarec's voice was casual. "I thought you'd be interested in meeting him."

They walked together, literally just three cottages down from where Cloarec was staying, to another cottage, a little larger and in a better state of repair. It was on the same side of the road and also looked out onto the ria. Pierre knocked confidently on the door, which was opened almost at once by a tall man with greying hair. Something about him looked serious, although the effect was offset by the flowery apron tied around his waist. He smiled warmly when he saw them, and invited them inside before there was time for introductions.

"Clémence, this is Richard," Pierre began. "Richard, this is Clémence Girard. She's working with me on the Hawthorne and Langley story." This made Clémence blink in surprise. She'd been instructed by Dubois – and in fact also by Pierre himself – not to mention to anyone what she was working on, or even that she was working on anything significant. She was so surprised she nearly failed to realise Pierre was still speaking.

"Not all the time," he went on. "She's also doing some smaller stories back in the office, but some of the time she's out here, helping me tidy things up."

Tidy things up? Now Clémence was caught, unsure whether to smile politely or to look as annoyed as she felt. Then she sensed a possible ally, as Brown's expression suggested he'd correctly read her dilemma.

"It sounds very exciting," he said, then added, tellingly, 'the very little that Pierre has told me about it." He smiled at her again, a disarming smile, very genuine.

"Come through, please. Perhaps a drink before we eat?"

He brought them into an open-plan kitchen-dining room, the decor modern, tasteful and relaxed. A simple wooden dining table was neatly set. The smell was frankly delicious, the salt-rich sweetness of roasting seafood. Despite her slight annoyance at having to break from working and her surprise at being brought over here, Clémence felt herself relaxing a little.

"What do you do, Monsieur Brown?"

"Richard, please." He smiled the same warm smile, turning to face her. "These days, the answer is not very much, which gives me time for simple pleasures like cooking." He indicated the apron still tied around his waist, which made it impossible for anything he said to sound pompous. "But I used to work in the diplomatic service for the American government. A very small cog in a very big machine." He held up a bottle of wine in each hand, one red one white, and indicated her glass.

"A little white. I'm working."

Pierre made a grunting noise, as if she were wrong about that.

"And for you, *mon ami*," – Brown turned to Pierre – "I thought you might appreciate this light and fruity Beaujolais, to complement the strong flavours of the fish."

"Sounds about right," Pierre nodded, and watched as Brown filled the glass nearly to the brim. Only then did he continue. "Where is the fish by the way? It smells amazing."

"Ah ha!" Brown's eyes danced, but he didn't answer.

The evening was cold – the nights were drawing in now – but the cottage was warmed by a glass-and-steel log-burner. Showing impressive flexibility for a man of his age, Brown squatted and carefully added three neatly chopped logs so that new flames flickered around them, giving out a comfortable heat and attractive light. They chatted easily; Brown was a good conversationalist, happy to answer questions about himself, but more interested in Clémence and the stories she'd written. And he seemed to have read every one she mentioned.

"He reads *Le Monde* every day; he sits in the café with his coffee," Pierre cut in at one point. He seemed almost an extra to the conversation, but not an uncomfortable one. Content to sit supping on his wine, showing off his friend.

"I enjoy it," Brown replied. "And it helps me greatly to keep my French up to date."

"It's very good. Your French," Clémence took the moment to say.

"Well, thank you. I try my best." He raised his glass in thanks, but also as if to acknowledge that the compliment had been generous.

"And now," – he seemed to be enjoying the opportunity to entertain – "*Le moment suprême.*" He invited them to sit at the table and opened the oven with a pair of thick gloves. He pulled out a tray and set it on the table, next to a simple salad. On the tray, the fish sat whole and entirely covered with a salt crust.

"I have wanted to try this recipe for some time," Brown explained, "but it's a little much for one. Plus I have never had the skill of Pierre for catching the correct fish." He paused, unsure how to break into the salted fish, but in the end he used the back of a large knife, knocking the salt away and revealing the white flesh of the fish inside.

They ate, Clémence eagerly accepting more when she'd cleared her plate, although she still felt a twinge of irritation as Brown told the story of how Pierre had caught it, a whole day apparently spent fishing while she hadn't taken a day off in weeks. But the fish tasted delicious, and Brown was such easy company, it was hard to stay annoyed.

"Do you live here all year round?" she asked, when the mood turned once more to conversation.

"At the moment. I keep a house in Boston too, but my boys

– they're about your age – they're both in Washington these days, so it feels lonely there."

"What do they do? Your sons?"

"Kevin – he's the older one – he's working as an aide for a senator, has been for a few years now. He's going down the politics route. Democrat, of course." He smiled. "Adam's taking a different path. He works for the World Bank, funding projects across Africa, health centres, wells. That sort of thing."

Clémence took a moment to try and imagine how they might look. She found she could easily image a younger version of Brown. Handsome and charming. It was a nice thought to hold in her mind. Bright, attractive young men, driving their careers, doing good for the world. She wondered if they were married or had girlfriends, and assumed that was probably the case, though Brown didn't mention it. She let the thought fade away, but returned to it several times over the course of the evening, perhaps because it reminded her of her own status as professionally single. Her working hours were too long to strike up or maintain a relationship. She thought too how she'd taken pains to hide this fact from Pierre, knowing that he'd see it as an opportunity to try his luck. It made her realise there was something about Brown that seemed the opposite of this. As if he came from a world where he was happy to exclude himself on the grounds of his age, accepting that he was from another generation. It was refreshing.

His cooking was good too. After the fish he brought out a *tarte au citron*, which was baked perfectly so that the pastry on the base was crisp but not overdone, and the balance of lemon to sugar to cream exquisite. Clémence was so focussed on enjoying it that she didn't notice the conversation had moved onto work matters.

"So do you have enough in your articles to bring down this Mancini family?" Brown had asked, causally aiming the question at them both. Pierre answered, with an easy shrug.

"Perhaps, perhaps not. Ultimately that will be a matter for the police. But it's..." – he paused, wiping a dab of cream from his lip with a napkin – "it's not really about the Mancinis. Sure, the reason I'm here – we're here – is out of some exaggerated sense of caution regarding them. But for the articles themselves, I want them to have a wider focus." He leaned forward, getting into his explanation. "I told you this is the largest ever leak – but there have been leaks before, as you probably know. And the problem every time is that the public find it difficult to identify with them. It's all so..." – he paused, searching for the right word – "*distant*. If you work every day in an office, if you're a teacher or a doctor, how do you relate to a story about how the one percent hide their millions? Let alone the one percent of the one percent, with their billions? What does the average man know of shell companies based on tropical islands?"

"I don't know," Brown replied. "Very little I imagine."

"It's about building a narrative." Pierre sounded focussed now, the way he did in the editorial meetings that Clémence had sat in on, too junior and frankly overawed to say much. "Not just reporting what these people are doing, but bringing it back to how much it's costing *you*, as a doctor, as an office worker. How much extra you're paying in tax, and how much these people – politicians, so-called celebrities – how much their failure to pay their fair share is costing *you*. We're trying to do something different this time."

Brown nodded. "I get it. I really do. And I'm profoundly glad that such an important story has come to such a fine journalist." He smiled at Pierre, but then glanced at Clémence as well. "Such a fine *pair* of journalists. I really do wish you the very best of luck with it." He raised his glass again, and Pierre nodded, accepting the compliment as if it had only been aimed at him.

"Now. I have coffee," Brown went on. "And a fine bottle of

cognac that I cannot bring myself to drink alone. Pierre, *mon ami*, could I ask you to throw another log on the fire?"

TWENTY-FOUR

The next day, the three of them met in the bar for their morning coffee. When Clémence arrived she'd already done two hours' work, while Pierre had decided instead to take a walk to clear his head. He hadn't shaved, and his jowly cheeks shone with alcohol-sweat from the night before. In contrast the American was clean shaven and looked refreshed in a cream linen suit. He mentioned, as they sipped their *cafés au laits*, that he was heading into the nearby town of Quimper and asked if he could pick anything up for them. Without really thinking – or rather because she *was* thinking about it – Clémence replied at once that they desperately needed a printer, and then she felt hotly embarrassed, because she hardly knew this man, and clearly he'd meant bread or a few groceries. Certainly not large, expensive electrical items. But he took it entirely in his stride, allowing only the briefest flicker of surprise to cross his face before nodding sagely and going on to discuss which attributes it should have – what colour ink and print type – as if it were a perfectly reasonable request. To cover her embarrassment she found herself over-explaining, telling him that it was easier to make sense of the wealth of data if it were printed out, but he waved away her concerns.

"Not at all, no need to explain, seriously. I'm actually delighted if I can help, even in a very small way." Then he paused, as if unsure whether it was appropriate for him to go on.

"Pardon me for the suggestion, but given the confidential nature of the work, would it be a sensible idea if I picked up a shredder as well? To be on the safe side?"

"Good idea." Pierre came to life and joined the discussion for the first time.

They finished their coffees, and Clémence watched Brown leave in a battered Peugeot 505 that generated a puff of light-blue smoke as it pulled away. Then Pierre got up heavily from the table saying something about how he had to get on, and left her with the bill.

Several hours later she was interrupted by a car horn outside the cottage; when she went to the window she saw Brown waving at her while lifting the tailgate of the old car and slipping out the first of several large boxes. The first contained a laser printer with two spare toner cartridges, the second a small shredder. The third and final box, tied with a ribbon, turned out to contain a selection of éclairs, which Pierre helped himself to while Clémence got the printer installed on the dining table. She was pleased when it was done; they had a much more professional set-up.

"Merci, monsieur," she smiled at the American, with his curious, accented French. "Please, how much do we owe you?" She feared for a moment he might insist on paying, which would reinforce her embarrassment, but instead he looked carefully through his wallet for the receipts, and handed them to her.

"I bought them with cash," he smiled easily. "I assumed it would be easier for you to claim back that way."

She felt a rush of relief that she had enough cash in her purse to reimburse him there and then, and gratefully folded the receipts into her bag. Then Brown delayed a moment, but seemed again to read her mood.

"Well, I'd best leave you both to it. I've taken up a lot of your time, and you have important work to do."

With the printer she was able to work more efficiently and didn't pause until eight that evening, when she made a simple meal with pasta. They ate balancing plates on piles of paperwork, and Clémence continued working until midnight. The next morning she worked straight through, missing the morning coffee break, but Pierre stepped out and returned forty-five minutes later. And then, at two, she hurried to the shelter where the local bus picked up, and climbed aboard. An hour after that she was on the TGV hurtling back towards Paris, her head down once again, her mind absorbed in the herculean task of unpicking the financial networks of the rich, the famous and the criminally corrupt.

TWENTY-FIVE

It was something of a relief for Pierre to get Clémence out of his hair. It wasn't that he didn't like the girl or respect her work – and it was pleasant to have a pretty young thing around the cottage, even if there seemed no prospect of them sleeping together, together with the lamentable fact she had such poor taste in clothes he was unable to get a good view of her breasts. But at the same time, he was a man who enjoyed his own space. And when it came to actually writing his articles – which he was now ready to do – he had a very particular style. He liked to work with the window wide open, the stronger the breeze outside the better, and he would bash hard at the keyboard while reciting out loud the words he was typing.

He still found time to break for coffee with Brown, and agreed at once when the American suggested they take dinner together that evening, recommending a seafood restaurant a few miles up the coast.

"There was something else I wanted to ask you," Pierre said, as they settled into their coffees.

"Oh yes?"

"I've been thinking, you look like a chess man; are you?"

At first Brown looked bemused, but then he smiled uncertainly.

"I'm not sure if that's a compliment or a grave insult?"

"Oh, it's very much the former. You see, I could do with a game. I like to play when I'm writing, it clears my head."

Brown's eyebrows went up in mild surprise. "I see. I haven't played in a while..."

"You can play with these computers these days," Pierre went on, more to himself than to Brown. "But they're impersonal, you know? Completely cold."

Again Brown looked nonplussed for a moment, but he nodded.

"Well I'd be delighted. I don't have a set though; do you?"

"Yes, I found one in the cottage. Maybe we could play after dinner?"

"Marvellous," Brown replied. "I'll bring the cognac."

By the time he broke for dinner Pierre had written drafts of the first two articles. It was difficult – as he'd expected – to give the words colour, to raise them above a mere catalogue of details on the movement of money. But there was a reason he was a senior journalist at one of the most prestigious newspapers in France. He had a knack for it. He'd managed to include almost as many human elements in the story as bare facts – the luxury items that the money had ultimately been spent on, and the curious fates of those luxury items. He'd also included brief details of some of the more unusual people who'd turned up in the data, apart from the better-known politicians and celebrities, the most serious of the organised criminals. He printed both drafts out before he left the cottage, meaning to cover them in red pen the next day before sending the final version to Dubois and her team of lawyers.

He was pleased enough with how things were going that he splashed out in the restaurant, ordering a lobster baked in butter and dressed with herbs. It was every bit as good as Brown had suggested, and he thanked his luck once more at finding such a companionable friend in a backwater like this. They split the bill, it was easier that way, and Pierre barely noticed that his own meal was more than three times the price of the *moules marinières* that Brown had eaten. If the American noticed he neither mentioned it nor seemed offended. On the contrary he also seemed to be on fine form.

"Are we still on with our chess game? You don't need to work, or rest?"

"Not at all. An international grudge match no less."

Brown drove them back, leaving the car outside Brown's cottage so he could collect the bottle of cognac. While Brown searched for glasses, Pierre lit his fire, now well-practised in doing so. He'd found the contents of the shredder made an excellent fire starter.

"I've set the game up," he said when Brown came back empty handed. He pointed at the dresser near the desk. "Glasses in there I think."

Brown went to look, quickly finding two heavy tumblers. As he returned, Pierre noticed how his friend's eyes went to the printed drafts of his article that he'd left on the desk. He looked just long enough to take in the title, but was respectful enough to not actually start reading. And Pierre wondered whether it would be useful to have a second pair of eyes on this piece, particularly given how much technical language it needed to pass the lawyer's judgements. And the American's French, while excellent, wasn't perfect, and perhaps would prove a good test? If he could read it easily, then your average Frenchman or woman would be able to. But he said nothing at this point.

"Shall we time the game?" Pierre enquired, sitting down on one side of the board.

"That sounds a little serious," Brown replied, which Pierre took as a good sign. Highly skilled players would be quite used to using a timer, and while he craved a decent game, he preferred to win.

"We don't need to bother then," he said, taking a pawn in each hand and mixing them up behind his back. He held both hands in front of him, and Brown chose the left.

"Black," Pierre said, satisfied. "I'll play white."

The game began excellently. Brown clearly had some idea of the game's finer points and his moves were well considered, but he was on the cautious side. Pierre was always able to stay one step ahead. He pressed an attack on the black queen, trapping it in a corner where Brown couldn't escape without sacrificing a rook. But then something strange happened. Out of nowhere Brown was able to launch an attack on the other side of the board, ignoring his queen completely, and placing Pierre one move away from checkmate three times in a row. It must have been sheer luck, because once Pierre had finally escaped from the danger, he was able to regain the upper hand and take the queen and the rook, leaving Brown with little choice but to resign. He played on for a few moves, apparently not yet seeing the inevitability of defeat. But then he sat back, shaking his head and smiling, and tipped over his king.

"Well played, *mon ami*," Brown said. "Good game."

"It *was* a good game, there's time for another though?"

"If it comes with another drink, perhaps," Brown replied. "And a bit of a break. I find chess can be rather intense." He stood and stretched his legs. And Pierre saw his eye wander to the desk again.

"I wrote the first of my articles today," Pierre began, speaking without really considering what he was going to say. But the decision had really been made weeks before. "Perhaps it would be interesting for you to read it?" He went on quickly, in case the American demurred due to his diplomatic reserve. "Actually, I'm being disingenuous. You would actually be doing me a great service; I would like to see how well what I've written connects with a reader who is unfamiliar with the data leak. An ordinary reader of the paper, if you will."

"Such as myself?" Brown gave a smile. "I would be delighted."

Pierre walked across and gathered the papers, shuffling them together.

"I've tried to make it interesting, a few titbits of colour in there." He felt a burst of nerves. Even now, in the later stages of his career, he got a buzz when people read his words. But then this was the article that would define that career. He shook his head lightly, tried to concentrate.

"Such as this." He pointed to a few lines midway down the first page. "We discovered fairly early on that the British serial killer Charles Sterling – you may have heard of him –was a client of Hawthorne and Langley's." Pierre glanced at Brown, whose face expressed no obvious recognition. "He died last year, I believe, but he was well known even here in France. There's a Netflix show about him." Pierre held out the paper to his friend. "You haven't seen it?"

"What was the name again?" Brown replied, his forehead slightly creased.

"Charles Sterling? He was a mathematics professor. A complete freak as well; he killed a string of women back in the nineties. And he's only famous now because he broke out of prison last year, escaping with this vast cryptocurrency fortune. I'm sure it was covered in *Le Monde*: you didn't read it?"

Brown hesitated. "I... guess I must have missed it." He forced a smile and Pierre suppressed a slight frown, wondering whether he'd erred by mentioning so much detail. Sterling wasn't really relevant to the story but he felt it added a dash of danger. But if the American hadn't heard of the murderer, then perhaps his readers wouldn't have either? On the other hand, perhaps the opposite was true. Perhaps the reason he enjoyed spending time with Brown was precisely because he *wasn't* like the average Frenchman with their sensationalist tastes. Either way, let Dubois decide whether to include it or not.

"Well, whatever," he said out loud. It was only one of many such references. There were others that he surely would have heard of. "Give it a read. I'm going to take a piss."

He left the American reading the article while he climbed the stairs to the cottage's little bathroom.

When he came back downstairs, Brown was sitting on the little sofa reading carefully, so Pierre tended the fire for a few minutes, and then reset the chess pieces. Finally Brown set down the papers.

"Well? What do you think?"

Brown said nothing for a while, then gave a half-smile. "It's interesting, very interesting." He looked thoughtful, his eyes still on the papers. Suddenly his gaze shifted, taking in Cloarec. He pushed himself up from the chair.

"Let me just grab a glass of water, and I'll give you my thoughts." He went to the kitchen. After a long wait, Pierre heard the tap run.

PART THREE

TWENTY-SIX

Outside the prison walls for the first time in twenty-five years, Charles Sterling took a few moments to breathe in the fresh air. Then he moved, following the memorised map that Barney Atkinson had drawn, showing where a red Ford Fiesta was parked. As arranged, the key was hidden in the driver's-side suspension spring. As Sterling climbed behind the wheel he took a moment to slow his beating heart. He hadn't driven a car in over a quarter of a century.

He stalled once, but then muscle memory balanced the clutch and accelerator and he pulled out of the parking space, glancing just once in the rear-view mirror at the huge walls of the jail.

He headed south, following another map that Atkinson had brought to his cell weeks before. And soon it was coming back to him. Turned out driving was just like riding a bike – though Sterling thought with a smile how he'd have to give that a go as well, to see if it was as easy as the saying suggested. Suddenly a tractor pulled out in front of him, its huge wheels throwing clods of mud into the road as it tried to match the speed of the traffic. Sterling braked hard, instantly alert but cautious. But with no cars waiting behind him he chose not to overtake, an unnecessary risk on such a narrow road. A few moments later he was rewarded when the tractor turned off, allowing him to carry on towards a small town about fifteen miles from the prison, where Atkinson had taken out a one-month let on a small furnished flat with a garage. The safe house. Sterling let himself in with the key from the car's glove box. He looked around cautiously.

The negotiations with Atkinson had been protracted, and while it was clear the prison guard neither liked nor trusted the multiple murderer he was helping to escape, Sterling held two points of leverage over him. Firstly, and most importantly, there was the money. In exchange for assisting Sterling, and blowing up his own life in the process, Atkinson would receive cryptocurrency to the value of around nine million pounds. It was Atkinson's understanding that this represented the lion's share of the Bitcoin that Sterling secretly held. This was incorrect, and it was important that the prison guard did not discover this until the escape was complete. It was important too that the Bitcoin be transferred in instalments – earlier, smaller amounts to prove that the wealth was real, and later, larger ones to transfer the bulk of the money only once Sterling was out and safe.

But that alone wouldn't have been enough, and the second lever that Sterling held was more subtle. Atkinson had spent a lifetime – like the men he guarded – inside the prison walls, and this no doubt contributed to the fact that his home life was not a happy one. His wife, who nagged him incessantly and with whom he'd fought physically on several occasions – had left for another man. They had no children, the son that Atkinson once dreamed of bringing up existed only in his now-bitter dreams. Sterling was able to wheedle away at this over many months, slowly persuading him to see for himself how badly he'd squandered the opportunities life had given him.

The second lever was the hope that it wasn't too late for Atkinson to change things. With the right amount of money, Sterling hinted, all was not lost. In the right location, specifically a country with no extradition treaty with the UK, Atkinson could still enjoy the life they both agreed he deserved. A country where a mature man with wealth could easily land himself a beautiful woman of child-bearing age, who would remain grateful for the opportunity he'd given her. And there would be little or no emotional cost. Sterling explained, as a Zen guru might to a young monk, that any actions Atkinson would take to make this new life a reality could not be blamed on him. Free will is but a compelling illusion. Morality a story, told by those who wield power over us to maintain that power. Sterling skilfully absolved the prison guard in advance from the responsibility of his future actions. He lined his lucrative honeypot with the psychological comfort that he could not have acted otherwise.

But such trickery could only be trusted so far. Sterling was free, but there was always the possibility that Atkinson had double-crossed him in some way. He wouldn't receive the final payment for a few days, but Sterling had already given him enough to leave the country and start his new life. And although Sterling had no doubts that Atkinson feared him, and would go on to fear him for as long as he lived – what better way to protect himself than by ensuring Sterling was recaptured only hours or days after the escape? Sterling knew he had to be careful.

And besides, even if Atkinson had done exactly as instructed, the escape was still only in its early stages. He might have found a way out of the most secure area of the UK's most secure prison, but that was the easy part. Getting away and living a free life – that was the real challenge.

. . .

On Sterling's instructions Atkinson had left several items in the safe house. There was food, make-up, hair dye, a selection of wigs and a bag of clothes – some purchased new, some from charity shops so that they looked lived in. There was a laptop computer connected to the Wi-Fi that also came with the flat. Most importantly there was a pile of cash. Sterling counted it, annoyed and concerned that it was three hundred pounds less than the one thousand he'd asked for. That was OK. He could get there for seven hundred. But it meant there wouldn't be enough for a plan B.

Atkinson and Sterling had discussed in great detail the movements they each planned to take after the escape, but now he was here, Sterling had no intention of doing what he'd said. Satisfied that the flat would suffice, he went to the kitchen, opened the drawers and tested the larger knives for sharpness. When he found one he liked, he returned to the Fiesta and drove it further south, towards the coast, and the home of his former colleague Dr Jeremiah Robbins. It was a visit he had fantasised about for decades, and it had nothing to do with Atkinson.

It was Robbins who'd stolen the brilliant mathematical formulas Sterling had created as a young man, passing them off as his own. Sterling had been powerless to complain, since Robbins had found out that Sterling had violently raped a young secretary and threatened to expose him for it. Later, when Sterling had been caught and imprisoned for crimes far worse than that, he'd been forced to watch as Robbins' fame and respect grew within the community from which Sterling had been shunned. He saw his work built upon so that it now under-pinned an emerging cryptocurrency industry which promised to one day replace the entire global banking system. Even from prison, Sterling was able to make millions of his own, buying and squirrelling away the mathematical computations that were now being sold as actual currencies. But he wasn't able to recover what Robbins had really stolen from him – the immortality of being the one to foresee (and build) this future – and that injustice couldn't be left unavenged. He found Robbins out on an evening walk and drove the knife deep into his stomach, twisting it round and round as he reminded the man why it was his time to die.

Two hours after Robbins' murder, and still the same day as the prison escape, Sterling was back in the safe house, washing the final traces of blood from under his fingernails in the first free shower he'd taken for twenty-five years. It was cathartic on many levels. He made himself a promise. Now he would focus on himself. On getting away, on getting hidden and staying hidden. There'd be no more violence: the risk was too great, and the need was gone too. Whatever rewards it had provided him with in the past was just that – in the past. Soon the water in the shower ran clean and clear. Sterling emerged with his conscience refreshed. Onwards and upwards. For a man sentenced to life with no chance of parole, the future was unexpectedly bright.

Atkinson himself had boarded a flight to Brazil on the day of the escape, using a false passport he'd purchased on the dark web. He'd also bought a second passport for Sterling, which he used to book a long series of flights that criss-crossed Europe and ended up in the Far East. But Sterling had never intended to use it; he knew the ports and airports would be on high alert, and would remain so for weeks or even months. Instead, he simply bided his time for nearly a week, using his disguises to buy food and the additional materials he hadn't asked Atkinson for.

Early on the sixth day after the prison-break, Charles Sterling made his move. He parked the red Fiesta by the river in the south-coast port of Littlehampton. He went to the vehicle's boot, opened it and removed a bag and a pair of folding aluminium oars. He shut the boot and locked the car. Around him the birds were just finishing up the dawn chorus.

The weather was perfect, neither so pleasant that many people would think of taking to the water, nor so bad that it would look strange to do so. The two yachts he'd identified on a previous reconnaissance trip seemed ideal too, around twenty-five foot long and moored on buoys near a large reed bed where they couldn't be easily observed from the bank. They were clearly used infrequently, yet both looked up to the trip.

With the oars over one shoulder, Sterling walked along the riverbank until he came to an area where a number of dinghies and yacht tenders were chained up to tree roots. Making sure no one was around, he used a pair of bolt cutters from the bag to chop through one of the chains, then pulled the boat down to the water's edge. He stepped inside and began rowing out towards his preferred yacht. He'd chosen a Beneteau that looked around fifteen years old. But as he approached it he heard voices from the open cabin of another yacht moored just astern. Suddenly a head appeared, a woman in her sixties. Sterling swore under his breath but paused his stroke to raise a friendly hand. Then he returned to the oars, adjusting his course slightly to make it look like he hadn't been heading for the Beneteau but had merely been pulled that way by the river's gentle currents. As he passed by the occupied boat he called out, his voice entirely natural.

"Hello there, lovely morning!"

The woman smiled and called a greeting back, then dipped back down into the cabin. Sterling noticed she wasn't yet dressed and had perhaps slept on board. It didn't matter; he kept rowing, aiming now for the second of his targets. Should this one also not prove suitable he might have a problem, but fortunately the few neighbouring boats were empty. Sterling looked behind him to be sure his actions weren't attracting any unwanted attention. There was no one there, just a few ducks chasing in and out of the reeds, the tide tugging at the yacht that sat obediently at its moorings in front of him.

He decided to proceed. He tied the dinghy to the stern of the boat, climbed carefully aboard, then pulled the dinghy to the mooring buoy and re-tied it so it wouldn't drift loose. He looked around, taking in the yacht's deck layout and the quality of its ropes and fittings. Everything looked a little tired and sun-bleached, but it would do. He set about breaking into the cabin. A wooden board sealing off the companionway was fitted with a simple Yale lock, yet it offered surprisingly strong resistance. Eventually it yielded and Sterling removed the smashed wood and took it with him down the steps. He checked the fuel levels – a slightly disappointing third of a tank – but with luck he wouldn't need it. He pressed the engine starter, hoping the owners had kept it well maintained. The big diesel turned over a few times before catching, but then it putted cheerily away, throbbing in a comforting manner through the fibreglass of the hull. He went back on deck, checked the side to see that water was running through the cooling system and then removed the covers from the mainsail, where it was flaked on the boom. He pulled in the few fenders that had been placed on the port side and stowed them in the cockpit lockers. He checked how the tide was flowing, assessed the wind, and he was ready. He went to the bow and slipped the yacht from its mooring, then returned to the cockpit and nudged the throttle handle forward with his foot, steering with his knees on the tiller. A few moments later he passed the yacht he'd rowed past earlier, and the woman raised a mug, acknowledging him as a fellow yacht owner. In response Sterling tipped the stupid sailor-hat that Atkinson had included in his bag of disguises. They both smiled, as if jointly acknowledging the ironic way he wore it. The morning sunlight scattered a billion diamonds on the water's surface, and Sterling drank in the salt air, the fresh breeze laden with spring flowers from the riverbank.

He'd sailed enough prior to his arrest for a cross-Channel trip not to be too big a challenge. The biggest danger was that the yacht's owner, or at least someone who knew that Sterling wasn't the owner, might spot him leaving. He'd done everything he could to mitigate this, but the danger couldn't be completely disregarded. But then, that was why he was going through all this – to be in a position where he would no longer be forced to take risks, even small ones, that threatened to tear his new world apart. And the most dangerous part still lay ahead.

Ten pleasant hours later he nosed the little boat into a visitor's berth in the public marina of Boulogne-sur-Mer, on the French side of the English Channel. He had been pleased to find a French flag which, as etiquette dictated, he flew from the yacht's starboard spreader, along with a yellow Q to indicate the yacht needed to clear customs. When he climbed off the boat and onto the pontoon, he left the radio playing, still tuned to BBC Radio Four, which just about reached this far across the Channel. This was to give the impression that someone was still aboard, or perhaps that the yacht's owner intended to be back at any moment. Which of course wasn't the case.

Carrying his few possessions he strode calmly along the pontoon to the shore, and then towards the marina's customs office. But instead of going inside as an arriving yachtsman should, he simply kept walking, and a few moments later found himself on a relatively busy street where an available taxi conveniently drove by. He hailed it and took it to the train station, where he bought a ticket on the second-to-last train of the day, destination Paris.

It was nearly midnight when he arrived in the French capital, where he checked into a cheap tourist hotel, one amongst many in that particular area. He paid cash in advance to avoid having to use his false passport. Exhausted, he fell straight asleep.

At eleven the next morning he bought another train ticket, this time heading for Switzerland. His plan was progressing perfectly.

TWENTY-SEVEN

Sterling entered the bank, feeling the security camera on his face but not looking up. He followed the guard's instructions, placing his laptop bag, along with a folded copy of *The Times*, onto the airport-style scanner before stepping through the metal detector, which stayed silent. Sterling nodded his thanks to the guard and headed for the tellers' desk. His mouth was dry.

This morning's meeting would go one of two ways: either he would cross a threshold into a new life of freedom and unimaginable wealth, or he would be recaptured and sent back to prison. It was hard to imagine any middle ground.

He was led to a large room with wood-panelled walls. Cream sofas were arranged beside a grand window with views over the lake and mountains. But the banker who arrived a moment later ushered Sterling to a table instead. Sterling felt the man looking him up and down, taking in his casual clothes and trainers – the best of what Atkinson had provided. Sterling had intended to first visit one of the excellent tailors in the Swiss town of Lugano, but money was short after paying for the travel and hotels. Perhaps this was why no coffee was offered.

"What type of account was it you wished to open, Mr

Smith?" the banker asked, clearly intimating that he didn't believe it was his real name, and was wondering whether the entire meeting was a waste of his time.

"I'm not sure exactly what you call it," Sterling replied. "I need to make use of your offshore-banking services."

The banker waited a moment, the slightest of amused smiles appeared on his lips.

"Of course. Could I first see some kind of identification? A passport or driving licence?"

The request came earlier than Sterling had expected, so before he replied he took a moment to adjust himself, rearranging his copy of *The Times* carefully on the table so the headline was clearly visible.

Serial Killer Charles Sterling Escapes, authorities discover surprise fortune.

"Actually I'm having a little problem with my passport." He leaned back now, waiting as the banker's eyes took in the first few lines of the article.

It's been revealed that the infamous serial killer Charles Sterling – who murdered seven women, including his wife and daughter – and who staged a dramatic escape from Highmoor Prison two days ago – was secretly in possession of a staggering six-hundred-million-pound Bitcoin fortune.

The article was accompanied by a photograph of a much younger Sterling. But he had done nothing that morning to disguise his appearance, and he hadn't changed significantly since the photograph was taken. The smile disappeared from the banker's face. Instead he looked confused, his expression changing again as he continued to read. Sterling kept his eyes on him and was pleased to see shock, and then... something else. Fear perhaps, but definitely laced with professional interest.

"Excuse me just a moment." The banker smiled, then stood and left the room. Sterling headed to the window to look out at beautiful Lake Lugano, the might of the Swiss Alps behind it.

Five minutes later he returned with another man, roughly ten years older but otherwise similar in appearance – sombre-suited and serious. The first man spoke to the second in hushed German which Sterling wouldn't have understood even if the first banker hadn't covered his mouth with his hand. The second man looked bemused as he listened, and then finally he approached the table, politely enquiring in English if he might take the newspaper. Sterling nodded and the second man read the entire article, his eyes flicking several times from the photograph to Sterling's face. Sterling sat again while he waited, his hands crossed in his lap. Eventually the second banker sat down opposite.

"Mr..." His eyes flicked to *The Times* again, and he didn't finish the sentence. "My colleague here says you are looking to open an account?"

"Correct."

"And your name is?"

"David Smith." Sterling let his head hang on one side.

"I see. But you don't have any documents confirming your identity as... David Smith?"

"I have a fake passport, but it's cheaply produced and unlikely to convince you." He smiled as if this were the type of irritation we all face from time to time. "I was actually hoping that this might be something else you could assist me with." Sterling moved his hand just slightly, so that his forefinger rested above the words 'six hundred million'. He tapped the paper casually a few times, then smiled again.

Six hundred million.

A veritable theatrical performance played out on the second

banker's face. A flutter of nerves passed through Sterling as he watched; this was his best shot – his only shot really, given he had no bank account, no documents or identity papers, and hadn't for decades. This in addition to the fact that he'd had no computer access in prison and his mail had always been checked before he could read it. He'd pushed Atkinson as far as he could, but there was a limit to how much one could wring from someone that stupid and probably disloyal.

"Actually I'm rather disappointed in the quality of the journalism," he said casually. "You'd think they'd check their figures. The actual number is closer to *nine* hundred million."

The implication of this correction was not lost on the banker, least of all the increase it represented for any possible commission. The tiniest of smiles played across his lips, but then he was back to cool, discreet professionalism.

"I see." He nodded once to the first banker Sterling had seen, sending the younger man a message that Sterling could only guess at.

"Mr... uh, Smith. If you'll just excuse me a moment?"

There was another wait after he left and the first banker stood by the door, as if Sterling/Smith might try to escape out the window. Sterling waited calmly, knowing that his fate would be decided in the next few moments. He estimated the odds at about fifty-fifty that the second banker would return with the security guard. If that happened, he was screwed. He'd spent years working out the best way to disappear should he ever escape from prison, and this was it. Having billions on a computer in Bitcoin was one thing, but you can't eat computer code. You can't buy a house with it either, nor even a train ticket. You needed cash in a bank, and connecting the two was the issue. Banks were required by law to know who their customers were. To have addresses on record, to confirm identities before accounts were opened. Atkinson had all that, so it was relatively easy for him to shift the Bitcoin Sterling had given him into dollars. But Sterling had no bank account, no viable identity documents, so no chance of opening an account. At least, not in a regular bank.

The second banker returned, holding the door open now while a third man entered. Sterling held his breath. But it wasn't the security guard he'd feared, but another man in formal grey suit. He was older, significantly larger, and clearly much more senior than the other bankers.

"Good morning, I'm Matthias Keller, Managing Director of Private Banking."

"Good morning." Sterling smiled, and waited while this man now read the article, looking up several times to compare the photograph with Sterling. Finally he spoke again.

"Swiss government regulations require us to view appropriate identification before we open any sort of account." Keller's eyes remained empty, difficult for Sterling to read.

"Of course." Sterling flashed a half-smile, still uncertain where this was going. "The issue is, I seem to have mislaid my passport. I was under the impression this was something the bank might be able to assist me with."

"In most cases if a client has a documentation issue, we would point them in the direction of the relevant embassy."

Sterling made a face. "I'm sure that's true. In most cases."

Keller gave a tiny smile, as if he sympathised, but only a little. But then he became thoughtful, turned to the door and barked something in German to the most junior banker, who retreated at once, shutting the door behind him.

Keller turned back to Sterling. "It's possible that something can be arranged – but it would come at a not-inconsiderable cost."

"How much?" Sterling asked, letting his head fall onto one side so he could better study the banker; the man's face was impressively impassive, but his eyes gave him away, falling again to the number in the headline.

"A replacement British passport, in the name of... David Smith," – his eyes were calculating – "would be at least five hundred thousand euros."

"Perfect." Sterling smiled. "Except my money is rather tied up in Bitcoin right now."

Keller waved away the objection at once. "That's fine, we have a facility for that."

Sterling allowed himself to begin to relax for the first time in several days. "OK. And how about the account?"

"There will be a fee for that as well."

"Naturally."

"A not-inconsiderable fee."

"Mr Keller, please understand I am both psychologically and financially prepared for you to name an outrageously high number. It will not be a problem."

This time Keller's smile deepened significantly. He moved his heavy bulk and leant back on his chair.

"Mr Smith, I do apologise, it seems my associates have neglected to offer you any refreshments. I myself often take a latte at about this time. And there is a pâtisserie nearby which does excellent *Luxemburgerli* – that's a type of small macaron filled with buttercream, in case you're unfamiliar." Keller's eyebrows went up questioningly, and on seeing Sterling smile he clicked his fingers. The remaining banker almost ran from the room in his haste to oblige.

The next few days were rather fun. The passport would take several days to arrange, but in the meantime the bank explained how things would work. The value held by Sterling in his Bitcoin wallet could only be accessed once it was linked to a legacy-currency bank account. But any attempt to transfer such a huge amount into any other currency would inevitably attract the attention of authorities across the world. So it had to be done gradually, and filtered through third parties. The solution was to use a law firm in the Cayman Islands, where the financial accounting laws were even more lax than in Switzerland. They would set up a number of shell companies – entirely legal – but whose ownership would be kept deliberately opaque. In turn these would be controlled by trusts, again legal, but with ownership papers concealed. The end result would be that Charles Sterling – or David Smith, or whoever he wanted to be – would have access not just to larger amounts, for property purchases for example, but also for day-to-day banking. He would have a credit card, a checking account. He could pay taxes and claim social security. To all intents and purposes he would be a regular citizen – of whatever country he desired. The only difference between him and a genuine regular Joe would be the secret access he would retain to the sort of fortune that only a few tens of thousands of people in the world could match.

The cost of all this was eye-watering – a ten per-cent levy on every dollar funnelled through the system. Sterling suspected this rate was made up on the spot and negotiated it down by gently reminding the bankers that he could – if pushed – walk across the street to one of their many competitors. But it was a delicate dance. Their other option was to put in a call to the Swiss authorities and have him re-arrested. They would gain the moral high ground by doing so, for a few weeks at least. But they would also be turning their noses up at probably the biggest payday of their entire careers.

TWENTY-EIGHT

The view from the window as the aircraft waited to take off was of thick, wet jungle bordering the airport, almost completely obscured by absurdly heavy tropical rain falling horizontally in huge curtains. The storm had threatened as the passengers waited in the departure lounge, a black cloud that had gathered and darkened the day almost to night as the aircraft's take-off slot approached. Despite the mix of languages in use, it was clear that most of the passengers were talking about it. Those who travelled alone, with no one to speak to, sent anxious glances out the window and embarrassed glances at each other, as if it were somehow humorous to be doubting whether it was safe to take off in such weather.

But apparently it was. The air crew seemed perhaps a little more tense than normal as they ran their cabin checks, securing the doors. And then the plane began its long trundle out to the runway. The familiarity of the terminal building slipped from view, lost in a mist of rain, and then the deluge finally began. Streams of water ran down the windows. The near-humour of the departure lounge was gone, the passengers now looked plain scared. Were they really going to take off?

The pilot's voice came over the intercom, but only to remind the passengers to turn off all devices. Unusually, there was a scramble to comply. More passengers than normal paid heed as the flight attendants went through their safety briefing, describing how to inflate a lifejacket, as if it would help in any way should they skid off the runway and explode into an inferno of ragged metal and jet fuel.

To some this perhaps felt the most likely outcome, yet the man in seat 13A felt no fear. He knew that what would happen would happen, and there was nothing he could do about it. Although that same philosophy hadn't prevented him from planning the events of the previous weeks in meticulous detail. He smiled now at the memory of it, but there was no time to luxuriate in his success as the engine note changed. A deepening whine now as the plane made its final turn onto the runway. They juddered to a sudden stop, as if the pilot himself were taking a breath. The noise increased to a roar, the body of the plane shook, and still the rash lashed at the windows. Then the wheel brakes released, and the heavy plane began to roll forwards, slow at first, then faster, and soon what felt much too fast for this weather.

The rivulets on the windows turned an abrupt corner and were pushed backwards then cleared off altogether, swept away by the rushing air. The engines screamed as if enjoying adding to the drama of the moment as the aircraft approached its point of no return. But then the wheels found a section of standing water on the tarmac and the whole plane slewed, one way then the other. At least three passengers screamed out loud, and many more reached out desperately for their arm rests, sometimes finding only the hands of their neighbours. Still the occupant of seat 13A relaxed, more deeply this time, almost willing the crash to occur. The irony of it would be delicious. But then there was a reduction in noise, a change of altitude, as the wheels lifted off and the plane and all the souls within it were held up only by its wings, bucking and twisting as they gripped and missed at the Swiss cheese of swirling air within the tropical rains.

The passengers on one side of the jet saw nothing but sky for a few moments, the other side nothing but jungle, and then the airport boundary – and then the wet city, already a hundred metres below as the aircraft leaned into a deep turn. Then there was nothing but thick grey cloud for some time, before finally they ascended into the bright sunshine above. Finally the flight smoothed and the sun shone into the cabin, helping settle the frayed nerves of the passengers. The plane began a more settled, steady ascent, west towards the Himalayas, the plains of western Asia and beyond. And, for the man in seat 13A, towards a new life in Europe.

The hospital room had felt almost like a prison. Yes, the view had been much improved from an *actual* prison – careful landscaping that had led the eye through lush gardens and down towards the broad expanse of the river – but he'd been unable to leave, not even to use the toilet. And the entire time he'd had to to keep up an act of being on the point of death, which had felt at times almost as exhausting as if it had been true.

"Sir!" A hand touched his shoulder lightly. He opened his eyes to see one of the flight attendants, in a fitted white blouse which might have been chosen to show off her slim build, the roundness of her small breasts. But he kept his eyes respectfully on her dark eyes – beautiful dark eyes – as he let her read out the full list of alcoholic and non-alcoholic drinks in the trolley. Then he asked for an orange juice. He watched her as she worked, the skin of her forearms smooth and dark. She had to lean over to hand the drink to him and he caught another European man glancing over at that exact moment, knew that he had waited to look, keen for a glimpse of how her skirt pulled tight against the curve of her backside. The man in seat 13A smiled again as the stewardess moved to the passengers in front of him. He didn't look at her as she bent forward; just sipped his orange juice.

In a way it had been sex that had led Charles Sterling to choose the Hoi An Clinic in Vietnam as the location for his death. Specifically, the rather sordid but undeniably popular sex between middle-aged – and older – European men and young South East Asian girls. It was an open secret that many men travelled regularly to cities like Bangkok or Hanoi to meet Asian girls, and sometimes Asian boys, and this had given him the seeds of the idea.

He had employed a private detective, a former police officer who advertised an anonymous and discreet service in the back of *Private Eye* magazine. He'd instructed the detective to search for doctors who held senior positions in high-end private medical centres somewhere in South East Asia, specifically those with a liking for very young Asian girls. The detective was sceptical, it wasn't a lot to go on, and the client – who was clearly using a false name – was unclear what he was supposed to do once he'd found this doctor, an outcome which in itself was doubtful. But Sterling had repeatedly reassured the detective that no harm would come to anyone and he offered to pay so handsomely – half in advance – that the detective took the job. A few weeks later he provided a shortlist of possible candidates. Number three was the head doctor of the Hoi An Clinic, a German man named Hans Guttenheim. He looked perfect.

Sterling instructed the detective to focus on Guttenheim, to see what more could be dug up. Soon he received photographs of the doctor receiving fellatio from several teenage girls, some of whom were unambiguously underage. The doctor himself had posted the images on a restricted chat room where such things were celebrated. Sterling was pleased, and he paid the second half of the fee to the detective. He selected another of his new identities and took a flight to Vietnam.

He watched Guttenheim for a couple of weeks before making his approach, satisfying himself that this was indeed his man. Then he took the seat next to him in a bar where he often drank alone, and quietly offered to buy him a drink. Guttenheim had been suspicious, but Sterling was calm and non-threatening. He explained that he had a need to disappear, and had heard that Guttenheim could make this happen. The German doctor had become angry, but at that point Sterling had handed him a thick envelope, requesting that he open it before coming to any rash decisions. The envelope contained the least incriminating of the photographs, along with ten thousand dollars in cash.

"There's plenty more where that came from," Sterling explained. "Money *and* photographs." He kept his voice entirely civil throughout, and reached out a hand to touch the man's shoulder.

"Dr Guttenheim, I have no desire to cause you any harm. I simply need your help. If you provide it, I am willing to pay you more money than you can earn in the next ten years."

"And if I don't?"

"Nothing. I walk away. But if I do – and you ever tell anyone about this moment – you will give me no choice but to send this photograph to the board of directors at your hospital." He met Guttenheim's eyes.

"But I don't want to do that. So let's talk."

They had talked, coming to a loose agreement, and then they'd met again the next day, this time accompanied by a lawyer who arranged for a large sum of money to be put in escrow, which would find its way into an account opened in the name of, and controlled by, Hans Guttenheim, once he'd performed the actions expected of him.

With Guttenheim enlisted, everything else had fallen

quickly into place. Sterling had been admitted to the clinic under another new identity, this time an Englishman named Jeremy Collins. A make-up artist was used to ensure Collins' appearance fitted the terminal cancer diagnosis he arrived with, which Guttenheim personally confirmed. Collins had requested that only Guttenheim would treat him, and while this was unusual, it wasn't unheard of for dying men to pin their remaining hopes on similarly absurd decisions. Either way, it made little difference. The notes and charts that Guttenheim created, the test results he took from other patients, all told a simple and convincing story. Collins was dying, and had chosen to do so in the tight privacy and comfortable luxury of the Hoi An Clinic, where he would be made comfortable, his every wish granted.

The fingerprint, dental and DNA samples were the most difficult. To begin with they looked clumsy, obviously doctored, but Guttenheim and Sterling had plenty of time and at this point no one suspected anything. A few thousand dollars here and a forged signature there, and everything was soon in place.

Over the course of Collins' stay his heath was seen to further deteriorate. This was achieved with a combination of ever more extreme make-up (applied by the make-up artist disguised as a nurse) and various drugs provided by Guttenheim. It was not hard to fool the nurses, who had no reason to suspect that the quietly dying Englishman was in fact faking the whole thing.

The death of Jeremy Collins was the most difficult part of the operation. When the time was right he was given more drugs to slow his heart and trigger alarms on the machines monitoring him. These drew nursing staff and other doctors, one of whom actually declared Collins deceased; a lucky bonus, since this was supposed to be Guttenheim's job. The German doctor had then taken over, accompanying the 'body' to the clinic's underground morgue, and informing his staff that Collins' wishes were that no autopsy be performed and his body should be cremated as soon as was practically possible. The critical moment took place in the morgue itself. Guttenheim had only a few minutes to deliver an injection of fast-acting steroids to wake Sterling up. He had then, somewhat groggily, vacated the casket in which he'd been placed and changed his clothes while Guttenheim filled the casket with two heavy sacks of medical waste. Dressed as a hospital orderly, Sterling had helped to seal shut his own casket, and then left the hospital by the staff entrance, where he'd found a further change of clothes hidden in some bushes.

Guttenheim had then issued the death certificate and requested authority to cremate as per the standard procedure. Some hours later permission was granted and the ovens were fired up. Less than six hours after his death, Jeremy Collins' remains were – or rather weren't – incinerated at the maximum temperature allowable. Two hours at 2100 degrees Fahrenheit reduced the bags of medical waste to a fine ash-like substance from which it would be impossible to obtain a DNA sample. These ashes were then scattered into the Thu Bồn River.

Twelve hours after that, the man who had briefly lived the death of Jeremy Collins settled down into seat 13A and sipped his orange juice.

TWENTY-NINE

Sterling spent a pleasant fortnight searching the property websites from a comfortable hotel in the city of Brest, far out in the west of Brittany. He'd chosen the area for a number of reasons. It was popular with British expats so a native English speaker wouldn't stand out, but also quiet, meaning he'd be able to settle down to a peaceful life. It was also, he had to admit, nice to think he would be just over the water from where Erica lived and worked, although he had no intention of contacting her or continuing his previous way of life. Now that he was dead, the plan was to stay that way, until he really did die.

Even after handing the bulk of his remaining fortune to Sands, he'd still been able to keep enough to see out his days in comfort, and having spent twenty-five years living in a fifteen by twelve-foot cell, his needs were modest. He would take coffee in a local bar, reading the newspaper each day. He would buy a fishing boat – nothing fancy – and on calm days he would anchor off a pretty headland and drop a line down. He would catch his own dinner. He would watch the tide flood into and ebb out of a little creek, and he would grow familiar with the sight of it, living a simple life around the clock of the tides.

He enjoyed the property search. First he made a shortlist, filling in the most precise search terms so that only those meeting his specific requirements were shown. Two bedrooms were enough, but the master had to look out over the water, and ideally close enough that the small garden backed onto the creek, river or beach. The cottage would be traditional, but either adapted or modern enough in design that it was light and comfortable. After twenty-five years without sunlight, this was important to him. A wood-burning stove was also essential. Woodland adjacent to the property – so he could coppice his own fuel – would be useful but not vital: he had enough money to fund the purchase of fuel, good-quality food and decent wine.

He arranged to view several properties with a local estate agent, a lovely middle-aged Frenchwoman called Eva. He used her to practise and refine an American twang to his French, which was rusty, or at least out of practice. He was used to reading in French, but it took a while for him to feel comfortable speaking it.

The first property was a definite no from the start. The particulars had failed to mention that it sat only a few metres from a busy road. He was viewing in mid-winter, so goodness knew what it would be like when summer arrived. Nevertheless he followed Eva as she led him through the downstairs rooms, admired the beautiful view out over a little estuary, with yachts bobbing at their mooring buoys, and then smiled to himself as she led him up the stairs to the bedrooms. He wondered what Eva would think if she knew that he wasn't really a former American diplomat, but a prison escapee who had murdered seven women.

"As you can see, the master bedroom has the same terrific view." Eva turned to him, but finally correctly interpreted his body language. "The road is too close, no?"

Sterling let himself draw in a deep breath then let it out, as if disappointed.

"A little. *Désolé, madame.*"

"No problem. I have one more, I wanted to save it for last."

He'd bought a car by then. A battered old Peugeot 505 in pale blue. It would be expensive to run, but it was just the sort of car that a francophile ex-pat American would drive, and in some ways he was now exactly that. Or at least that was who he genuinely intended to become. He drove it now, following the estate agent's Citroën, watching through the rear window as the curls of her hair tumbled down and kissed the softness of her neck.

They drove for forty minutes, eventually entering a small village. Eva led him first past a wide, sweeping beach that looked out west to the open expanse of the Atlantic, and then a small fishing harbour, clearly still in operation from the colourful boats unloading boxes of silvery fish. There was a bar, a hotel. They pulled up outside a row of small, picturesque cottages, the sparkle of the water visible in the gaps between them.

"I took you via the beach; there are a number of excellent restaurants very close by too." Eva paused a moment, and Sterling wondered why she'd mentioned that – was she hoping he might invite her to one of them? He shook his head, enjoying the thought, but allowing his focus to widen to the actual property. It was a pretty cottage, modernised, and from the outside it looked perfect. He followed Eva up the path, enjoying the swing of her hips, and sensing that this was the one.

It was so light inside. The previous owner – Eva explained – had converted the downstairs into one open space, but Sterling barely listened. Instead he was drawn to the property's large rear windows that looked out over a small garden and then the wide ria. There was a small wooden landing stage. The tide was in, and calm water flowed gently through the wooden posts. The kitchen was brand new, and clean in the way that only a never-used space could be. The master bedroom also looked out over the ria, only from higher up. The second bedroom had a view of the village and, behind it, the beach they'd driven by. The price – of course – was absurd, and had Sterling been bothered to ask, Eva would have told him that the owners might be willing to reduce it slightly should the right buyer come along. But he didn't care to negotiate. He nodded earnestly.

"Please tell me, when's the quickest I can move in?"

Eva told him a month, but Sterling made the money available the next day, which sped things up. In the end it was just over fourteen days before Sterling got the keys to the small cottage in Plourec. Where he planned to build a new life, and disappear forever.

But even the best-laid plans sometimes go awry.

THIRTY

It took a little longer than expected to feel at home. It was a small village, and Sterling quickly learned that everyone knew everyone. Or at least those from the village (or the nearby area) knew all the other locals, but held a subtle but noticeable contempt for anyone else – *outsiders*. A part of this, no doubt, came from the fact that roughly half the houses in the village weren't lived in full-time, but served either as holiday homes for wealthy Parisians or were rented out to a steady stream of tourists. The economics of this arrangement meant that many of the menial workers from the village could no longer afford to live there. But Sterling hadn't bought the largest or flashiest house in the village. He drove a battered Peugeot and he was polite and respectful whenever he used the facilities, such as the small shop which sold groceries, fresh bread and a few newspapers. In the bar he always left a tip, and once he'd finished reading his copy of *Le Monde*, he always made a point of leaving it on the bar for others to read.

Still it took time to move beyond a simple and final 'good morning' from the barman to learning his name and discovering he was the nephew of the hotel owner and brother of an attractive young woman who taught in the local school.

But this time was useful; it gave Sterling the space he needed to settle into his new personality. If he were to be successful in disappearing from the world, he had to appear somewhere as well – and so he researched his new persona, an American who'd retired early from the diplomatic service. And there were early mistakes, innocent questions that he was unable to answer, but in the first weeks he was able to cover them up by pretending he'd failed to understand the question, what with his imperfect French.

It was more likely that the villagers accepted his story because they weren't particularly interested in it. They accepted him for what he was: an oddity. An eccentric, but not an especially unwelcome addition to their rural lives. He took a big step a couple of months after he'd arrived when he began to enquire about purchasing a small fishing boat, something simple to operate that could be moored to the wooden dock at the end of his garden. It turned out that wouldn't be possible – the sea was too shallow at low tide – but that was fine, and he purchased a mooring further out for a few hundred euros a year.

He drew up a shortlist, and several volunteers were willing to escort him on his search, commenting knowledgeably about the advantages and drawbacks of the various boats he looked at. He insisted upon paying them a finder's fee when he finally selected a small, semi-open wooden boat with a blue-painted hull and a diesel engine that was apparently very reliable, even though it had to be started with a wrench. Its top speed was fast enough to beat the strong tidal flows. It was perfect, and once it was his, he'd perhaps graduated to that strange place in the village hierarchy where he was not one of them – a true local – but a part of their lives nonetheless.

. . .

It was nearly a year later when Sterling first noticed the newcomer. The man was at the bar sipping coffee while Sterling was at his regular table. He saw strangers every day – tourists with their guidebooks and their maps and, depending on the weather, their sun hats or anoraks. But this man looked different. He wore neither the workmanlike clothes of the locals, nor the leisure wear of the passing trade. And something about the way he held himself wouldn't have looked out of place in a Parisian café – a style that Sterling himself was going to some effort to emulate. He was careful not to draw any attention to himself, but he imprinted an image of the man's face into his memory, just in case.

And when, the next day – and the day after that – the man was there again, it pulled at Sterling's mind. He pretended to read his newspaper while tugging at the puzzle's threads. And then he got it, in a flash that both alarmed and intrigued him in equal measure. The uncomfortable-looking visitor was none other than *Le Monde* journalist Pierre Cloarec – his photograph sometimes accompanied the more serious articles in Sterling's now-daily paper. That got his attention.

Once Sterling had identified Cloarec, it became necessary to find out why he was there. There was no reason to suspect it had anything to do with Sterling himself, but on the other hand, he didn't seem to be on holiday there.

And so, cautiously, he set about his next move. One day, after he felt that Cloarec *had* noticed him, he finished his coffee and casually stood, as if to leave. But then he moved towards the bar to leave his copy of *Le Monde*, as was now his custom. And when he passed Cloarec it would have been impolite not to offer the newspaper to him. As he spoke he carefully mispronounced his French, advertising himself as an American. He was pleased when this drew a comment and an opening from the journalist. He took a gamble and admitted that he recognised Cloarec's name and praised his work – noting the pride this provoked. Then he backed off, allowing Cloarec to make the next move, if he wanted to.

Sterling left the bar and pretended to stroll up the street, but in fact waited out of sight until he saw Cloarec leave. Then he followed him, careful not to be observed, and discovered the journalist was staying in a small cottage only a few doors down from his own. Further observations indicated he was indeed working on something there, but what it was, Sterling did not know.

He might have found a way to ask him, but the next day Cloarec appeared in the café with a girl. She was slim, in her late twenties, with blonde hair and an elegant neck. She pecked at a notebook computer, as if trying to interest Cloarec. But he seemed distracted, perhaps wondering whether Sterling had noticed how attractive his young companion was. Sterling *had* noticed, and he raised a hand in greeting – but chose not to disturb them.

The girl was there again the next day and, spying from behind his newspaper, Sterling wondered about her. The body language was wrong for them to be lovers; their ages were just about right for father and daughter – but that was clearly wrong too. Colleagues then. But if so, what were they working on? Why were they here? What was it about this village – besides himself – that might attract not one but two Parisian journalists?

Sterling sat at his table biding his time, but knowing he couldn't do so for ever.

The next day she was gone, and Cloarec seemed a little lost without her. Sterling sensed the time was right and he quietly steeled himself for a prolonged spell of his American-accented French.

"*Bonjour*," said Cloarec when Sterling headed to the bar on the pretence of returning his newspaper a second time. "May I?"

"Of course. Although I'd have thought you've already read it." Sterling's smile reminded Cloarec of his own importance.

When Cloarec invited Sterling to join him for a glass of wine he pretended to hesitate, but then casually responded to the journalist's numerous questions about his presence in the village. It was a good test, both of the general plausibility of the cover story he'd prepared –Cloarec would know many people similar to the fictional Richard Brown – but also whether he could ascertain whether Cloarec's presence had any connection to Sterling. It was inconclusive. The journalist was vague, and Sterling was too cautious to press.

However, Cloarec did seem to need a friend, and Sterling was only too happy to provide. He offered to help start his car, and from there he suggested they go out for a meal together. Over the next week he did his best to charm the journalist and give the impression he was reciprocating the obvious 'bromance' that was developing in one direction.

Soon they were chatting every day over coffee about a range of topics, but never the exact nature of Cloarec's work. They dined together too, which made a genuinely pleasant change for Sterling from eating alone. He talked freely – but carefully – about his own fictional life, making up two sons and a failed marriage, all of which he committed to his impressive memory so he wouldn't be tripped up later. He was always ready with an explanation for why little to nothing could be found about him on the internet: his natural aversion to publicity and his profession which required – literally – diplomacy. But it seemed Cloarec was too disinterested, or perhaps too foolishly trusting, to even look. Indeed, it became increasingly clear that Cloarec wanted most of all to talk about himself. Apart from, rather frustratingly, the reason he was there in the first place.

It almost became a problem – but then a solution presented itself. A day's fishing would provide the space, time and privacy for Cloarec to spill his guts. And for Sterling – as Brown – to listen while maintaining his non-stereotypical and decidedly un-American reserve. He had one of the restaurants pack them a fine lunch, and took a cool box of beers and some excellent local ciders. No reason not to enjoy a day of work.

The fish weren't biting, but Cloarec was embarrassingly impatient to impale himself upon the hook. He explained about a leak of confidential data from a Cayman Islands firm named Hawthorne and Langley. And as he did so, the journalist was engaged enough in his own story not to notice the sense of shock that swept over Sterling when he heard the name. Although he hadn't paid that much attention to the lawyers who'd set up the structures to move and hide his money, he certainly remembered their name: the very same Hawthorne and Langley, based in the Cayman Islands.

It didn't appear to be an immediate disaster – they clearly had hundreds – perhaps thousands – of other clients, and Cloarec's focus was on exposing the hypocrisy of the sort of politician or celebrity who claimed to be men (and very occasionally women) of the people, while using sometimes legal-but-immoral – and other times plainly illegal – methods to shelter their huge fortunes from the taxman. Or – and it turned out this was the chief reason for Cloarec's presence in the village – the exposure of actual criminals, organised gangs of drug smugglers and modern-day mafiosi, such as the Mancini family.

Gently, Sterling dug deeper. He discovered that the data dump was vast and had been gathered in a somewhat haphazard manner, without the system within which it had been filed in the law firm's accounts. This meant that working through the data dump was an enormous task, being carried out simultaneously by *Le Monde* and other leading newspapers across Europe and America. He discovered that Cloarec and his part-time assistant Clémence (now Sterling had a name for the girl with the elegant neck, who was apparently coming back the next day to continue the work) had been working on the data dump for several months, and were now close to writing the first of their articles, which would doubtless become a huge, world-wide news story.

Finally they ran into some fish, and Cloarec took evident delight in reeling in the biggest of the day. Sterling was almost too stunned to act as if he cared.

On the one hand, it seemed the most incredible coincidence. But after some consideration Sterling revised this understanding. Hawthorne and Langley would have – and the files clearly demonstrated this – assisted tens of thousands of wealthy people to shelter their money over many decades. So the fact that one of the many journalists writing this story had come into contact with one of Hawthorne and Langley's clients was perhaps not the freak of chance it seemed at first glance. But from his point of view – that *he* was the sole client who had lucked upon advance warning of the negative publicity to come – that was nothing short of extraordinary.

It was less clear what he should do with the knowledge. The one piece of good news from the day was that Cloarec seemed to have no knowledge of or interest in clients such as Sterling, and it seemed highly likely it would stay this way. All he could do was continue to monitor the situation, and once the story was finally printed it would impact celebrities and politicians but have absolutely no effect on the new life Sterling had built from himself.

That, at least, was the hope.

THIRTY-ONE

The girl arrived again the next evening and Sterling invited them both to dinner. The stated reason was to do justice to the huge sea bass the journalist had landed, but of course his true purpose was to see what else he could discover now he knew the unsettling truth about Cloarec's work.

Once he had everything prepared, Sterling spent a long time meditating but, unusually for him, found it impossible to keep his mind clear. He found thoughts persistently inter-rupting him, images that refused to fade away. Some were of Cloarec himself, suggesting that Sterling was beginning to tire of his friendship with the Frenchman. He pictured the unpleasant way the man's distended stomach had stretched against the material of his shirt as he'd sat back against the cush-ions on Sterling's fishing boat – a space where Sterling himself normally relaxed.

But other thoughts came too, and after a while Sterling noticed they centred upon the girl, Clémence. In the end he gave up and simply thought about her. He had clearly seen suspicion in her face when he'd called out a friendly greeting to Cloarec in the bar. For a long time he assumed this was what was bothering him, but then he saw the obvious, the simple reality that he should have noticed at the very beginning. Clémence closely resembled Sterling's victims, all those years ago: the same body shape, the same shade of blonde hair that he'd always found himself drawn to, She was around the same age too. But really it was in the way she carried herself where he saw the similarities. Clearly she was well aware of how attractive she was, and the effect this had on men. And the way she used this power angered him, again echoes of how he'd felt as a younger man. He allowed an image of her to fill his mind as he sat cross-legged on the floor. The curve of her neck, the lustrous shine of her hair. The way she'd noticed him in the bar but slid her eyes away to avoid any chance of contact, dismissing him as beneath her interest. He could teach her a lesson for that. He could wipe that complacent smile from those pretty, painted lips...

No! He angrily swept the thought away. Those days were gone, he had no desire to return to being that man again, and no intention of doing so. And at once the sense of calm he had sought and failed to find arrived at last. He breathed, deep and slow. He had no interest in Clémence other than to dismiss the unlikely possibility that her and Cloarec's work posed any threat to him. He was not going to hurt her. There was no possibility and simply no need for him to peer into her soul while he choked the life from that elegant neck. Charles Sterling may have been a killer, but Richard Brown was not. He got up, his meditation over, and went for a shower.

They arrived that evening, Pierre already jolly, and Sterling could smell that he'd already started on the wine. He poured him another, filling the glass generously but not so high that it might have suggested he wanted him drunk. Clémence was cagey though, and it became apparent that Cloarec had failed to provide her with much advance warning of the dinner appointment. This was disappointing, but it also gave Sterling an opportunity. Subtly he set about allowing a contrast to form between himself and Pierre, not putting too much pressure on the senior journalist, who had to be kept onside as well, but highlighting that where he was casually sexist, Richard Brown found such attitudes distasteful. Where Cloarec had a slight tendency to oafishness, which was amplified when he drank, Richard Brown possessed a natural, disarming grace. It was a fine line to avoid offending Cloarec, but as the evening wore on, Sterling found himself ever more able to walk it. He even found himself enjoying the dance.

By the time dessert was finished – a very successful *tarte au citron* – he felt ready to send her an important message; her senior colleague had made the mistake of being loose-lipped, not just with him but potentially any number of his well-connected friends.

"So do you have enough in your articles to bring down this Mancini family?" Sterling asked. Pierre answered with some bullshit about building a story that connected with ordinary people. But Sterling kept his eyes on Clémence, seeing the flash of surprise as Pierre droned on. He redoubled his efforts to coax her fears away.

"Well, I think you're both very brave," he said, changing the subject to give the impression he wasn't all that interested. He twisted the screw into the cork of another bottle of wine.

THIRTY-TWO

The next morning Sterling met Pierre and Clémence again for coffee, and he was delighted when his offer to pick up some groceries was slightly misinterpreted by Clémence when she asked him for a printer. It gave him the opportunity to contribute something to the journalistic mission, which he felt sure would be rewarded at some point with more information. He still wasn't that worried. He'd learned that data on thousands, perhaps tens of thousands, of individuals had been leaked, and the chances of his name being noticed seemed almost impossibly remote. But it wouldn't hurt to be sure.

He was disappointed to learn that Clémence was leaving that same day, and he let it show. After all, it was only natural that he would enjoy the presence of the pretty young woman, and her polite interest in him and his family. But he made a play of pretending that he would also enjoy spending time alone with Pierre. The man had – out of the blue – challenged him to a game of chess, which of course Sterling had accepted, while warning that he hadn't played in years. Which wasn't entirely true. They arranged to play that evening, after dining again together in a nearby fish restaurant.

.   .   .

Sterling spent the afternoon meditating – a little more successfully this time – before picking Cloarec up for the short drive to the restaurant. It was immediately clear that the journalist was pleased with himself. At first Sterling pretended not to notice, before eventually asking what had gone so well. It turned out that Cloarec had made progress on writing the first of the articles that would appear in *Le Monde*. He hinted too, clumsily, that he would ask Sterling to read it, but stopped short of doing so. This irritated Sterling, and he was even more irritated when the Frenchman ordered a whole lobster but then assumed they'd simply split the bill. Even more so because he'd previously told him that *Le Monde* was picking up all his expenses while he was in Plourec. The truth was that the sudden absence of Clémence from their meetings had left a greater hole in his enjoyment of the proceedings than Sterling had anticipated. He wondered whether it would be possible to unravel some of the blossoming friendship he'd cultivated with this man, at least until the next visit of the lovely Clémence.

Cloarec set up the pieces for the game, clearly noticing Sterling's brief glance at the drafts, printed out and left on the desk in the corner of the sitting room. Still the fat fool said nothing, and Sterling sat down to play. He was unsure what to do. His pride urged him to crush Pierre, but Richard Brown probably wouldn't have done so and he let himself be gradually manoeuvred into a terrible position where his queen was pinned into a corner. Then the smirk on Pierre's lips pushed him too far and for a few moves he fought back, unleashing a terrible attack on the opposite side, almost resulting in a checkmate before Sterling regained control and remembered he was supposed to be losing. He placed his bishop in a ridiculous position and clapped a hand to his mouth as if unable to believe how clumsy he'd been. Greedily the Frenchman took the piece, as if Brown might ask to take it back.

"I hoped you might not see that," Sterling commented. "But maybe all is not lost."

But he made sure it was.

"Well played, *mon ami*." Sterling chose to resign rather than waiting for the fool to actually find a checkmate, and he knew this was the moment.

"Good game, good game." Cloarec hesitated but then went on, his eyes on the print-outs.

"Perhaps it would be interesting for you to read them?" he asked. "Actually, I'm being disingenuous. You would be doing me a great service; I'd like to see how well what I've written connects with a reader unfamiliar with the data leak. An ordinary reader of the paper, if you will."

The patronising French fuck.

"Such as myself? I would be delighted," Sterling replied. That part was true at least. For a moment he marvelled at how easy it was to see through this man. With such transparency there was simply nothing for him to fear. But then the journalist went on, and Sterling's brain went into freefall.

"I've tried to make it interesting, a few titbits of colour in there," Pierre said. "We discovered fairly early on that the British serial killer Charles Sterling – you may have heard of him? He was a client of Hawthorne and Langley's. He died last year, I believe, but he was well known even here in France. There's a Netflix show on him."

"Who?" Sterling managed to reply, his voice hollow.

"Charles Sterling? He was a mathematics professor. A complete freak as well; he killed a string of women back in the nineties. And he's really only famous now because he broke out of prison last year, escaping with this vast cryptocurrency fortune. I'm sure it was covered in *Le Monde*: you didn't read it?"

Sterling's mind spun, like disconnected gears.

"I... I guess I must have missed it." He managed to force a smile.

"Well, whatever." Cloarec had seemed mildly annoyed at this. "Give it a read. I'm going to take a piss."

Sterling did so, swallowing when he came to his own name and trying desperately to think. He heard the toilet flush upstairs and a moment later Pierre reappeared, glancing at him and then tending to the fire. He then set about replacing the chess pieces in their original positions, as if the world hadn't shifted and his life didn't hang in the balance. Still Sterling forced his mind to think through the implications of this surprise, and his best response to it.

"Well? What do you think?"

Sterling said nothing for a while; he still didn't trust his voice.

"It's interesting, very interesting." He managed a half smile, but still needed more time. He pushed himself up from the chair.

"Let me just grab a glass of water, and I'll give you my thoughts." Sterling forced his legs – suddenly stiff and awkward – to rise and carry him to the kitchen, where he stared at the tap for some time before finally setting a glass underneath and turning it on. His hand shook as he took a sip. Then he noticed two kitchen towels hanging on the handle of the oven. Without conscious thought he took one and ran it through his fingers. Next he took the other and knotted them together. He tested the knot by pulling at it, hard. Then he held the towels behind his back as he returned to the little sitting room.

"Well what do you think?" Cloarec asked a second time. "Did it connect with you?"

For the first time Sterling managed a genuine smile.

"Yes, I think so," he replied. For a few moments he felt conflicted. Regret – not for what was about to happen to his new French friend, but for himself, for the huge amount of work he'd put in to no longer being a killer.

"Yes, I really think it did," he said, cooly walking behind Cloarec so that the journalist had to twist his neck to keep his eyes on him. As Pierre turned the other way – as Sterling anticipated he would – he smoothly slipped the towels around his fat neck. He pulled both ends tight, and with a violent lunge wrenched him off the chair and onto the floor where he put his knee into the man's back, preventing him from struggling. As expected, Cloarec's hands went uselessly to the towels, trying to claw his fingers underneath the material which was now pulled so tight it was preventing him from taking in air. Pierre flipped, twisting and writhing like the fish they'd caught together only a few days before. Sterling breathed deeply as the Frenchman's body quickly used up the small amount of oxygen it had stored and the carbon dioxide built up in his system. He began to meditate again as Cloarec's struggles quietened and turned into mere twitches.

Only then did Sterling release the pressure on the man's neck.

THIRTY-THREE

Never once did Sterling lose control. He calibrated the pressure he'd applied with the utmost care, and released Cloarec just before he approached the point of no return. He left him there, slumped unconscious on the floor in front of the fire, while he returned to the kitchen to see what other useful items he could find. He was about to take a kitchen knife from the drawer when he noticed an old metal toolbox on the ground near the back door. He put it on the table, opened it and saw with satisfaction that it contained a good assortment of tools, mostly with a rough film of rust where they'd been mistreated over the years. He rummaged until he found a pair of pliers and checked them for sharpness. They were blunt, but he smiled at the thought of how impossible it would be to cut cleanly with such blades. Then he set about finding some rope, zip-ties or good-quality tape. That was harder. All he found was a length of string which didn't look terribly reliable. But there was a lot of it, and when he combined it with the power cable from the printer he'd bought, he could tie Cloarec's hands and legs to a chair, matching the still-unconscious man's body to the contours of the furniture so he could knot his hands, feet and neck securely. He was soon satisfied it was impossible for him to escape.

Then he waited, sitting in an armchair opposite Cloarec and sipping on the last of the cognac until the Frenchman came to.

And then he set to work.

THIRTY-FOUR

When Pierre came round he found himself tied to a chair, his hands bound to the armrests. Another cord was wrapped around his belly and the backrest of the chair. His neck hurt and breathing was difficult, so much so that he felt a flutter of fear that he might not be drawing in enough oxygen. But for a moment that fear subsided when he saw his friend Richard Brown sitting opposite him. And then he remembered.

"What..." he began, but the word cut into his sore throat; he tried to lift a hand to touch it but ended up only highlighting how tightly he was bound. Brown watched, no expression on his face. Pierre swallowed as gently as he was able.

"Why?" he asked this time. His voice was rough, rasping.

Brown pursed his lips, apparently considering. Pierre noticed a small pile of equipment on the table in front of him, tape, a hammer, a pair of pliers from the rusty toolbox in the kitchen. Next to them was a satsuma. It was this he picked up, throwing it thoughtfully from one hand to another.

"Open wide," he said finally.

When Cloarec didn't reply, Brown quickly grabbed his hair and yanked his head backwards, briefly pulling Cloarec's mouth open. It was all Brown needed, and he jammed the satsuma whole into Cloarec's mouth, using the heel of his palm to push it in past his teeth. The sharp tang of the fruit's skin filled Cloarec's mouth. He missed the opportunity to fight back, to bite down on Brown's fingers, and then again he missed the chance to spit the fruit out because Brown then wound the tape around his mouth and the back of his head. Cloarec moved his head first one way and then the other, as if this would stop the sensation of gagging and the renewed assault on his ability to breathe. Somehow the fruit shifted just enough for him to breathe, but his jaw hurt intensely where it had been stretched open.

"I'll be the one asking questions from now on," Brown said. His American accent was gone; he now sounded English.

Pierre felt a trickle of saliva creep down his gullet and managed a half swallow to clear it. He closed his eyes for a moment of relief, hoping that when he reopened them the view would be different, the situation improved. When it wasn't, his mind began to work quickly. He tried to find an explanation for his predicament. The only one that fitted was that this was somehow related to the Mancinis. And yet – how or why would they recruit a former American diplomat?

"I gave all this up, you know," Brown continued. His face was grim. "I went to a lot of effort and spent a lot of money to leave this all behind me, and you've forced me right back. That makes me angry. So if I get ahead of myself, if I cause you more pain that I really need to, you have to remember this is your fault. Not mine." He shook his head.

Cloarec strained to listen, to analyse the words for a trace of Italian, and another possibility exploded, again with a burst of relief. This was a joke. An ill-judged joke, to be sure, but at any moment Brown would release the knots that bound his hands and they would have a good laugh together. And then he would throw this lunatic out of the cottage, and maybe get in the little Peugeot and get the hell out of here.

But Brown didn't release the knots. Instead he took the pliers, carefully positioned himself to one side of the chair and took hold of Cloarec's index finger. For a second Pierre let him, still thinking this was a joke and he wouldn't hurt him for real, but then panic set in and he scrabbled to pull his finger away. And for a few moments it was comical. They scrabbled together, Brown trying to prise the finger loose, Cloarec doing everything he could to keep it hidden. After twenty seconds it seemed that Brown had it, only for Cloarec to pull it free again. This time Brown lost patience and went back to the table, picked up the small hammer and without a moment's hesitation swung it down onto the back of Cloarec's hand.

The pain arrived a second after the small metal head of the hammer punched down into the hand, clearly breaking two of the bones that led to the fingers. Cloarec's scream was muffled by the satsuma, which was ejected forward and was only prevented from escaping completely by the tape that held it in place. The initial wave of agony passed, followed by a second, more focussed signal that his brain was able to pinpoint to his suddenly shattered hand. Cloarec made no further attempt to hide his extended fingers. Five seconds later Brown had him, the tip of the finger caught between the jaws of the pliers. Brown relaxed visibly now, drawing in a deep breath and keeping just enough pressure on the handles so there was no way Cloarec could withdraw his finger.

Brown leaned forward and pulled the satsuma out of his mouth. He gave him a look to warn him it would go back in if he didn't keep quiet.

"Now. We're going to do some light editing to that article of yours."

PART FOUR

THIRTY-FIVE

Detective Sergeant Luke Golding knocked twice on the open office door, then waited until his boss called him inside, not looking up from the papers she was studying on her desk.

"Morning, ma'am," he said, his eyes glancing around the room.

There was a half-grunted response from DCI Sands, who still didn't look up.

Golding waited, until finally Sands was forced to stop what she was doing.

"What is it? What do you want?" She glanced up at last, looking impatient.

"I, uh, just wondered if you had any questions about the files," Golding replied. He indicated a stack of pale-yellow folders placed neatly on her desk. Placed by him in exactly that spot, three days earlier. "The case files the department's working on."

"Oh." Sands glanced at them too, then shoved them lightly, as if moving them a little would make it slightly less obvious she hadn't touched them.

"No. They seem... all good."

"Right, yeah." Golding nodded, but hesitated. "I mean I know they're not the biggest cases we've ever worked, but I wanted to be sure you were happy with how they were going?"

"Yes, of course." Sands suddenly looked serious. She seemed to observe her deputy a while before continuing, "No, I'm quite happy."

Still Golding hesitated. "There was, um... one more thing." He moved closer to her desk and the stack of files, but waited.

"What is it?" Sands frowned now. Golding was now standing right by her desk and could see she was reading. Though he couldn't read Vietnamese, there was little doubt what case she was working on.

"It's uh..." – Golding made himself sound embarrassed – "It's just I wrote a birthday card for my niece. I think it might have slipped into the files somehow." He picked the top one up and flicked through it. A moment later he pulled out a birthday card, with the words "Congratulations! You are SIX!" printed on the front. He flapped it against his hand.

"Probably better if this doesn't go to the CPS. And have a copy sent to the defence lawyers..."

Sands stared at the card with a deep frown on her face. She sat back in her chair.

"I was going to ask how old she was." For a second Luke almost fell for her bluff, before showing her the six in giant letters.

"That was actually a joke, Luke. Didn't you tell me I needed to make more jokes?"

He gave a half smile, half shrug, then waited. Sands sat back in her chair.

"So you didn't leave that in there by accident," she said after a while.

"Not a real accident. No."

"You actually thought," Sands continued, 'that if I gave the card back it would have meant I'd seen it, which would have meant I'd looked through the files. But since I didn't give it back, it means I'd ignored them?"

Golding's eyes moved to the office wall, where a world map had been pinned on a whiteboard, with dozens of tiny notes attached. Some in Brazil, but the majority in the Far East. Vietnam featured strongly.

"Something like that," he said eventually.

"Well, maybe you've neglected to consider that I might actually just trust you? Or that maybe I was going to take them home tonight to look at them?"

"Yeah, maybe." He glanced at her. "Were you?"

Sands looked away this time, drawing in a deep breath.

"*Fuck.* Do I need to?"

Luke smiled again. "I don't think so. I think we're fine. I'm just... I dunno." He lifted his hands in another half shrug.

"Shit, I'm..." It took Sands some time to form the words, and then they came out strangled. "I *apologise* Luke, I should have given them more attention."

"It's fine. Really it is. I understand." He considered his words. "I sort of understand. And I sort of don't." She sent him a glance at this.

He felt uncomfortable pushing her. But surely they both knew this level of obsession couldn't be sustained. Not if it meant she wasn't doing her day job.

"How's it going by the way?" Golding asked her, the question almost surprising him. He pointed towards the paper she was reading. "How's the Vietnamese coming?"

"It's not," she replied. "At least, not easily. But I want to speak to the locals who work at the clinic again, and I don't trust the translators."

Golding nodded. "This is the clinic where he died?" As soon as he spoke he bit his lip, wishing he could rephrase. Sands' head jerked up to stare at him.

"I mean, where he *might have* died. Where you think he faked his death..."

Sands seemed on the verge of rebuking him, but the speed at which he corrected himself apparently gave her pause.

"That's right," she said slowly.

Golding nodded, considering. He thought about saying more but decided against it. He tapped the birthday card against his hand again, as if reminding them both of the real reason he'd come in.

"Oh, there was one more thing," he said. "Did you hear about Susan Hunter?"

The name seemed to mean something to Sands, but clearly she couldn't place it.

"The woman in the coma? DI Karim's case? He was going for an attempted murder charge, saying her husband pushed her down the stairs. But you... let's say you tore him a new one because he didn't have the basics right. You said we'd be better off waiting till she wakes up and asking her if he did it?"

"Oh. Yes. What about her?"

Golding flashed a smile. "She woke up."

"Oh."

For the first time in the conversation Golding felt he had her attention, or most of it.

"What state's she in?" Sands asked.

"I haven't heard. Apparently Karim's in quite a state though. I think he was hoping she went the other way, so he could upgrade the case to murder."

The details appeared to come back to Sands, but more slowly than Golding was used to.

"She was the... sleep-walker, correct? With spinal injuries... and a brain injury? She'll need rehab to learn to walk again, maybe even to speak." She fell quiet. Golding wondered if she was considering her own time in hospital, recovering from being shot and blown up. Something about that, some element of caring about her and worrying about her, made him go on.

"How long do you reckon you're going to be looking into this?" he asked.

"Looking into what?" Sands asked. She didn't seem to follow him.

"All this. Sterling," Golding replied. He waved a hand towards the whiteboard, the documents in Vietnamese on her desk. He offered a half smile to show he meant the question in a supportive way.

"Until I find him," Sands replied, but she wouldn't meet his eye. He waited a beat and then went on.

"But what if he really is dead? What if there's nothing to find?" It was a question he'd wanted to ask for some time, and now he had, the words began to flow. "It's been, what? A year now? And you don't have any actual proof he didn't die, it's just a hunch." Golding shrugged. "I just don't see where it ends. What if he really did die from cancer, and you spend your whole life trying to prove otherwise?"

Sands shook her head quickly, but she seemed less certain than usual, less aggressive. "If he really did die, why not let us see his body? Then we'd know for sure."

"The guy from Interpol, Briggs? Didn't he have a theory about that? Sterling had his body burned so you'd spend your life not knowing for sure. Like it was his last act of defiance against you?"

This time Sands looked away, and there was an awkward silence in the little office.

"And what about the money? If he wasn't dead, would he really have given away nearly half a billion pounds?" Golding shook his head again. "That's the part I struggle with. I know he was different, but how many people on earth would give away that much money?"

"It doesn't prove anything. Certainly not that he's dead,"

Sands insisted. "Sterling didn't care about money; it would have been easy for him to give it away, knowing the effect it would have on me."

Golding glanced at her, seemingly about to say something, but then he stopped himself.

"What?" Sands asked sharply.

"Nothing."

"Spit it out."

"It's just... You've told me before how easy it would be to give up half a billion, so..." He paused.

"So what?"

Golding bit his lip. "So how come you haven't? Given it away I mean. You've said how you're going to give the money away, to charities or whatever – but you haven't actually done so. So maybe it *isn't* that easy?" He drew in a deep breath, preparing himself for an onslaught that was now surely coming his way. But Sands didn't rebuke him the way he expected.

"I haven't decided what to do with it yet. I'm not *spending* it."

"I'm not saying you are. But you must have heard people talking, around the department. Christ, everyone here is tracking the price of Bitcoin, trying to work out when their boss is officially going to become a billionaire. If it was so easy to give it away, you'd have done so by now."

"Do you want it?" Sands stared right at him. "Is that what this is about? Because if so just say the word, and it's yours. I'll hand it over right now, and you can figure out what to do with it."

Golding swallowed, shook his head.

"I don't want your money."

"Well then? Doesn't that hole your theory below the water-line? If you won't take it?"

He considered. "Not really. Not if you were never actually going to give it to me."

For a moment they stared at each other. Then Sands buried her head in her hands before suddenly jumping off her seat and moving to the whiteboard. On the left was a print-out of a spreadsheet.

"Look. This is a track of the value of his assets, after he escaped. This is how much he left to me, and this is an estimate I've put together of how much it would have cost him to get to Vietnam, with estimates for the false paperwork et cetera. This is how much he paid for the clinic. I've calculated that he would have had *millions* more than he left to me. Millions of pounds, Luke, unaccounted for. Almost certainly he *didn't* give his whole fortune to me, he kept some. Doesn't that tell you he's still alive?"

Golding studied it, not seeing exactly what she did but knowing her well enough to trust what she said. But he was saved from answering by a knock at the door.

THIRTY-SIX

"Not interrupting am I?" Superintendent Yorke hesitated at the doorway of Sands' office. She stopped what she was doing, then moved away from the whiteboard.

"No, come in."

He tried to close the door behind him; she normally left it wedged open with a doorstop and he had to struggle for a moment to get it to move. When it finally shut it changed the feel of the room. Golding felt uncomfortable, unsure if the superintendent had registered that he was there.

"I was just finished..." he began, but Yorke waved a hand.

"Actually this concerns you as well, Luke, if you're not too busy?"

"No, sure." He shook his head, and Yorke indicated the single chair facing Sands' desk.

"Have a seat," he said to Golding while he perched on the table. Sands sat down too, in her chair behind the desk.

"What's this about?" she asked.

Yorke took a while to answer, as if he were searching for the correct way to start.

"It's about the way things are being run at the moment," he said after a while. "And the fact they can't go on this way."

Sands muttered something under her breath; to Golding it sounded like 'another one'. Then she shook her head with a firm smile. "What's the problem exactly?"

"The first problem is that I have Detective Sergeant Golding here practically running the department, while you—"

"I trust Luke, sir. He's doing an excellent job."

"I don't doubt that, but it's not the point."

"And I'm supervising him. I'm up to speed on all the current cases." Sands picked up the pile of folders that Golding had left on her desk, and which she still hadn't looked at. She held them in the air for a moment, then let them fall with a heavy thump.

"Again, I don't doubt it, Erica. But it's hardly the point. I've asked you to handle those cases, and you're not doing so. Instead you're..." – he waved a hand at the whiteboard, but didn't seem to want to actually look at it – "chasing ghosts."

There was a silence.

"He's not a ghost. If I could be certain he was dead, I wouldn't be chasing—"

"Except he might be dead."

Golding decided to intervene.

"I don't have a problem with the workload at the moment sir," he began. "It's not like we have any major cases."

"Yes, well maybe that's about to change," Yorke replied, half under his breath.

"What does that mean?" Sands asked.

"You remember DI Karim's case? Susan Hunter? The woman who may or may not have been pushed down the stairs by her husband? In the middle of the night after an argument?"

"Yes." Sands avoided Golding's eye.

"She came out of her coma last week, and from what she's

been able to say so far, she's confirmed what her husband has been saying all along. That she tripped while sleep-walking."

Sands seemed to consider for a second, then shrugged. "So how does that equal a major case?"

"Because Karim followed your advice, that's why. He checked with the television streaming company to see if they really had been watching a series involving an argument that night. And they hadn't been. He took sound readings from their apartment – everything you suggested. He based his whole case on what you told him, and then charged the husband with attempted murder. Now that's fallen apart, we're looking at a civil case. Wrongful arrest without probable cause." There was another silence, during which Golding thought he noticed Sands glancing wistfully at the documents on her desk.

"I hardly see how it's my problem sir, if I was the one pushing for a more thorough investigation."

"It's your problem if this department is about to get sued," Yorke snapped back.

He got to his feet, walked over to the whiteboard and studied it for a few moments. Then he turned back to Sands, rubbing his chin.

"Look, Erica, this isn't an official visit. But I have to tell you, the next one will be. This has to stop." He waved at the whiteboard. "What you do in your free time is up to you, but when you're at work you cannot be investigating the possible whereabouts of the late Charles Sterling. Not any more. Not at the expense of everything else."

Golding considered interrupting as the superintendent went on to outline how he'd been running the team despite not being fully qualified, and certainly not being fully paid, to do so.

"Fine," Sands said suddenly, surprising Yorke into silence.

"Fine what?" he asked.

"I'll step down."

The superintendent didn't seem to understand.

"Step down from what?"

"From the job. I don't need it any more anyway. I certainly don't need the money. Sergeant Golding has just informed me the whole department is aware of that."

"Erica, that's not what I'm saying," Yorke sighed. "That's not what I'm here for…"

"No, actually it's fine. I've been considering handing in my notice for a while. If I'm going to make sense of what happened in that clinic in Vietnam I need to be there. I still have suspicions about that German doctor, Guttenheim. He's disappeared since I last spoke with him, which suggests he was involved in faking Sterling's death—"

"Erica!"

"What?"

"I can't let you leave!" Yorke sounded incredulous. "What else are you going to do? This is your life."

Sands was silent a moment as she glanced around the tiny office. Not for the first time, Golding wondered what sort of a life it was.

"OK, how about a leave of absence? I'll take six months off. Unpaid."

Yorke looked away. To Golding's surprise he seemed to be considering it.

"What if you can't prove he's alive in six months?"

"A year then. However long it takes."

Yorke stared at her. "Who runs the department while you're gone?"

"I don't know. That's your problem. Luke's doing a pretty good job of it. My point is, I understand this isn't sustainable. I realise I've pushed my luck." She stood. "I'm no fool, I know you can't allow this to continue, but see it from my perspective. I *need* certainty on this. And I won't get it here if I'm distracted trying to find out if Paul Hunter did or did not push his wife down the stairs."

She stopped, visibly breathing hard now.

"You're actually serious?" Yorke said.

"Yes."

There was an awkward silence.

Yorke broke it. "I'd ask what you're going to live on, but I guess that's not a problem."

Sands shook her head. "I had savings even before Sterling left me the money," she replied. "But I guess I can dip into it. If I use his money to find him, there's a poetic justice to it. Even if that's what he wanted all along."

Golding looked from one of them to the other.

"What will you actually do?" he asked.

"I don't know. If I can track down Guttenheim, maybe I can get something out of him." Golding thought she'd go on, tell them she had a better lead than that. But instead her voice faded away. Yorke sighed, his shoulders slumped.

"I can't not make this official," he said. "If you take a leave of absence, that's what it will be. You'll lose your office; I doubt you'll be able to come back to this position."

"Fine. Agreed. Actually it'll be a relief. For Luke as well, I'm sure." As if to demonstrate this she began gathering together the documents in front of her into a pile, as if about to sweep them into her bag and leave.

"You're actually serious?" Yorke said. "This isn't what I wanted when I came in here. To lose the best detective this department has."

She glanced at Golding before replying.

"You still have the second best."

THIRTY-SEVEN

One month later, and the changes at the Murder Investigation Department had bedded in. A new DCI from London had agreed to head the department, and though his style was rather different to that of Sands, the fact that he was actually engaged with the work was a definite improvement. For Golding at least, who now only had to do the job he was paid for. So when his phone rang, mid-afternoon on a quiet Wednesday, he answered it in an upbeat voice.

"DS Golding, how can I help?"

The woman on the other end of the line sounded hesitant, her voice heavily accented. French perhaps?

"I was... I am trying to reach Detective Chief Inspector Sands? Erica Sands?"

It wasn't the first call that had come in for Sands since she'd left, and Golding pursed his lips.

"She's uh... she's on a leave of absence. But maybe I can help? What's it about?"

"I was told she was leading the investigation into Charles Sterling, the serial killer who escaped from—"

Golding sat up a little straighter at his desk.

"I... I know who he is. Who's speaking please?"

"Um, my name is Clémence Girard, I'm a reporter for *Le Monde* newspaper, here in Paris. This is just a..." – she hesitated, as if searching for the right phrase – "courtesy call?"

"What about?"

She went on, but now it sounded as though she were reading from a script. "We are investigating a large data leak from an offshore financial firm based in the Cayman Islands. It involves the financial information of thousands of individuals. Part of my job is to notify law enforcement where those individuals are or were of interest to the police."

Golding had done his best to follow, but he blinked in confusion. "I'm sorry, I don't understand."

There was a slight sigh, as if the woman had explained this many times without quite finding the right way to do so.

"Charles Sterling's name appears in the files. It seems he used the firm we are investigating to move and hide money. We have a duty of care to let you know, because of your investigation into him. It is our intention to name him in the articles when they are published—"

"Whoa, whoa!" Golding found himself almost laughing at the sudden absurdity of the call. "Sterling's dead, there is no investigation."

"Yes, I'm aware of that. I spoke to a man at Interpol." There was a delay, apparently while she checked something. "A man named Jonathan Briggs. He was leading their case into Sterling. It was Mr Briggs who gave me the name of Detective Sands. He said that I ought to speak to her. But as I said, this is just a courtesy call. If there is no investigation into Charles Sterling, then there is nothing to be done. I am simply – I think you say dotting the i and crossing the t..."

"Where are you?" Golding interrupted.

"I am in Paris. Why do you ask?"

"Can I come and see you?"

A pause.

"I'm sorry, why would you do that?"

Golding considered before answering. The real reason was that if he passed this onto Sands, she'd probably be in Paris within the hour, probably not-too-subtly interrogating a journalist from a major newspaper. The role he'd just played in sorting out the fallout from Paul Hunter's wrongful arrest had given him a fresh understanding of the need for subtlety in media relations, and he didn't want a new shitstorm to calm. And if he *didn't* pass this onto Sands... well he didn't like to think what might happen then.

"There are a few loose ends regarding Charles Sterling," he said eventually. "This might be the break we've been waiting for."

"Loose ends?" She sounded unsure about this.

"It's nothing to worry about. But if we could meet up, maybe you could show me what you've got? I'll know then if it's going to help us."

Clémence didn't reply.

"What was your name again?" Golding asked. "Can I call you back?"

Golding got her details and jogged up the stairs to Yorke's office.

"Sands was following the money," he concluded after he'd explained the call. "She thinks that's the best way to prove if he's dead or alive. If this proves he's dead, then maybe we can convince her? Maybe we can get her off this self-destruction route."

Yorke sat still for a while, considering. "Are you talking about telling her?" he asked in the end. "Taking her to Paris to speak with this journalist?"

"Absolutely not. I'm talking about going there to find out if there's anything she needs to know about. So that she doesn't end up going herself. Maybe we'll tell her later – if it helps her put this whole thing behind her."

Yorke spent a few moments stroking his chin. His eyes darted to a whiteboard which displayed a neat chart summarising the departmental workload. Without needing to read it he knew Golding wasn't overly busy at that time. He pulled in a deep breath.

"OK. Go to Paris. Talk to them and find out what this is about. But don't say anything to Sands."

THIRTY-EIGHT

The Eurostar swept Golding quickly across the wide, flat expanses of northern France, and then slowed into Gare du Nord station. He disembarked and followed the directions on his phone, down the steps into the Métro. He had to change trains at a station called Montparnasse-Bienvenüe, eventually looking up at the glass and steel offices of *Le Monde* feeling like he'd somehow landed a bit part in a spy movie. Inside the building the feeling grew, as a receptionist of unclear gender telephoned Clémence while eyeing Golding with cool disinterest. When the journalist appeared, Golding felt like he'd suddenly been promoted to the movie's lead role. Clémence Girard was strikingly beautiful, with wavy blonde hair and deep blue eyes.

"I have booked one of our meeting rooms," she said, tossing her hair as she said something in rapid French to the receptionist, who typed Golding's details in and printed out a plastic name badge.

"*Voilà*," they said, handing it to him.

"*Merci*." Golding's attempt at French didn't evoke a smile.

"How was your trip?" Clémence asked as he followed her up a flight of marble stairs.

"It was fine," Golding replied. He was still a little taken aback. The journey had given him time to plan for this meeting. He wanted to understand as much as possible about the documents the newspaper had on Charles Sterling. But the moment he'd seen Clémence he found himself instantly distracted. "*Attracted to*" would be a better description, he admitted privately. He was unable to prevent his eyes followed the curves of her body as she walked up the steps ahead of him, gripped tightly by a dark-blue woollen dress, her legs sheathed in sheer tights.

"Have you been to Paris before?" She turned her head to glance at him and he quickly lifted his eyes to her face. She unlocked the door to a small glass-walled meeting room, pulled out a chair at the table but waited until he sat before doing the same.

"No." He prepared to smile, but the young Frenchwoman was already concentrating on her paperwork, which she'd been carrying under her arm. Golding was powerless to not take the moment to study her. She was about his age, maybe a few years younger. He inhaled lightly but deeply, trying to draw in the perfume she was wearing.

When she looked up she was frowning, pressing dimples into her cheeks. "There is actually very little mention of Charles Sterling in the papers," she explained, looking at him in a way that seemed to say there was no reason for him coming all this way. But then she began to explain.

"It seems in his case the situation is complicated. He was using a false name, and also required false identity papers in this name." She shook her head, frowning again at the papers, as if unable to make full sense of them. For a second Golding's mind refused to concentrate, but he forced himself to listen.

"My colleague has led the work on this section of the

papers," Clémence went on. "I am not so familiar with the case personally... He tells me that Sterling's real name was used in an email from a banker in Switzerland, explaining that his... background was the reason for the unusual arrangements."

"This bank knew he was a convicted murderer? That didn't concern them?"

"Many of the clients of these firms are engaged in criminal activity, including drug smuggling and organised crime. If the sums of money involved are large enough, they are not put off by violence." For the first time she offered a smile, albeit a cool one.

Golding sat back. "Wow," he said.

"Yes," Clémence replied. This time she looked him square in the eyes. For a few moments neither of them looked away.

"Can you tell me what name he used?" Golding asked, glancing down now. "The false identity?"

He waited while she studied her papers, and tried not to study her.

"I can see he was initially referred to as David Smith. Later he's Jeremy Collins, but he may have used other names. As I say, I'm not personally familiar with the details, they were tracked by my colleague."

Golding turned his head, trying to see what she was reading, but she'd laid her arm over the document, keeping it hidden from him.

"No, that's fine," Golding said. He leaned in closer, still trying to see.

"So how much money did he move? Do you know that?"

She shook her head, her golden hair catching the light from the window, which Golding only now noticed offered a beautiful view of the city's grey slate roofs.

"Not in detail, *non*." The French caught at his mind, reminding him where he was. "It is enough for us to show that Sterling used the firm. He is..." She searched for a word again, this time turning away so Golding was left looking into the bright white of the sides of her eyes. She looked back. "Colour. For the articles."

Golding narrowed his eyes, for the first time not understanding.

"We have literally millions of documents, and no key to make sense of them. To work through them, to track a transaction, it takes many days, perhaps weeks of work, and even then we might be missing a crucial document. We are most concerned with the politicians or famous people who have used this firm to break our tax laws. Hypocritical people, who say one thing in public and do another in secret. You understand?"

"Yeah, I think so. Sterling isn't a priority."

"Exactly." Again she smiled at him, more warmly this time. Golding couldn't help but smile back. For a second time she held his gaze, as if she too was a little unsettled by the meeting. Then she looked away again.

"Can I get a copy of those papers?" Golding asked.

"*Non,*" Clémence replied at once, shaking her head. "That will not be possible. I can share with you this summary, but I cannot reveal the source of the information. I cannot share with you the documents. I hope you understand the ethical reasons for this." She placed her arms over the paperwork and looked up at him, blinking her blue eyes.

"Actually, I'm not sure I do..."

"But you must have been expecting this?" Clémence went on. She looked genuinely confused, and he had to smile again, she damn near melted his heart.

"You have similar rules for press freedom in the United Kingdom, no?"

He had no idea, and should have checked before getting here. "I guess we do."

"And Mr Sterling is deceased, no? So there is no actual investigation regarding him?"

That part was right. "Yeah."

"Then you will understand," she said firmly. But she went on. "Actually, I am not sure exactly why it is you are here, Detective Golding."

"I'm not exactly sure myself," Golding replied, and for a moment he enjoyed the way this made her face crumple again with confusion. "My boss is..." – he stopped – "My former boss, Erica Sands – the woman you were trying to get in touch with – she's kind of obsessed with this case. I wanted to come out here so that she doesn't."

"Doesn't what?"

"Come out here." Golding paused again. He was aware that he was telling this young woman more that he ought to, given her status as a journalist. But he owed her an explanation, for letting him come out to see her. And much more than that, he was enjoying speaking to her. He glanced down at her hands to see if she wore a ring, and she caught him looking. She folded her slender, unadorned hands one on top of the other. Hiding them, or maybe drawing his attention?

"Why is she obsessed?"

Golding laughed at that, and looked away. "That's a long story."

"Is it an interesting story?" she enquired pointedly, and then after a pause she continued, her voice normal again. "One that perhaps could be incorporated into the article we are writing?"

"No. I don't think so," Golding shook his head. "No, that wouldn't be helpful." He smiled, again telling himself to focus. It still didn't quite work.

"What exactly are you planning to say about Sterling in your article?" he asked.

She seemed to tighten up briefly at the question, but soon relaxed again. "As I understand it, very little. He is simply mentioned as a person who has used the services of this firm to launder money. Mostly the article will focus on other people. A politician, and a television presenter who is very famous here in France. I cannot give you their names, I am very sorry."

That's fine, Golding thought. He hoped Sands would never see the article. He wondered if that would be better.

"When will it come out?"

"We are going to run the first exposé next Sunday. My boss..." – she winced at the word, wrinkling her nose – "He is writing the first of them at the moment."

"OK." Another thought occurred to Golding. "Does that mean you're phoning police forces all over the world, telling them about the criminals using this firm?"

She shook her head. *"Non.* Only those people who will appear in the article. There are millions of documents, covering tens of thousands of clients. It would not be possible for us to alert the authorities to every one of them."

Golding nodded, it was making sense now.

"Any chance I could see the article, before it goes out?"

She hesitated, and he sensed she was on the verge of saying no, but something stopped her. He smiled again, thinking that maybe he knew why.

"Perhaps I could do that. I would have to check with my boss."

"Would you mind? It could help me with *my* boss." He smiled again, and the idea seemed to hang in the air between them. A connection made.

"OK." Golding tapped his fingers on the desk, wondering whether there was more he could do, having come all this way. "You say you haven't tried to track Sterling's money. Is there any chance you could? Now, I mean?" As he spoke he wasn't sure if his intention was to find out more about Sterling, or the journalist sitting in front of him. And when she answered he got the clear sense she was similarly conflicted.

"Non." She shook her hair again. "Impossible. I have too

much work to do this afternoon. But..." She glanced up at him, hesitated and then seemed to come to a decision.

"Perhaps if you could meet me when I finish work? It is possible that I could look through the files then? I cannot promise anything, but perhaps there is something I can tell you?"

Golding nodded happily. He very much hoped so.

Golding was left with three hours to kill. At first he walked at random, but after seeing the distinctive outline of the Eiffel Tower framed between two buildings, as if cut out from a poster and dropped in front of him, he began walking towards it, and finally stood underneath the giant steel structure. Lines of tourists queued to gain access but he didn't bother joining them. Instead he carried on through the Champs de Mars gardens, where couples lounged on the grass. He was asked by three German girls if he'd take their photograph. They were young, students perhaps, and they giggled as the girl who handed him her phone blushed. He did his best to frame them with the iconic tower in the background. And as he handed the phone back the girls glancing approvingly at him. They were pretty, but not nearly as attractive as the journalist he was due to meet in – he checked his watch – forty-five minutes.

He realised suddenly that he'd thought of little else the entire time he'd been walking.

THIRTY-NINE

He spotted her as she left the *Le Monde* offices. The building, and those around it, were discharging a steady flow of workers. After his walk, and the earlier journey from England, Golding felt the muscles in his legs ache, but she led him at a brisk pace through the already darkening streets. Fast enough that it crossed his mind that she was keen that no one should see them together.

"Are you hungry?" she asked at one point.

"Actually, yes."

They had already passed many cafés and restaurants, and Clémence led him past several more before she pushed open the door to a wine bar named Les Papilles.

"This will be quiet, we can talk here without being overheard."

A waiter appeared and Clémence spoke to him in impenetrable, vowel-filled French. The man nodded and led them to a table in the corner, briefly disappearing before returning with a large bottle of sparkling water. He opened it and poured them each a glass. If Clémence had asked the waiter about food, he seemed to have forgotten.

The bar was mostly empty, but Clémence still looked around carefully before pulling her laptop from a bag and placing it on the table in front of her.

"We must be careful," she said. "Some of the people who are implicated in this data leak are dangerous."

"Sterling among them," Golding replied.

"I don't think so..." – she shook her golden hair – "not any more." He frowned at this, and she gave him a curious expression. "He is dead, no?" Her head tipped just slightly onto one side.

"Yes, of course." Golding frowned slightly at his lack of professionalism. Of course Sterling was dead. He took a sip of his water as he thought about that. For nearly a year Sands had tried to convince him this wasn't the case. And while everyone else seemed quite convinced she was wrong, her insistence, and the high regard he held her in, made it hard to be completely certain.

He waited while she typed into her computer. He realised after a while that she was searching in a database of some kind, but it didn't seem to be going well.

"*Non,*" she said after a while.

"'*Non*' what?" he asked, before telling himself not to attempt her accent. "What does that mean exactly?"

"*Non,* I will have to speak with my boss. The files..." – her nose wrinkled again as she went on – "The data leak is very large – enormous. I assumed it would be possible to see why my boss had included Sterling's name, but... it is strange..." Her voice tailed off. "I am sorry, it appears I have wasted your time."

"No, no," Golding heard himself reply at once, but he was frustrated too, a little intrigued. "So you don't have anything there about Charles Sterling?"

"I have millions of files on tens of thousands of clients, but it is not so easy to access the documents which are about Sterling.

I am sorry." She shrugged and glanced towards the door, as if she were thinking about leaving. He didn't want that.

"Could you call your boss? To find out? Would you be able to do that?"

She shook her hair again, and he got another waft of the perfume from her shampoo.

"Is he... difficult? Your boss?" He offered an understanding smile.

"It is not that. He is not here in Paris. And where he is there is no reception on his mobile telephone. I could send him an email," – she was thinking aloud now – "but it is unlikely he will reply." Suddenly she looked directly in his eyes.

"How long are you staying in Paris?"

The honest answer was that Golding didn't know. His expectation had been to travel here and return on the same day. But he'd bought an open ticket, allowing him to travel on any train. And while he'd been waiting for her, he'd found out there were any number of hotels he could check into at any time, should their business meeting run later than the trains.

"That depends," he said. "If I need to stay a day or so to get the information I need, that's not a problem."

"In that case I will ask him now." She looked down at the screen, and he watched as her elegant fingers tapped out a message. Finally she hit send and closed the lid. The action seemed to signal the end of the professional part of the meeting. The atmosphere briefly threatened to turn awkward.

"It must be exciting, working on stories like this?" Golding asked. Clémence took a while to answer; she touched a hand to her neck, and the light gold chain that hung around it. He sensed she was deciding whether to stay, or make her excuses and leave.

"It probably sounds more exciting that the reality," she said at last.

"Why's that?"

"Mostly what we do is chase paper trails," she replied. "But it is... exhilarating." She seemed to make a decision, and relaxed a little. "I like that what we do can be important. It can make the world a better place. It must be similar with yourself. Working for the police?"

Golding shrugged. "I don't know. We do a lot of chasing paper trails too. Watching hours of CCTV footage. But it has its moments." He smiled at what he'd just said. "Like this one."

She frowned now, her nose crumpling. She hadn't got his reference.

"Sending me to Paris, I mean. Meeting exotic journalists who are publishing stories that are making the world better."

The compliment was well judged, the praise for her work allowing her to ignore his subtle reference to her beauty. "*I* am not publishing the story. My boss will be taking all the credit. He's making very sure of that."

"Well, I hope you get some," Golding replied. Again the conversation paused, but this time it was less awkward.

"Are you hungry?" she asked for the second time. "The food here is quite good."

Golding glanced at his watch before replying. He frowned for a few seconds, pretending to consider his options.

"I don't have anything else on," he replied.

She laughed for the first time while they were studying the menus and it became obvious how little French he understood. Then he turned the card over and saw an English translation on the other side, but retained some pride by pointing out how poor it was. In the end she ordered for both of them. And while they waited they talked about her role at the newspaper and how she'd got the job in the first place, working initially as an unpaid intern. She asked him about his family and he described his sister, working as an artist on the Isle of Wight, a place she'd never heard of.

"So you've never been to England," he asked after a while.

"Never," she replied, as if challenging him. "Why would I?"

"Because it's only twenty miles over the English Channel," he replied.

"La Manche," Clémence rebuked him. "It is only the English Channel to the English. To the rest of the world it is La Manche. And besides, you told me you had never been to Paris before? How is it possible you could avoid the most beautiful city in the world?"

"I never had any reason to come before." They were flirting now. Or rather *he* was flirting, but there was no doubt she was beginning to respond.

"Your English is very good," he said. "Where did you learn it?"

"In school." She gave a casual shrug. "And from watching TV, and I studied in Berlin for a year." She was quiet a moment and he felt a pang of utterly irrational jealousy for anyone she might have met out there.

"And your French is terrible," she interrupted him. "How is it that so many English cannot speak another language?" She watched as he topped up their glasses with wine; the bottle was nearly empty.

He apologised on behalf of his nation, and she gave him a rebuking look but then took on a more serious tone.

"Tell me, Mr Policeman, when you talked about your boss before, you said you were worried she might come here. Why does that worry you?" It wasn't a topic that Golding particularly wanted to return to. But he was happy to tackle any subject that interested her. He considered how to reply.

"She's an interesting person, Erica Sands," he said. "She's kind of obsessive. Kind of brilliant too, but she's not subtle."

"Brilliant?"

"Yes, I'd say so."

"That's not a term many people use to describe their bosses."

"You wouldn't use it to describe your boss?"

She thought about this, turning away so he could admire her profile for a moment.

"Actually, yes, in a way. He is a great journalist. A very good writer, but perhaps not a great person."

"Why not?"

"He's old-fashioned. He comes from a generation where he expects certain things. For example, that a younger female colleague would want to sleep with him."

"I can see how that might be awkward."

"I think English men are different, no? You do not have the expectation that every young woman will want to be your mistress?"

"I can't speak for every Englishman," Golding replied, 'but not personally."

She held his gaze for a moment, before looking away.

The restaurant had filled up while they were eating their main course, but was now emptying again. They finished their desserts and the waiter brought the bill.

"It's late," Clémence said, looking around as if suddenly noticing. A further realisation seemed to hit her. "Where will you stay?"

Golding gave her a white lie. "I booked into a hotel earlier."

She seemed to consider this. "And then you will go back to England tomorrow. Over – or under – La Manche – and I will never see you again?"

He didn't answer, but put his credit card down. She glanced at it, and after a moment added hers. She spoke quickly to the waiter, who split the bill across the two cards. Golding didn't complain.

When they left the restaurant the night was cold. When he helped her into her coat, she seemed to struggle just a little more than she needed to, so that their bodies brushed together. Golding felt hot pulses of electricity flowing around his body. He held his breath as she took his hand and led him across the road to a row of taxis. Leaning in close to the window she gave instructions to the driver, and then opened the rear door. She climbed in, and – giving him a look – pulled him onto the seat next to her. Neither of them spoke, and she held onto his hand. Golding saw the driver glancing repeatedly at them in the rear-view mirror as he drove them through the now-quiet streets.

They arrived at what he guessed was her apartment build-ing, and this time Clémence paid the fare. Still holding his hand she led him through the front door and into a marble-floored lobby. A bank of mailboxes was fixed on one side, a giant mirror on the other. With some sense of disbelief he watched their reflections as Clémence led him further inside the building, to a tiny lift. They had to wait while it descended, and still she held his hand. But the moment the lift door closed behind them, she pulled him close and wrapped her hands behind his head, drawing him towards her and kissing him hard on the mouth. Thirty seconds later the lift stopped and so did she. She led him down a dark corridor to a dark-stained door. She used her keys to open it and pulled it open. She went to pull him inside, but this time he stopped her. Not wanting to, but wanting to be clear on one point.

"This can't go anywhere," he said. "Not with you here, and me in England."

She paused, her fingers toying with his hand. She regarded it for a few moments, then looked up into his face.

"Then let's make the most of now." She let herself fall back-wards so that she was leaning against the wall on the inside of her apartment, still holding onto his hand. She pulled him lightly towards her and he closed the front door behind him. The cliché of it struck him as he kissed her in the hallway of her apartment, not knowing or caring if she had any flatmates. But as she unbuckled the belt of his trousers he guessed she didn't and began working on opening her blouse. Eventually they moved together through the nearest doorway, which turned out to be her bedroom. He allowed himself one more thought before giving in to the desire he felt: *Sometimes, life comes at you fast.*

He didn't know how true this would turn out to be.

FORTY

She woke him with a groan. When he remembered where he was and how he'd got there, he tried to read her expression; she was watching him with deep blue eyes that were both captivating but somehow suspicious.

"I have to work," she said. "I'm going to take a shower." She reached for a towel on the chair beside the bed and used it to cover herself as she stepped out of bed and into the bathroom. He considered asking to join her, but decided instead to try to make coffee. He got out of bed, found his trousers and shirt and walked barefoot to the kitchen. The fridge was nearly empty, but he found a coffee maker on the stove and filled it, then stood by the window, gazing at a view she must enjoy every morning, the quiet side-streets of Paris slowly waking up. When the coffee was made he carried two cups back to the bedroom. He found her with the towel wrapped around her, drying her hair.

"*Merci*," she smiled at him now; the suspicion in her eyes seemed to have disappeared.

"*De rien*," he replied.

"I wondered if you would take the opportunity to sneak away."

Golding frowned, genuinely not understanding. "Why would I do that?"

She simply shrugged and sipped elegantly at her coffee. When her phone chimed from the bedside table she ignored it, instead placing her coffee cup neatly next to it. Golding's own phone was still in his trouser pocket. Its battery must be almost completely drained by now: a little awkward as his Eurostar ticket was electronic only. But the thought of that, of a train taking him away from her, made Golding want to move closer now. He slipped his hand behind her head, pulling her gently towards him, meaning to kiss her again, but she pushed him away. But instead of letting go completely she held onto him.

"*Désolée.* I have to work." She bit her lip, their heads close together.

"What do we do about this?" Golding asked. But she shook her head and then gave a little shrug. She seemed about to answer when her phone sounded again, a call this time.

"*Merde.*"

She pushed him away properly this time and rolled across the bed to accept the call, now sitting on the bed facing away from him. Golding watched as he caught a stream of French on the other end, a man's voice. He tried to work out what he was going to do next. Should he use the Eurostar ticket? Was there any way he could stay and spend more time with Clémence?

"*Quoi?*" she said, her tone suddenly different. She said something else, far too fast for him to catch the words, let alone understand. Then she listened again for a while. She stood up abruptly, pulling the phone lead from the wall as she did so. She spoke again, striding quickly to the window and pulling the towel closer around her. Golding saw that her hand was shaking. When she ended the call and turned to face him her whole body was trembling.

"What is it?" Golding asked. It took her a long time to reply.

"Pierre Cloarec... my boss," she began. "He was found murdered this morning."

FORTY-ONE

They travelled again by taxi back to the offices of *Le Monde*, where Clémence was met by a woman she introduced as Lucille Dubois: the chief editor – or something similar. With the clear shock written on the faces of everyone he met there, plus the language barrier, it was difficult to make sense of what was going on. Clémence introduced him as a British policeman interested in one of the people identified in the article. And while Dubois seemed to register there was something odd about that, perhaps wondering why he was there so early in the day, any real curiosity seemed subsumed by her sense of shock.

"The police are upstairs," Dubois said, after the two women had hugged and stood for a while in the marble lobby. She spoke English, and after a moment Golding realised she was addressing him.

"They want to speak with Clémence – the police. So perhaps you could wait here?" She gestured to a couple of sofas and a low coffee table opposite the reception desk. The receptionist from before – now looking distinctly more feminine than masculine – stared this time with open hostility, as if Golding who brought these horrific events into the very heart of the newspaper. Golding waited, unsure whether to stay or leave, but his decision was made when he saw Clémence walking down the stairs, all the colour and life drained from her face.

"Can you come with me?" she asked. "I will explain".

They went to a coffee bar opposite, where Clémence ordered café au lait for them both.

"His body was found by the mother of the editor," she began, glancing at him. "This is a complicated story." She waited, just long enough for the drinks to be placed in front of them.

"Pierre was staying in a cottage in Brittany to complete his research and write the articles. He was there because there was a risk, a very small risk – or that's what we thought – that there might be some danger to him. One of the clients of the firm where the documents were leaked from is an organised crime family." She glanced around, lowering her voice. "The Mancini family?"

Golding shook his head. "I don't know them."

"No matter." She sipped her drink absent-mindedly. "My editor had a tip-off that they might be aware of the leak – nothing certain – but that it might be safer to send Pierre away. But really it was more about him working on the story without interruptions. Even if the Mancinis did know, it seemed inconceivable that they would do anything like this." She stopped and shook her head. For a moment it seemed she might start crying, but instead she gathered herself to focus on telling the story as clearly as she could. "The cottage belonged to my editor, Lucille Dubois – the woman you met this morning. Her mother visited the cottage this morning because she had seen the curtains were drawn, and had been drawn the whole day. She found him tied to a chair. He'd been strangled. His fingers had been cut off and left on the keyboard of his laptop computer."

She fell silent and tore the corner off a sugar sachet. She

poured it into the coffee, then stirred it around. But when she touched the cup to her lips she recoiled.

"Cold," she said, putting the cup back down. "*Merde.*" She looked away, there were tears forming in her blue eyes.

"Do you know what happens now?" he asked her. "The murder was in Brittany? Presumably the local police will have jurisdiction?"

She turned back, seemingly glad for an excuse to concentrate. "*Non.* Here in France serious crime is investigated by the Police judiciaire – the case has been escalated to them already, because Pierre is so well known."

"Is that who you spoke to today?"

"*Non.*" She shook her head, but then opened her hands, as if acknowledging the complexity. "*Oui*, the same force, but not the same people. Today I spoke with officers from Paris. They were simply establishing the preliminary facts. They said the case will be investigated from their regional headquarters in Brest. It's a city in Brittany, the largest place near to where the murder happened." She stopped talking and shook her head, but then went on. "But you know how this all works. You are a detective? You are used to this?"

Golding shook his head. "I'm not used to how it works here." But he found himself visualising how the crime scene might look, a pretty cottage in Brittany – that was easy to picture. And the mess and gore of a violent death scene. He'd seen enough of those too.

"What can I do to help?" She cut into his thoughts, suddenly forceful. "I want to help, I want to catch these bastards." She stared at him, her blue eyes pleading. "You understand these things, what can I do?"

Golding considered; it felt like he'd been punched sideways by the events of the previous twenty-four hours. He was no longer sure he trusted what appeared in his mind. The correct answer, if someone asked him the same question in the UK, was to do nothing. To stay where they could easily be found if that's what the investigation team required, but basically to let the police do their job. But Clémence knew about the data leak that Cloarec had been researching. Perhaps more than anyone. The police would definitely want to speak with her, in some detail.

"The police who spoke to you this morning, did they tell you to stay put?"

She shook her head. "*Non*, they were just informing us, and establishing the basic facts. But they said the team from Brest will need to speak with me again. That I should stay in contact."

Golding nodded. "Can you go there?" He didn't really want her to; it might mean the end of them. If there'd ever been any chance of a "them". But she'd asked him what she could do. Clémence nodded.

"That's what my editor said as well." But her next words surprised him. "Will you come with me? I do not want to be alone."

She reached out, and laid her hand on his.

They travelled together, on the same TGV train Clémence had used only the week before. They didn't speak much, but as the French countryside flashed by, her phone rang and a commissioner from the Judicial Police, Julien Morel, spoke to her at length and told her he'd meet them off the train in Brest. They walked out of the station and saw a dark-blue car waiting just outside, a blue light on its roof. As Clémence and Golding approached, the door opened and a man in his fifties stepped out.

"Clémence Girard?" She nodded and gestured to Luke.

"Luke Golding is a British detective," Clémence explained.

"And why is he here?" Morel asked.

"He's investigating the British serial killer Charles Sterling."

"I understand what you're saying, but not why you're saying it. Is this man Sterling linked to the case somehow?"

Golding watched while Clémence told Morel in French how she'd contacted Golding.

"He says Sterling is not relevant," Clémence cut in suddenly in English. "He wants to speak with me at the regional headquarters, but you should wait there for me."

Golding nodded.

When they arrived at the nearby headquarters, Golding was shown to a basic waiting room where he sat for over two hours, completely ignored, before Clémence finally re-emerged.

"Well?" he asked, as she stepped into the room. She looked exhausted.

"Come. I am hungry. We will eat and I will tell you."

They'd both skipped breakfast and lunch, but eventually Clémence found a creperie that was open all day, and she ordered for them both.

"They say the murder is the work of the Mancini crime family," she began as soon as they'd ordered. She drew in a deep breath, as if trying to get used to the words, and how they were now associated with her former boss. "The manner of... what they did to Pierre, and the way they changed the article, they removed all reference to the Mancinis – but they did not do a good job. They left his notes."

Golding nodded. From the little he knew of the case, the conclusion seemed reasonable. But at the same time, he felt uncomfortable.

"They didn't want to speak to me?" The answer was obvious since they hadn't asked to do so, but he preferred to hear it explained in a language he understood.

"*Non*," she shrugged. "Why would they? As you told me, Charles Sterling is dead. This has nothing to do with him."

Golding nodded again, not really doubting it. What she said was true. Sterling was dead; at least, Golding was almost certain that was the case. But even if not, it seemed completely impossible that he could now be implicated in a French journalist's exposé of financial crime. Investigating this connection to the Mancini family was clearly the right path.

"Are you in danger?" he asked suddenly.

Her eyes glanced up at him, her shoulders gave a shrug.

"They think not. Apparently this is not the first time the Mancini family commit murders like this. They do not believe the primary intention was to destroy any evidence that the family uses this firm to move and hide its money – that would be impossible. But they did it to warn us off featuring them in the articles. They will wait now, to see what we do. If we feature them in the articles."

"And will you?"

"Yes. Absolutely." Clémence's jaw was set firm, but then she looked away. "At least, I hope so. It will be the decision of my editor. I don't actually know."

"But the article was scheduled for this weekend? That won't happen now?"

Clémence shook her head, falling silent as their food arrived. The smell and sight of it reminded Golding of the feeling of finally eating after a long hangover.

"Yes. No. I don't know. Everything is up in the air – do you say this?"

Absently Golding nodded, watching the steam from his crepe coil upwards from the plate.

"Yeah. I guess we do."

That night they booked into a hotel in Brest. There was no discussion between them, but they took two single rooms which, either by accident or because Clémence had requested it from the receptionist, were next door to one another. They didn't kiss as they parted, but Clémence held him close for a few moments before saying she had to sleep. Golding thought about insisting he check her room first, but it seemed like overkill. They had seen nothing suspicious. The hotel had been chosen at random. He let her go and went into his own room, where he stood at the window watching the street outside. There was nothing to see, no hoodlums waiting in parked cars. No killers stalking through the night. He was about to get into bed when a knock sounded on his door. When he answered it Clémence was there.

"Is it OK if I come in?"

Golding knew, at least from the moment he woke the next day and probably earlier, that he could no longer keep this from Sands. Whether or not the original articles would now mention Sterling, the news would soon break that a journalist had been murdered in relation to a leak of financial documents. Eventually Sands would find out that her father had also been named in the documents, and if she also found out that Golding had kept this from her, she would probably kill him. There was also the tiniest chance that Sterling himself was somehow involved in the murder.

Over breakfast Clémence received a message that Morel had more questions, and she agreed to meet him in the same office as before. The police still had no interest in speaking with Golding, so he stayed at the hotel. After several false starts, he dialled Sands' number.

"Luke." Sands' voice sounded cautiously hopeful. As if she were pleased he was calling, and hoping it wasn't an attempt to convince her to go back to work.

"Boss." He bit his lip.

"What do you want?"

Golding glanced around the bland decor of the hotel room.

He wondered how to explain all this to her without her becoming furious with him for not telling her sooner.

"I'm in France," he said eventually.

"That's nice," Sands replied, then her voice hardened. "Why?"

He hesitated. "I might have a lead on Charles Sterling."

FORTY-TWO

Sands listened with increasing disbelief as Golding explained where he was and what he'd been doing. She felt an almost overpowering urge to immediately reach the conclusion that the journalist must have been killed by Sterling. But she stopped short of saying it. She was well aware that her conduct over the previous year had been viewed as obsessive, and that to some extent that criticism was valid. Obviously not every suspicious death could be attributed to her father. Furthermore this was a case she knew nothing about. But as she listened she recognised the urge within her as something akin to hope. Up to now she'd only been investigating Sterling's movements *before* the date he'd supposedly died. If he'd killed in the last week, it would be certain proof his death had been faked. It would also be proof she wasn't insane. She didn't hope that Sterling had killed again, or at least not quite. But perhaps it was reasonable to hope this was the break she'd been waiting for.

Overlaying these thoughts was fury at Golding for not telling her earlier. And she was less successful in holding this in, less capable of nuance. But as he explained how he'd received permission from Superintendent Yorke to travel to France, she was able to bite back her anger a little. She held the two posi-tions simultaneously: anger at not being told at once, alongside a grudging gratitude that he'd taken it seriously enough to go in the first place.

"Where are you now?" she cut in when she felt he'd explained enough. There was a hesitation before he replied.

"I'm in a hotel in Brest. But I have to get back because—"

"What's the name?"

He paused, a little reluctant to give it.

"Hôtel Central, but—"

"Stay where you are. I'll be with you later today." She ended the call and checked her watch. She had a grab bag packed and hanging in her coat cupboard. Three days' worth of fresh clothes, cash. Latex gloves and forensic coveralls. She hooked it over her arm, took her passport from a drawer, then slipped it into a second bag with her laptop and charger. Then she jogged lightly down the stairwell of her apartment building and across the street to where the Alfa was parked.

The traffic on the M25 motorway around London was appalling. At one point she was stopped for a full twenty minutes, during which time she established that the Eurostar was fully booked, and instead bought a ticket on the Dover to Calais ferry.

Later she sat at the front of the ferry, watching the French coast pull closer agonisingly slowly and taking thoughtful bites from a baguette. Back in the Alfa and she soon left the French port behind her. Once the roads were clear she pushed the big car fast, calculating as she did so. Five hundred and thirty kilo-metres, averaging say 140 km per hour. She glanced at the clock on the dash. She ought to be there by eight that evening. She pulled up outside the Hôtel Central at seven-thirty.

She'd phoned Golding as she hit the outskirts of the city and he was waiting in the lobby when she walked in. He looked tired – but there something else as well, an expression on his face she couldn't read, as if he were worried about something else.

"Have there been any developments?" she asked as she walked across.

He shook his head. "How was your trip?"

"Slow," she replied. She looked around for somewhere to sit. He seemed to sense what she wanted and led her through into the hotel bar, where a young man with a goatee beard was listening to French rap while he polished glasses.

"*Deux expressos.*" Sands ordered for them both, not asking Golding whether he wanted anything. Then she turned back to the bar. "And turn the music down."

The barman responded by squinting at her, as if he hadn't understood.

"*Baissez la musique.*" She stared at him; the French words formed in her mind a little slowly but were still there, despite her not having studied the language for several years. For a moment she thought she was going to get the opportunity to practise a little more, but then the man did what she'd asked.

They took the coffees to a table by the window and sat down.

"So?" Sands repeated. She still felt impatient, aware of the time she'd spent just getting here. "What can you tell me?"

"Actually not that much." Golding looked uncertainly at his coffee, as if he hadn't wanted it in the first place, while Sands sipped at hers, the first she'd had since the boat.

"Who's running the case?" she asked. "What do they think of the possibility that Sterling might be involved?"

The fact that two questions came at him at once seemed to prevent Golding answering, and Sands felt her fragile resolve not to be angry with him waver a little.

"I don't know exactly."

"You don't know what?"

Golding looked away, clearly troubled.

"You don't know who's investigating? But surely you're working with the Police Judiciaire? I assume they're handling the case?"

"Yes, but..." Golding shrugged, and almost winced as Sands stared at him. "No."

"*Yes but no?* What the hell does that mean?"

Golding glanced towards the doorway of the bar before he answered. "I know the name of the lead officer. It's a Commissioner Julien Morel. But he's not interested in us working together. He's convinced Cloarec was assassinated by a hit squad from the Mancini crime family. I did try to get him to look at Sterling, but he's listed as deceased, so..."

Sands squeezed her hand into a fist, frustrated but not surprised. She took another sip of coffee. Then nodded.

"OK. But if you're not working with Morel, what are you actually doing here?"

Rather than reply Golding looked towards the doorway again, then got to his feet.

"Excuse me a moment."

As Sands watched he walked across the bar's carpeted floor to the entrance, where a young woman had appeared. She was clearly attractive, although she looked tired and downbeat. Her expression changed though as she noticed Golding, a small smile flashing across her lips. And then she reached out to him as if expecting him to embrace her, but he twisted subtly out of it and turned to point out Sands, still sat at the table. The woman's expression darkened now, as Golding spoke to her. And then he led her back across the room. Sands felt her expression darken too.

"Erica, this is Clémence Girard. She's... the journalist with *Le Monde*. The one who told me about Sterling in the data leak. She was a colleague of the man who was killed."

Sands said nothing, but inspected the woman further now that she could see her better.

"Clémence, this is... my old boss, Erica Sands."

"Luke has told me about you," the woman said in heavily accented English.

"He has?" Sands replied.

"He told me about your father. How you do not accept he is dead."

Sands felt her reserve of understanding take another hit. She turned to Golding and spoke in a voice loud enough for all of them to hear. "You discussed that with a member of the press?"

"I didn't exactly... I was trying to explain the case—"

"It is public record, not a secret," Clémence cut in. "And anyway, it is not a story that would interest anybody here in France." She shrugged and turned to Golding. "Luke, I am very tired. I have been speaking with the commissioner all afternoon. Perhaps we could find somewhere to eat?"

Sands smoothed her eyebrow with a finger, watching the two of them.

"You met the Police Judiciaire? Today?"

Clémence turned to Sands, a little weary. "Yes. I have been explaining the operation run by the Mancini family to him, it is complicated."

"Do they have physical evidence connecting this Mancini family to the killing?"

Clémence paused, her mouth hanging half-open in a way that reminded Sands of a fish.

"Boss, Clémence's had a rough couple of days," Golding said. "She's lost a colleague and a friend." Sands stared at him, and then back at the Frenchwoman. There was something between them that she didn't understand. Or perhaps didn't want to understand.

"You are the journalist that first contacted the British police, attempting to notify us that Charles Sterling appeared in this data leak?"

Clémence nodded.

"Attempting to notify me, but DS Golding took the call instead?"

"Yes, that's correct."

"And do you two know each other? Apart from that?" Sands pointed her finger at each of them in turn, then watched for the response. Golding glanced at the woman, who looked down at the table.

"No," Golding replied, his voice suddenly firm. Clémence looked suddenly up at him, but he carried on speaking. "But I've travelled here to assist her where I can. I think we're going to find somewhere to eat..." It was quite clear that he was trying to excuse himself.

"Fine," Sands snapped. "I'm hungry as well. I'll come too."

FORTY-THREE

The meal didn't go well. After declaring herself too tired to head out again Clémence had agreed to eat in the hotel dining room, but it had been quite obvious that she hadn't meant for Sands to accompany them. Golding's further hints that the journalist was exhausted after a day of interrogation had apparently been missed by Sands, who had then carried out her own interrogation during the meal, trying to establish what Clémence knew of the crime scene, the questions the French police had asked her, and what answers she'd given. Finally, without finishing her main course, Clémence had stood up, announcing that she was tired, and then stared at Golding, clearly indicating that she expected him to accompany her upstairs. Now he was sitting on her bed, still unsure why she'd invited him into her room.

"She is not even your boss now!" asked Clémence. "Why do you let her treat you like that?"

The response "like what" came to Golding's mind, but he nodded slowly instead. "She's a difficult person, I know. But she's also... brilliant. I think she could help."

"Help how? Clearly she thinks Pierre was murdered by a

man who died last year from cancer. And she's completely ignoring the evidence that he was killed by professional assassins. To me that is stupid. She is stupid." She stood before him and took his hand. He could see her chest rise and fall under her blouse.

"I do not want to make love tonight. Do you understand?"

Golding blinked in surprise, since the thought hadn't crossed his mind. In response he simply nodded.

When Golding came down for breakfast the next morning Sands was sitting at a table in the breakfast hall, sipping coffee. The plates in front of her indicated that she'd finished eating some time earlier.

"Luke." She raised a hand and called out, giving him no choice but to sit with her. He held up a finger to say he'd be right there, tossed a pair of croissants on a plate and filled a cup with black coffee.

"We need to speak with Commissioner Morel," Sands began the moment Golding sat down. "I would like to examine the crime scene, and I need to be briefed on the physical evidence that has already been collected there. From what your girlfriend said yesterday it's clearly the case that they need to do more to rule out Sterling's involvement..."

Golding stopped what he was doing, tearing the croissant into soft pieces.

"My girlfriend?"

"Yes." Sands looked perplexed, or pretended to. "Or would you not say that's what she is? Clearly you are sleeping together."

Golding swallowed. He wanted to tell her that they hadn't slept together, at least not the night just gone, but her assumption provoked him further.

"What business is that of yours?"

Sands looked affronted.

"That you're having sex with an important witness, and potentially even a suspect, in a serious crime? No business at all. It *irritates* me that there's literally nobody in my department that I can fully trust, but I'm hardly surprised." She turned to stare at him, clearly a challenging look. For a few seconds Golding let his brain try to supply a response, well aware that his mind didn't work as fast as hers. But that didn't mean she was always right.

"It's not a case that you're investigating though. And it's not your department. You walked away to chase the ghost of your father."

If he'd expected this to anger her further, the opposite happened.

"Well someone had to. If I hadn't, this murder would be chalked up to a couple of phantom assassins while the real killer gets away with it. That might still happen if you don't get on board and start helping me."

"Helping you do what? You're not even a police officer at the moment. What makes you think the commissioner is going to listen to you? Why should *I* even listen to you?"

Golding was suddenly aware he'd raised his voice; he glanced around the restaurant, catching the eye of a pair of French businessmen who quickly looked away. He warned himself to cool it.

Sands took advantage of the moment to press her hand against her forehead in frustration. After a few seconds she turned back.

"I'm well aware I have no jurisdiction here, Luke. I was aware when I handed in my resignation that I would likely have no jurisdiction wherever Sterling turned up, if that's what's happened. But I had no choice, because I was being prevented from investigating him when I was leading the department.

What would you have had me do? Just let him get away with it?"

"Get away with what? Dying?"

Sands pulled a tight face. She sipped at her coffee.

"I don't believe he's dead."

"Clearly not. But what if he is?"

"I don't think he is."

Golding took a deep breath, but decided to just keep at it. Ask the same question over and over again. Force a response at last.

"But what if he is? How do you let it go? How do you let *him* go?"

Sands shook her head.

"I don't. I won't."

"But you have to admit he *might* be dead? How are you going to live your life, insisting that he's somehow behind every murder that has even the most tenuous link?"

"You think this is tenuous?"

"Yeah." Golding tried to take stock of the conversation. "I do. Sterling used the same bank. That's pretty much it. Before he died he used the same bank, along with thousands of other people, some of them violent criminals prepared to kill to keep their secret."

When Sands didn't reply Golding shook his head. Then the moment passed as Clémence entered the breakfast hall. Her neutral expression changed to a slight smile when she saw him, and then went the other way as she registered Sands. Her head bowed as she walked straight to the table and sat down, not stopping to pick up any food.

"*Bonjour*." She offered a tight smile for Golding, and her eyes flicked quickly to where Sands sat. She gave the slightest of nods.

Golding nodded back, well aware of the tension in the air. "Hi, how'd you sleep?"

"Fine." She glanced around, as if only now noticing the buffet.

"Can I get you anything?" Golding went on. "Coffee, croissant?"

She nodded again, and then he regretted offering because he had to get up and leave the two of them together while he fetched the food. When he came back they still weren't speaking.

"You're seeing the commissioner again this morning?" Sands asked through thin lips.

"Yes, but not for long. Monsieur Morel said he has just a few more questions for me."

"And after that, has he asked you to stay here?"

Clémence shook her head. "*Non*, I can return to Paris."

"And will you?"

"I don't know."

"I understand from Luke that you have access to the leaked database?"

"Yes. But I cannot allow you have access to it."

"Who could authorise that?"

Clémence gave a slight, exasperated shake of the head.

"For that you would need to speak to my editor. But she will give you the same answer."

"Lucille Dubois?"

There was a flicker of surprise in Clémence's eyes, but she hid it well.

"*Oui*."

Sands nodded thoughtfully. "OK. Good. What time are you meeting the commissioner? I'll drive you both there."

It was more of a command than an offer and when Sands stood to leave, Golding said they'd meet her in the lobby when they were finished.

FORTY-FOUR

The meeting with the commissioner did not go well either. When they arrived at the Police Judiciaire headquarters Clémence was told to wait until Morel was ready for her. In the meantime Sands spoke with a young officer on the reception desk, explaining that she also needed to meet with the commissioner. It was a whole hour before Clémence was called to speak with Morel, and then only for a short while, and only to repeat the information she'd provided the day before. When she returned they waited again, with Sands making several trips to the reception desk to reiterate her desire to speak with Morel. Finally he appeared with another uniformed officer and led them to a meeting room.

"Chief Inspector Sands?" Morel began, gesturing to a chair and waiting until she sat down. "Or to be precise, *former* Chief Inspector. How can I assist you?"

"What is your primary line of inquiry in the murder of Pierre Cloarec?" Sands replied, as if she hadn't noticed the tone of his voice or had been made to wait the whole morning. But he shook his head.

"That's not something I'm prepared to share with a member of the public."

"Then are you prepared to share it with my sergeant here? Show him your badge, Luke." Golding wasn't about to do so, but Morel waved the idea away anyway.

"There's no need. I've already spoken with Detective Golding, and he's told me about your concerns. We welcome the offer of assistance, but it's not necessary at this time." At the mention of time he glanced at his watch, as if conscious of how much of it he was wasting.

"I understand you're investigating a possible Italian link?" Sands tried again. "Are you working with Interpol? Could I recommend you contact Agent Jonathan Briggs; he's familiar with some aspects of the Charles Sterling case and would be able to keep me informed—"

"Interpol, no," the Commissioner interrupted. "The Italian authorities have agreed to work directly in partnership with us. And from the evidence we've found so far, there's no need to involve the British authorities. No... there are no British subjects involved. Now, if there is nothing else?"

Sands paused a moment, clearly frustrated with how this was going. "Yes. It's vital you examine the database in close detail to establish if there is any way that Charles Sterling could have been aware his name was about to be published. If he is involved, it's highly likely this would have been the trigger for him to act—"

"*Non.*"

"Excuse me?"

"This is not necessary." Morel shook his head.

"I'm telling you it *is* necessary."

"*Non.* I disagree. Charles Sterling is not involved in this case."

Sands scoffed. "We don't know that. I accept it's not *clear* that he is, but it's critical to be sure—"

"He is dead, no?" Morel interrupted. "He died in..." – the commissioner paused and lifted his glasses up to his forehead to better study something on his mobile phone – "Vietnam? You have been there investigating his death?"

"Yes. I have good reason to believe that he did not die, but faked his death there in order to disappear—"

"And is that reason linked to Charles Sterling being your father?"

"No." Sands drew her lips tightly together. "Not at all. There were a number of irregularities in Vietnam which point to the likelihood that Sterling is not in fact dead, not least the fact that his body was never—"

"Then you have plenty of work to do, *non?*" Morel interrupted. "Investigating those *irregularities?*" He put just enough emphasis on the word to make it clear he didn't consider them as such. "So I suggest that you return to Vietnam and spend your time annoying the authorities there? Meanwhile you let the French police investigate this very unpleasant murder of a French citizen? Yes? Now if there really is nothing else?" He dropped his glasses back down over his eyes. And when Sands didn't respond he rose to his feet. Without another word he left the room. A few moments later a uniformed officer arrived to escort them to the reception area.

Golding had to work hard not to say "That went well', the phrase ringing out in his mind. Instead he settled for a less caustic "Now what?" after they'd left the building. Sands glanced at him, but apparently decided the question wasn't intended for her and led the way back to her car.

"I have to return to Paris," Clémence said as they followed her. "Now I have been released by the commissioner, I have to work. And I suppose there is nothing more for you to do here, you must return to England as well?" It was awkward having this conversation with Sands just ahead of them, and Golding noticed her glancing back. But she didn't seem concerned.

"I guess so," Golding said. "I should speak to my superintendent, but I imagine he'll be keen to get me back." It felt as though a very strange break from his normal life was coming to an end, and he suspected he would never see her again. He didn't like the idea of that, but had no idea how to prevent it.

"Luke isn't going back to England," Sands said suddenly.

"Excuse me?" Clémence asked.

"You'll probably need to stay too. At least for a while."

"*What?* You cannot simply order me around."

Sands sighed. She stopped and spoke to them as they approached the car as if addressing particularly stupid children. "If the French police are unwilling to entertainment the possibility of Sterling's involvement, then *we* will have to do it. The three of us. And in any case it's quite clear that neither of you wants to separate, so it's an outcome that serves all our needs. I'll need you to start by explaining exactly how Sterling's name appeared in this data leak." She checked her watch. "We can do it over lunch." Sands pulled open the rear door and waited beside it until Clémence sighed and got in. Golding walked around to the passenger door.

"Do you know anywhere good to eat?" Sands turned round to ask Clémence once she'd climbed behind the wheel. "The hotel food last night was very poor."

"*Non*," Clémence replied. "This is not my city."

"No problem, I saw a place as I drove in yesterday." Sands started the engine and pulled away so rapidly that Golding reached for his seatbelt.

FORTY-FIVE

The place that Sands had noticed turned out to be on the outskirts of Brest. It had been doing good business, but the lunchtime rush was now slowing down. Sands used the Alfa's horn to encourage an elderly couple in their Renault to leave a little more quickly. Then she slid the car into the space they'd just vacated. Inside the restaurant she snapped instructions to the waiter in French that Golding didn't understand. The man looked momentarily taken aback, but then nodded sharply and took them to a table by the window. Sands sat down, moving the chair next to her away so that Golding and Clémence had no choice but to sit facing her, almost as if they were interviewing her for a job. Or perhaps it was the other way round.

When they'd ordered, and Sands noticed a young waitress walking past carrying two plates of what looked like omelette, she looked almost happy for the first time since she'd arrived in France. She spoke to Clémence. "Now, I need you to give me the data. I need to understand exactly how Charles Sterling appeared in these files." She leant forwards on her elbows, waiting expectantly.

"*Non.*" Clémence shook her head. "I told you, this I cannot do. It would not be ethical to share the data. I also explain this to Luke already."

"That was before your colleague's murder?"

"Of course. But the situation is still the same. I have an obligation to protect the source of the leak."

Sands shook her head.

"But you've already spent three days discussing this with the Police Judiciaire?"

"French law requires me to cooperate with the investigating authorities. But I have only spoken about the Mancini family, not the other people who are named in the data."

"Because that's all they're interested in?"

Clémence didn't respond to this.

"Just to be clear," Sands continued, 'you are placing journalistic integrity before the possibility of discovering who murdered an actual journalist?"

"*Non.* I am protecting the source. These files were shared with *Le Monde*, and the source agreed they could be seen by journalists from other newspapers, but we expressly agreed they would not be shared more widely."

"Nonsense. That might once have been the case, but now your colleague's been murdered, and the local police are refusing to explore the possibility that Charles Sterling was the killer. At this point you have no choice but to tell me how his name appears in the database." As Sands spoke the waitress returned with two bottles of sparkling water; while she filled their glasses the table was silent.

"I do not understand what is happening here," Clémence said at last. She turned to Golding. "I do not understand why she is here, why you are listening to her?" She shook her head, her golden hair catching in the light. Sands was silent and both women kept their eyes on Golding. He chose to reply, torn between his loyalties to them both.

"I... Look, I get that this must seem strange. But Erica might be right. Somehow. It wouldn't be the whole data leak we'd need access to, but if we could see how Sterling's name appears, we can rule out the slim possibility that he had any involvement in Pierre's death."

Clémence seemed about to answer, but then swung her head away, muttering under her breath.

They were interrupted again, this time by the young waitress with their food. She served Clémence first, setting a salad of green leaves in front of her. Then she served Sands a large steak which Golding looked at with weary envy as he thanked the girl for his omelette. Sands began cutting into the meat at once, checking it was done to her liking. Clémence didn't touch her food. She looked at Golding as if he had betrayed her.

"I cannot make this decision alone. I will need to speak to my editor."

"Good. Great." Sands held out her fork in the direction of Clémence's purse while she finished her mouthful. "You have a phone in there? Go and use it."

It felt like a dismissal and Clémence certainly took it that way, taking her phone to the other side of the restaurant to make the call. While she did so Golding took a bite of the omelette. It was filled with goats' cheese, which he was either mildly allergic or just intolerant to. He pushed it away in frustration.

"Boss," he began, catching Sands eyeing him sharply. He kept his mouth open to speak, but didn't know what to say. In the end he just shook his head.

"Just go easy on her, OK?"

Sands stared at him for a few seconds, as if she had no idea what he was talking about.

"Why? You like her?"

Golding was too surprised by the comment to answer, and only when Clémence returned to the table did it occur to him that Sands might only have said that because she felt a degree of jealousy. He was further knocked sideways by this thought as Clémence cleared her throat.

"My editor says she must meet you in person before she can decide."

Sands shifted her gaze from Golding.

"Excellent. Then we'll go to Paris." She looked around the restaurant and clicked her fingers for the waitress to return.

"Eat up, I'll get this."

FORTY-SIX

The trip back to Paris began with palpable tension in the car. Clémence demurred when Golding offered Clémence the front seat, and after they joined the motorway he glanced behind and saw that she was asleep, her head resting against the window. He didn't take the opportunity to speak with Sands, instead letting her drive in silence, pushing the big car twenty kilometres an hour over the speed limit. As they flashed past various signs indicating speed cameras he quietly hoped they might get stopped and fined. But it didn't happen. As they approached the outskirts of Paris the traffic increased and Sands had to slow down, but she followed the directions from the car's GPS to the *Le Monde* offices.

Dubois didn't keep them waiting long, but instead of seeing them in her office she led them along a corridor to a meeting room. She showed Golding and Sands inside, but then stayed outside for a few moments to speak with Clémence in private. A young man served them coffee before Dubois and Clémence entered and sat on one side of the table with Golding and Sands on the other, the lines clearly drawn.

"I understand you wish to have access to the information

that Pierre was working on?" Dubois addressed her question to Sands.

"Not all of it. I only wish to understand more clearly why your journalists felt the need to contact the British police regarding Charles Sterling. He is of interest to us not because of the multiple crimes he has committed in the UK, but he is also listed on Interpol's red list as an internationally wanted fugitive. It is also in your interest to rule him out as a suspect in the murder of Pierre Cloarec."

Dubois seemed to consider this carefully.

"But Monsieur Sterling is dead?"

Sands didn't hesitate. "It's possible, but it's also possible that he is not. Which is why we need to understand the data in your possession."

"But surely you agree that the Mancini family are the most likely suspects?"

"It's not for me to say. Unfortunately it won't be possible for the French police to answer this either, since they refuse to consider the possibility that Sterling was involved. This could very well be your one shot of getting to the truth."

Dubois leaned close to Clémence and whispered in her ear.

They talked for a while longer, but Golding found himself tuning out, the arguments familiar now. Moreover he reasoned that Sands would win; if the editor had no intention of letting them see the data, then surely she wouldn't have agreed for them to come to Paris. And sure enough, after about fifteen minutes Dubois rose to her feet and summoned Clémence outside. Soon afterwards the editor stepped back into the room.

"Ms Sands, Detective Golding," Dubois began, "I sent Pierre to stay in Plourec. He was killed in my family's cottage. He has a wife and a daughter, and I must do everything I can to bring them justice. I will allow Clémence to explain the data to you in detail, but you will not be allowed copies, and I will remain in the room while she does so." Then they waited in silence until Clémence came back into the room, this time carrying her laptop.

"I don't know how much you know about these kinds of documents," Clémence began once she'd set up.

"Assume we know nothing," Sands replied. Now that she'd got what she wanted she seemed less self-assured. Golding guessed why: she'd won a battle but the files might still show nothing.

"OK. When the files came to us, it was simply a dump of millions of different documents, without any clear way of understanding how they were organised. It was agreed to work with other journalists at other newspapers, the *Guardian*, *El País*." She stopped and glanced at Dubois, who nodded for her to continue.

"And obviously there's a huge security risk, with many different journalists all having their own copies. These files have been leaked once; if that happened again it would risk everything that we're doing. And clearly the data can be dangerous." She clicked a button and the screen showed a clumsy-looking page with boxes of text.

"So we created a secure server, held here in the *Le Monde* offices, and everyone who accesses these documents has to do so from here. They cannot make copies. Everything is held within this database. Every time it's accessed a log entry is made."

Sands nodded, her eyes fixed on the screen.

"Who created the database?"

"We have a team of technicians in house," Dubois cut in. "It was then security-checked using dummy information. The *Guardian* and *The Washington Post*'s tech guys tried to break in. Unsuccessfully." She gave a tight smile. "Only then did we fill it with the real data."

"OK. And have there been any breaches, or attempted breaches, of the data? Since it was added?"

"No. None at all."

Sands nodded again. She turned back to Clémence. "Fine. Continue."

"As I said there are millions of documents. And in the beginning it was almost impossible for us to follow one name through the files, to de-tangle the web of shell companies and hidden identities. But eventually we realised that this was also true for the lawyers who were working for these clients. So they appear to have created what we have called index documents."

"What are they?"

"Exactly as they sound. They allowed the lawyers to keep track of exactly who owns what and how, even if the company structures themselves are deliberately designed to be opaque or impenetrable. They're like maps. But never intended to be made public." Clémence stopped again.

"Surely *none* of this was intended to be made public?" Golding heard himself ask.

Clémence shook her head. "No, some of it was. The company ownership papers, the records of transactions – they're designed to be filed with governmental bodies. Then there are bank statements, which have to be released to tax authorities, but the overall purpose is to confuse. To conceal what is really happening and who is the ultimate beneficiary. The problem is it's almost too effective; it was necessary for the lawyers to create these index documents so that they don't get lost themselves."

Sands nodded again as if this made perfect sense to her. "And when you spoke with Commissioner Morel, you were going through the index document for the Mancini family?"

Clémence glanced at Dubois before answering, but the older woman did nothing to stop her.

"Yes. Showing it to him, but also explaining exactly what it means. It was highly complex."

There was a pause.

"So you'll have an index document for Charles Sterling?"

Clémence glanced again at Dubois.

"Yes. There must be."

"Can I see it?"

Clémence didn't answer but instead got to work. For a while there was silence apart from the sound of her fingers tapping rapidly at the keys.

Gradually however, a frown appeared on her face. She kept working, her eyes fixed on the screen, but she was apparently unable to find what she wanted. After a while Dubois joined her, occasionally pointing and muttering something in French far too fast and low for Golding to understand. Eventually Clémence sighed loudly and looked up.

"What is it?" Sands asked.

Clémence looked pained and glanced at her editor, who eventually nodded her assent for Clémence to explain.

"Charles Sterling is mentioned only once in the files – a banker in Switzerland gives his name, but also mentions a false name that Sterling apparently asked to go by. We're able to track that name for a while in the documents..." She stopped. She frowned again and broke off her explanation to speak with Dubois who was now working on the keyboard, but shaking her head. Clémence went on.

"We're able to see that he used a number of shell companies to launder money though, money which originally derived from cryptocurrency. It would seem that this is why Pierre decided to include him in his article, and why he therefore wanted me to inform the British police, as a courtesy. However..." She broke off and frowned again.

"There are then several other identities that seem to have

been used to continue to move the money around; there's no way of knowing whether they're real people or not."

"I see," Sands said. She sat very still, staring thoughtfully at the wall.

"*I* don't," Golding interrupted. "I don't see at all. Can someone explain it to me?"

Clémence turned to face him, looking more worried than he'd ever seen her.

"There's no index document for Sterling. Nor for any of his false names." She sat back in her chair, biting her lip. "He just disappears. He disappears into the data."

FORTY-SEVEN

"Does that mean it's been removed?" Golding asked. "Does that mean it was never there?" He shrugged. "What are you telling us?"

"I'm not sure," Dubois replied. "We have several million documents, but we do not have a complete copy of all the files held by the firm. It's not unheard of for the chains of paperwork to be missing some elements, and we have to piece things together."

"But you do that using the index documents?" Sands came in, clarifying. "And that's what you don't have here?"

"Yes."

Sands pushed her chair back, drumming both her hands on the tabletop.

"So how many other people have you not found an index document for?"

Everybody looked to Clémence, who rubbed her face with her hands.

"None," she said. "But that doesn't mean there's necessarily anything strange here. There are hundreds of thousands of people named in the files. So far Pierre and I are looking at the higher-profile names; it's possible that some of the smaller clients also have missing index documents..." She stopped, then bit her lip.

"*Were* looking," she corrected herself. "We *were* looking at higher-profile names."

"Could it be that the files have been changed?" Sands asked eventually. "The index document removed?"

Dubois shook her head firmly.

"Impossible. The database has been set up so that any changes are not allowed. And any attempt to make changes would be logged. We'd see who did it, when it was done and what was changed." She looked confident, but Golding kept his eyes on Sands.

"What about if the change log was also changed?" Erica said.

The tiniest of frowns appeared on the editor's brow.

"That would be very difficult to do..." Dubois seemed to think for a few moments. "You'd need to be highly technical, and everything is encrypted and password protected." She began to shake her head, dismissing the idea, but Sands persisted.

"It's not particularly technical to execute an SQL script." Sands waved away the first objection, but the second seemed to make her think.

"Could someone have gained access using Cloarec's password?" she asked. "His fingers were removed. I think we have to assume he was tortured. With Cloarec's password, would it be possible to unlock the encryption and make changes to the data, deleting an index file and then clearing any evidence of that in the change logs?"

This time when Dubois spoke her voice was hoarse.

"Pierre was the lead on this story. He had access to everything."

Sands looked away for a moment and swore under her breath.

"What?" Golding pressed, trying to keep up. "Is that a yes? With Cloarec's password someone could do all that? What she just said?"

Again he looked at Clémence, who gave a small half shrug.

"Are there any copies of this data?" Sands asked. "Anything we can compare the information on Sterling with, to see if anything has been changed?"

Clémence looked up at her editor, a slight trace of hope on her face.

"No. For security purposes this is the only copy that exists."

This time Sands didn't look away.

"Then we're fucked," she said. "We're never going to know."

They tried for some time, without the index document, to trace the path that Charles Sterling and his money had taken through the labyrinth of accounts, shell companies and asset-protection trusts, but without a map or a key to what was actually happening, the truth was protected behind an impenetrable veil of security. After an hour Dubois left them too it, saying she had to continue working, and half an hour later the same young man brought in a tray of baguettes and more coffee. Golding took a sandwich and ate it while watching the two women hunched over the laptop. Half the time they were speaking to each other in French, the other half using descriptions of financial transactions that meant nothing to him. But he let them work, waiting until they reached a resolution. Finally Clémence sat back, rolling her head around on her neck and letting out an exasperated sigh.

"It is not possible."

Golding took the opportunity to ask, "I got the basics before, but what exactly is not possible now?"

"We are trying to see if any of Sterling's money or assets were moved or accessed after his death in Vietnam," Clémence answered. "This would demonstrate, or at least give a strong indication, that he didn't die."

"And?"

"It's not possible. Here," – she turned the laptop towards him – "the money is split into three smaller amounts and put into different names – this is before his death – but this document does not tell us what those names are. We cannot search the rest of the data to see what happened next, because we do not know what name to search for."

"So what do we do? Do we need more time? Can we get more people on it?" asked Golding.

"No. Without the names, without the index document, we would never know if we had found the correct papers. It is impossible, a complete dead end."

Golding glanced at Sands, still not quite understanding – or at least only following at the most superficial of levels, but also not quite prepared to believe it unless he heard it from his former boss. But she seemed to have retreated into herself, apparently deep in thought.

"This is hopeless," she said after a while, and seemingly not to either Golding or Clémence. She picked up one of the sandwiches, looked blankly at the contents and put it back down on the plate.

"Most likely Cloarec was killed by the Mancini family," she went on, apparently paying no heed to Golding's head snapping up in surprise.

"I can see no way that Sterling, even if he is alive, could possibly have become aware of Cloarec and what he was doing. At the same time, the French secret service saw fit to alert *Le Monde* that one of their journalists might be in danger because the Mancinis were aware of the data leak. It's therefore much more likely, just thinking logically, that Cloarec was murdered by the Italians."

"Is that it?" Golding asked. "Are you giving up? Are you going back to England?"

It took Sands a long time to answer, and seemingly a long time to decide.

"No," she replied in the end. "I'm going to Brittany. I want to see what I can find there for myself."

For a moment Golding though she was going to ask him to come with her, but she had other ideas.

"You should get back. Yorke doesn't have infinite patience for his officers running around chasing ghosts; I think we've established that."

Golding nodded, a little relieved. Then he watched while Sands made her way awkwardly to the door, where she stopped.

"Thank you for all your help," she said. For a few seconds she hesitated, then held out her hand for Clémence to shake.

"I'm sorry if I was rude." Her eyes flicked to Golding again. "Luke is a good officer, and a decent man." She looked embarrassed and wasn't able to keep her eyes on Clémence. After a moment she turned to look at Golding instead.

"The last Eurostar leaves for London at nine. If you go now you'll catch it. I'll let you know if I find anything." She didn't sound optimistic.

FORTY-EIGHT

"Sands is right," Golding said to Clémence after Erica had left the room. "I do have to get back." He bit his lip as he watched how she would take this. He wondered if he should promise to phone her or try and visit Paris again in the near future, not even knowing if she'd want him to.

Clémence didn't reply, but she glanced up, meeting his eyes and not looking away. He glanced at his watch. Seven pm. Clémence looked away suddenly and nodded her head.

"Of course."

"Maybe we can..." Golding began. He meant to say 'stay in touch' but the words sounded inadequate in his head. Insulting almost. Clémence shrugged, as if she knew what he was going to say and it made little difference to her.

"I have leave due. Maybe I could come and..." – this time he said it out loud – "I could visit you?"

When she finally looked at him her expression had changed. It didn't seem to match the way he was feeling.

"What?" he said, trying to read her face.

"I have..." She hesitated, then held out her hand for his. "Come with me. Maybe I have an idea."

FORTY-NINE

The long journey out west settled Sands somewhat. For once she didn't push the car too hard. It was already late, and there was nothing she could do to investigate Pierre Cloarec's murder until the following day. But another thought kept her foot light on the accelerator – that there was nothing she could realistically do when she reached Plourec. With no jurisdiction in France, and no chance of the Police Judiciaire allowing her access, she wouldn't be able to see the crime scene, she wouldn't be given access to any forensic reports. Sure, there was nothing stopping her from speaking to people, asking them questions as a private citizen. But what was she really hoping to achieve?

It had long since fallen dark and the French countryside flashed past unseen, except for the clusters of lights in the distance that marked out towns and villages. The autoroute was quiet; occasionally she came up behind a lumbering lorry and indicated to occupy the fast lane and then cruised past before returning to the right-hand lane, her full beams illuminating the empty road ahead. She kept the interior cool, the stereo silent while she used the time to think.

After a while she admitted to herself that there was another reason for the mood she found herself in. This one made little sense. She'd barely seen Luke in months, and when they were working together she'd almost completely ignored him, heaping work on him she should have been doing herself. But still, it was clear she was affected by the sight of him with the pretty French journalist. She found herself wondering whether anything would come of it, whether anything *could* come of it. It seemed unlikely, given the physical distance between them, but then, something about the way they looked together made her think otherwise. The thought gnawed at her and, to her growing discomfort, a phrase kept returning to her mind. Words that she would normally have disregarded as imprecise and meaningless: *They looked good together*.

At midnight she pulled off the motorway and followed the GPS to the soulless travel hotel she'd selected earlier. The bed and curtains in her room were a vibrant orange plastic and smelt of body odour, only partially masked by chemicals. It did little to boost her hope that this was a trip worth taking.

It was raining the next morning when she left the hotel, and raining harder still when she pulled into Plourec's main street just over an hour later.

The village was not big. Nor, in the rain, did it appear particularly attractive. She let the Alfa coast along the main street, ticking off in her mind the slim pickings of its attractions. There was a small bar, closed. A few shops looked like they sold paintings and beach goods, but probably not until spring returned. The largest building was a small hotel, and at least that did look open. Beyond that it was mostly small cottages and a few rows of terraced houses. With the rain still falling, she drove on. A little way past the village centre was a small but clearly still working port. Separated from it by a heavy concrete wall stretched a long sandy beach. The rocks on either side had been smoothed by the elements. A lone fisherman stood, apparently oblivious to the still falling rain.

Sands decided to start there. She crossed into the shelter of the fish-processing building and began to ask the orange-jacketed workers there if they knew anything of Cloarec. But either the journalist had kept to himself, or none of the few, tough-looking men wanted to speak to her about him. She suspected probably both.

She had better luck an hour later in locating the cottage where Cloarec had been killed, half a mile inland along the ria from the port. There was no one about but the gate giving access to the tiny front garden had been secured with police tape. Sands inspected the yard carefully before ducking under the tape and looking through a small gap between the curtains in the front window. The cottage looked much as she'd expected it to: traditional, cosy – if you liked that sort of thing – but left in a state of familiar chaos by the evidence-collecting process. At least that appeared to have been completed. Hoping it had been left unlocked she tried the front door, but no luck. Two neat lines of rocks marked out the little path, big enough to break a window or even the door itself. She eyed them wistfully, but decided against it. Instead she walked around the side, noticing that the row of cottages backed onto the shore of the ria. The back door, annoyingly, was also locked.

She walked back round through the rain to the front and knocked on the doors of the two neighbouring cottages. Then widened her search to their neighbours, but none of them drew a response. Only one even looked like it was lived in full time, and as she glanced around she realised many of the properties in the village were rented out as holiday homes. The whole place had a feel of somewhere that people only visited on vacation, never seeing it when it was cold and wet and grey. She glanced up again. The rain was falling even harder. She gave up, climbed back into the Alfa and drove the hundred metres down to the hotel.

Sands ordered a coffee at the bar from a young man with

tattoos on both his arms; he nodded silently before putting down the mobile phone he'd been looking at and picking up a cup. He turned to work the large espresso machine that dominated the back of the bar.

"Did you know the man who was killed here?" she asked in French, not really expecting much of a response. He stopped what he was doing and slowly turned round.

"Are you another journalist?"

"No. I'm from the British police," Sands replied, then repeated the line she'd refined over the course of the day, smoothing over her less than flawless French. "I'm working on a private case, following some loose ends. Can you tell me about it?"

The man looked thoughtful, disappointed.

"The press offer better tips."

She glanced up at him, surprised. After a few seconds she reached into her pocket and drew out a small zipped purse. She inspected the euro notes inside.

"How much do they offer?" she asked.

Now the waiter looked surprised, perhaps even a little unsettled. He shrugged. "Maybe a hundred euros?"

Sands nodded thoughtfully. After a few moments she selected a fifty-euro note from the purse and pulled it out, moving it back and forth between her fingers. Then she took another one out.

"I'll double this if you can me tell me anything useful."

The barman went back to what he was doing, heating milk and then pouring it into the coffee.

"What do you want to know?" He slid the coffee in front of her.

"Did he ever come in here?"

"No. I don't think so. There was a woman though, another journalist. She stayed here a few times. I think she was working with him."

"Pretty? Blonde?"

The barman shrugged, pretending he hadn't noticed. But Sands already knew who he meant.

"You see him with anyone else?"

"*Non.*"

"You know anything else?"

"*Non.*"

Sands resisted the urge to sigh loudly. She hunted in her mind for another question.

"Have you had any Italians staying here?"

"That's what the local police asked me," the young man smiled.

"And what did you tell them?"

"The truth." He shrugged. "That I didn't see anything. I don't know anything." He looked suddenly perturbed, as if he realised that admitting this might disqualify him from collecting the money.

"There is another bar in the village," he went on. "The guy who died, I think he went there most mornings. Maybe they could tell you more?"

"The bar that's closed?"

"Yeah." He seemed to sense the problem. "But the man who works there, I know him. His name's Jacques. I can tell you where to find him? If that would help?"

This time Sands did sigh. "OK, where can I find him?"

"He likes to fish. He'll be down at the port, at the end of the pier."

Sands took a sip from her coffee, considering. After a few moments she handed over the two fifty notes, along with a caustic smile.

"That's all I have. *Désolé.*"

. . .

For the second time that day Sands drove down to the little port. The rain had stopped now, and although the sky was still thickly matted with clouds, there were breaks where the sun was dipping towards the horizon, giving flashes of colour amid the grey. She parked the Alfa overlooking the basin where four large fishing boats were protected from the weather by thousands of tonnes of ugly concrete wall. Even this far from where the sea worried and swirled at the defences, the boats were jostled and bumped together in the oily water. She turned up the collar of her jacket as she set off to walk along the arm of the harbour wall, towards where a giant green bollard held up a light that was already flashing green with the approaching darkness. At the very end sat the fisherman she'd seen previously, watching his lines. As she approached she felt him watching her, perhaps noting that she didn't look like the usual tourists who'd walk out here to catch a view of the pretty village laid out behind him.

"Jacques? From the bar?"

The fisherman squinted at her in the dim light. He pulled a drag from a cigarette he held between his lips.

"Who are you?"

Sands felt a pang for her police identity card, but spoke quickly instead.

"I'm with the police. I'm following up some leads regarding the man who died here this week."

Jacques nodded. "How did you know I was here?" he asked.

Sands ignored the question. "You knew him, I understand? You served him in the bar?"

"Yes." He shrugged. "Not often."

"How often? How frequently would he come in?"

"I guess most mornings." He tapped the ash from his cigarette into a bucket beside him of what looked like fish guts. "Every morning."

Sands regarded him for a few moments, wondering why anyone would want to spend time in a place like this.

"You speak to him?"

"No. Not much. He said good morning." Again the shrug. Jacques seemed nervous, but no more nervous than Sands would expect.

"Did he say what he was doing here?"

He shook his head.

"Did he speak to anyone else?"

"*Non.*" He took another drag from the cigarette and flicked the butt into the black water. Sands tried to suppress her frustration. Clearly this whole day had been a waste of time; there was nothing for her to do, nothing here to discover. The swirl of doubts she'd felt driving down here was flooding back. Frustration at her decision to leave her job – but what else could she have done?

"Except the American. He spoke with him quite a bit. Most mornings in fact."

It took a moment, but Sands' brain cleared, allowing her to focus on this new detail. "What American?"

"I don't know." He thought for a minute. "Richard, I think his name is. He lives in the village. Near to Cloarec, the cottage with the white door. They were friends, you could maybe try talking to him?"

"What do you know about him?"

The look he gave her was hard to read in the failing light. But the shrug helped.

"He drinks coffee at eleven. Beyond that, not really anything. No more than I've told you."

Sands glanced at her watch. She nodded a thank-you to the fisherman. Perhaps the day hadn't been a complete waste after all, but Cloarec's American friend would have to wait until tomorrow.

FIFTY

"What's the idea?" Golding asked.

"It's a long shot," Clémence replied, leading them back towards Dubois' office where she spoke rapidly with the editor's receptionist, who then picked up her phone, presumably to see if her boss was willing to see them. After a while she nodded and replied to Clémence in French.

"She says we can go in." Clémence held his gaze a moment, and then pushed open the door.

"What is it?" Dubois said in English, looking to Clémence for an explanation.

"We need another copy of the data," she began. "We need to see if any changes have been made by whoever killed Pierre. But we don't have any copies."

"No one has a copy. I told you." Dubois' brow furrowed. "We specifically agreed not to create any copies to minimise the risk of leaks."

"But there are still the original copies? At the law firm?"

Dubois still looked confused. "What are you saying? You want me to put you on a plane to the Cayman Islands? That's not going to happen. Even if I did, there's no way to get them—"

"*Non.* I'm thinking about the source who got them in the first place. Pierre told me about her."

Dubois fell silent. She glanced at Golding, clearly uncomfortable at having to listen to this. She replied in French, but Clémence interrupted her again, still sticking to English.

"He didn't give me her name, but he said she was a cleaner, and she'd approached him because she knew who he was. She respected him as a journalist, because of the award he'd won?"

"Yes." Dubois spoke slowly. "I suppose that's true. And very like Pierre to focus on that detail. But what of it?"

"Well," – Clémence's eyes flashed as she spoke – "if I was her, and if I'd been smart enough and brave enough to steal this data... And to bring it halfway around the world to walk in here and give it to a famous journalist, then there's no way I wouldn't make a copy of it first."

"I cannot give you her name."

"I'm not asking for it. I'm asking if you can contact her. Explain to her what's happened to Pierre – as a direct result of this data – and see if she can help. If she's come this far, then I don't see why she wouldn't let me look through the data and see if it's been changed. She's brave. She wants the truth to come out."

"That can only happen *if* she has the data. She told us she was handing over the only copy..."

"And you believed her?"

Dubois drew in a deep breath.

"And him,"– she glanced at Golding – "What is he still doing here? Why has he not returned to England?"

"I don't know," Clémence replied. "After Pierre, I feel safer with him around."

Dubois considered this for a while, then stood. "Wait outside."

. . .

For fifteen minutes Golding waited with Clémence outside Dubois' office before she called them back in.

"As a precaution the source agreed to take an unlisted mobile phone in case there was a need to contact her. I've called it and spoken to her. She's very shocked to learn of Pierre's death... But she has agreed to meet you. She's insistent that you don't see where she lives, not even which city, but she will meet you in the café of the Musée Gadagne in Lyon."

"Does she have a copy of the data?" Clémence asked.

"I don't know. She wouldn't say. But a TGV train will get you there in two hours."

Fifteen minutes later the sleek train was gaining speed as it left the outskirts of Paris behind them. Golding sat opposite Clémence, wondering at the strange sequence of events that had led him here, with her. He emailed Yorke a summary of everything that had happened, and of this final lead he needed to chase down. Five minutes later Yorke called, Golding having to stand in the passageway to take it, his tone hushed so he wouldn't be overheard. Yorke made it clear he considered that Golding had been infected with the same maddening obsession as Sands, but he stopped short of ordering him to stop what he was doing and return to England.

The one positive was that the Susan Hunter case had been resolved. The wrongly accused husband had accepted a deal to keep the case out of the courts. By the time the call ended the landscape outside the train windows was already changing, from the wide-open fields and low rolling hills of France's central plains to the industrial outskirts of its second city. Golding made his way back to his seat to find Clémence poring over her laptop, again checking if she could find Sterling in the data.

Clémence bought two entrance tickets for the museum. They were twenty minutes early but entered the café anyway. Dubois had told the cleaner they'd be sitting in a window booth and Clémence would be wearing an orange scarf, but the place was so quiet there was little need. Half an hour later a short woman in her sixties approached them. She wore a headscarf and her eyes were nervous, darting around and sizing them both up. She said nothing but stood in front of them. Clémence got to her feet.

"My name is Clémence Girard. I am a journalist." She spoke in English and kept her voice low. "I worked with Pierre Cloarec." She paused. "I'm sorry, I do not know your name."

"My name isn't important," the woman replied.

"Of course. I didn't mean..." Clémence looked momentarily flustered. "My editor told me you speak good English. My colleague here is from the British police. Detective Luke Golding. He doesn't speak French."

"I speak English," the woman replied. "I lived thirty years on Grand Cayman." She nodded. "We sit." She said it as a command.

"Do you, err... could I get you a drink?" Clémence asked, but the woman ignored her

"Mister Cloarec is dead because of the files I take?" Her eyes, a little milky from cataracts, stared into Clémence's.

"Not directly. Not as a result of anything you did," Clémence replied.

"How you know this?"

Golding replied for her. "We don't know. Not really. That's why we have come to see you. We're hoping you kept an original copy of the files. That might be the only way we can find out who killed Pierre, and why."

She didn't move. "I knew no good would come of those files. No good people in that place." She shook her head.

"Did you keep a copy? Of the files?" Clémence pushed.

"Lotta no good people in the world." The woman glanced around again at the near-empty café. A couple of elderly tourists sat examining a flyer on the opposite side of the room.

Behind the counter a girl no older than seventeen sat on a stool and browsed her phone. The woman looked back at Golding, and he stared into her misty eyes.

"Too many bad people."

"That's why we need to see the original files. We think whoever killed Pierre might have edited them. If you have an original copy, we may be able to see how it's been changed and work out who did it."

"Not them mobsters from Italy? I would see them every month. Coming over with their designer suits and their gold watches. Sports bags filled with bank notes. I never liked them. Never trusted them."

"The Mancini family?" Clémence asked.

The cleaner's eyes slid across to Clémence, but she didn't answer.

"The police here think it was them. But Detective Golding has another idea. That's why this is so important," Clémence went on. "We think a British man might be involved. A very bad British man."

"Do you have an original copy of the data?" Golding asked again. The woman's milky eyes flashed onto his, but then she looked away.

"Pierre Cloarec told me I had to delete everything I had; the editor woman too. Dubois. But I don't know. In person he wasn't quite as impressive as I thought he would be." She turned to Clémence now, her head on one side. "You know what I mean?"

Clémence considered a moment. "I think so, yes."

The older woman nodded thoughtfully. Then, slowly, she reached into the pocket of her jacket, fumbled a moment, and finally pulled her hand out. She kept something hidden in her fingers for a few moments, as if still deciding, then opened her hand on the table in front of them. On her palm was a small pen drive. She placed it down on the table and pushed it towards Clémence.

"Thank you," Clémence seemed to nearly well up with tears, but with a glance at Golding she quickly reached into her computer bag and slid out her laptop. She took the pen drive and slid it into the port on the side of the computer. Golding watched the screen as she navigated to the new drive. The first thing she did was check the size of the files it contained.

"Nine hundred eighty-two gigabytes." She nodded to Golding, her voice suddenly brighter. "That's the same size as the files I've been working with."

"Then you have what you need." The woman stood up bleakly. "I hope you will do the right thing with it." With that she turned from them and walked away.

"How long will it take you to find the information?" Golding asked after he'd watched Clémence work for some minutes. "To see if anything's been changed?"

She replied without taking her eyes from the screen. "If we didn't know what we were looking for it would take weeks, years even to compare it by hand." She worked as she spoke, her fingers pressing quietly on the keys. "But we *do* know what we're looking for. At least we have a very good idea." She went quiet for a while, and Golding did nothing to interrupt her. Finally she pressed the return key and the laptop began to hum as it worked on the task she'd set it, searching the millions of documents.

"We're looking to see if Sterling – or someone – removed the index file allowing the lawyers to keep track of the movements of money."

"So you run a search for "Sterling" and "index file"?" Golding asked. She looked at him suddenly,

"It's not quite that simple." She gave an apologetic smile. Then her eyes slid back to the screen. Her face changed.

"*Merde.*" She looked up at him, the colour drained suddenly from her face. "It's here. The index file."

Golding shifted on his chair to better see the screen.

"What does that mean? That someone deleted it from the files at *Le Monde*?"

Her silence confirmed the answer.

"Can you click on it? Open it?"

Silently she did so, and the display changed to what looked like a Microsoft Word document displaying a table filled with text. It was in English, but still made little sense to Golding. Clémence however seemed to follow it with relative ease as she scan-read the boxes, her lips moving as she did so. She scrolled down. Suddenly she stopped.

"Here." She pointed to the screen.

"What does that mean?" Golding asked. But it took a while for Clémence to answer. She seemed to be double-checking she was right.

"The dates. You told me Sterling was reported dead nearly a year ago? This money was moved in April, three months after he died. A substantial amount too..." – she traced the screen with her finger – "for a property transaction. This suggests that he did not die, no?"

Her hand went back to the trackpad as she continued to interrogate the file. "Oh shit. Oh no." And then her hand went to her mouth. She looked at Golding, the colour again draining from her face.

"What is it, Clémence? Tell me what it says."

"The property was a house. In Brittany. In Plourec. Oh shit. I *met* him Luke, I had dinner with him. The house was bought in the name of Richard Brown."

· · ·

It seemed to take Clémence a few seconds to realise that the name meant nothing to Golding, and then she started trying to explain, but so quickly that he had to tell her to slow down.

"He's an American. He was Pierre's friend, I thought he must have known him for years because of how close they seemed. But I didn't understand why he was there, living in Plourec."

Golding's mouth opened and closed like a fish.

"He was... charming," Clémence continued. "I liked him..."

"Sterling's *living* in Plourec? Under the name Richard Brown?"

"Yes." She nodded. "He must be."

"And he's near to where Cloarec was killed?"

"*Yes*, he's in the cottage. Almost next door."

"Shit." Golding calculated for a few seconds. Sands had left two days ago. She would surely go door-to-door on the houses near where the murder happened. Which meant there was a good chance she'd knock on the door of Sterling's house. He pulled out his phone.

"Come on, come on," he muttered as the call took an age to connect. Clémence watched as he worked, face pale and eyes wide.

"*Shit*," he swore again, when the line failed.

"When I was there I had to walk down to the port to get a signal," Clémence said, her voice hoarse. "There's no cell-phone signal near Pierre's cottage.

FIFTY-ONE

"I'll be right down, come in out of the rain." The voice was friendly, unmistakably East Coast USA but softened by what sounded like extended stints in Washington, or its enclaves around the world. Sands peered in the doorway, not understanding at first where the voice was coming from. Then she saw a pair of feet at the top of the stairs.

"I'm just finishing up shaving. Jacques said you were looking for me. Seriously, come on in, it's lashing down." The feet disappeared out of view, back up the stairs. Sands hesitated. She'd meant to get a decent night's sleep and then catch the American when he went for his morning coffee, but her hotel was an hour from Plourec and the traffic that morning had been awful. As a result she hadn't arrived until nearly midday, when the rain appeared to redouble its efforts to wash the village away entirely.

Her jacket was half soaked just getting from her car to the cottage, and when she knocked on the door it swung inwards, revealing a dry, warm-looking interior. She heard the American whistling upstairs as he worked.

"Seriously, come in, no need to get soaked."

Sands looked around. "It's fine. I'll wait here."

"Come on! It's chucking it down," the American continued. "Hey, I'm sorry if you tried to catch me yesterday, I was outta town." The tap was turned on, the sound of running water and the whistling continued.

"That's fine," Sands replied. The cottage, traditional on the outside, had clearly seen a lot of work inside, but nicely done. It was bright and comfortable, the walls knocked through to create one wide-open space. The kitchen area was clean and looked new. A French press was brewing on the worktop, she could pick up the aroma. She moved a step further into the cottage, glanced at the stairs from where she could still hear running water. The rear windows provided a perfectly framed view of the ria. The cottage had its own small jetty that reached out into the water, its surface dappled and pockmarked as the rain continued to fall.

"Help yourself to coffee," the American said, his voice much closer now. Somehow he'd got downstairs without her hearing, but when she spun round to see him his back was turned and he was drying his hair with a towel as he closed the front door. When he turned again, his face was still partially obscured by the towel.

"It's Ethiopian. Freshly roasted beans. I was stationed there and I got a taste for it." He was wearing a pink flannel shirt and chinos, his feet still bare. He draped the towel around his neck and stepped sideways into the kitchen area, where he pulled a cupboard open. Keeping his back to her he placed one, then two heavy stone mugs on the marble work surface.

"Typical Brittany weather," he said. "On a clear day you can see all the way to the other side."

Sands didn't look back at the window, instead fixing her gaze on his hand and the back of his shoulders. She hadn't registered on a conscious level that she still hadn't seen his face, but her senses told her something was wrong. But not precisely what.

"I'm here because of what happened to Pierre Cloarec," she said, watching to see if his shoulders stiffened. They didn't.

"Poor man. I was speaking to the police about it yesterday." The cupboard door was still open; this seemed strange to Sands but she was far too relaxed, the casual act he was putting on not making her feel directly threatened, only curious. And it seemed that at any moment she'd finally see what the American looked like, freshly shaven and ready for her. The cupboard door began to close.

"Oh, look at that, it's clearing up." Against her will – not caring at all about the weather – she glanced momentarily towards the window, and the rain-streaked ria.

He crossed the distance between them with impressive speed. The first mug – which had never left his hand – connected with her head, sending her crashing into the wall and window, nearly rendering her senseless. Then the second mug hit her, this one breaking, perhaps because it struck the wall at the same time as connecting with her forehead. Although the attack came as a complete surprise, Sands somehow found herself, at the very moment it happened, expecting it. But she was so far behind that there was nothing she could do. Her hands went up to protect her head, fighting far too late as his hands found her neck and expertly cut off her air supply. He whistled again as he waited the few seconds he needed for Sands' body to react to the sudden restriction in oxygen. She moved her hands to his wrists, knowing already that the fight was over. She tried a punch to his stomach but she had no power; her vision was closing in and it was as much as she could do to realise he was fine-tuning his work, reducing the pressure just enough to stop her from losing consciousness. She gagged, trying to prise his fingers away from her throat, but when he just grinned at her she began to panic, flailing, her vision flared, black and white spots in her periphery swelling and swirling and closing in.

"Come on now, Angel." She heard his voice. No longer with the American accent.

"Come, my Angel. Come to Daddy."

There was nothing to do, no way to fight it. She felt herself go limp before her mind switched off.

FIFTY-TWO

She drifted back into consciousness, not yet thinking but aware of a painful tightness in her throat that came and went with every breath. Sometime later, not long, she tried to touch her neck but couldn't move her hands, and then she realised they were lashed together behind her back, secured to the dining chair she was sitting on. She tried to kick her legs but they were tied to the front legs of the chair, and when she tried to shuffle her body she discovered a belt had been wrapped around her and the chair's upright back. Finally she tried to open her eyes, finding to her surprise she wasn't blindfolded. It was the same room where she'd been attacked. And in front of her, calmly reading a book in an armchair just a couple of metres away, was her father, Charles Sterling. He glanced up, noticing her stirring and gave a small smile. Then he raised a finger in the air, as if asking her to hold on while he finished the page. Finally he picked up a bookmark from the table beside him and slipped it into the book. He put it down, then took a sip from the ceramic coffee mug he'd hit her with.

"Detective Erica Sands," he said, touching a finger to his eyebrow and smoothing it down.

Sands opened her mouth to speak, but just breathing hurt enough.

"I suppose congratulations are in order. Of sorts," he went on. "You found me." He raised his fingers in the air and waggled them, smiling at the childishness of it. As if the last year and a half had been nothing but a giant game for them both.

"But it would probably be premature to say that you *win*. Although none of us can predict the future..." – he bit his lower lip – "I would hazard a guess that yours isn't looking too bright." He smiled, showing her his white, American teeth. But the smile didn't last long.

"All the same, this is an extremely irritating outcome for me too." He took another sip of coffee.

"This *is* Ethiopian by the way. I never served there – as you know – but I do subscribe to a rather brilliant mail-order service that sends me freshly roasted beans every week. A little foil packet, with a different type of bean each time. It's just one of the little touches I've set up for my life here that I was really beginning to enjoy." He placed the mug carefully back down on the table.

"Of course that was before you fucked the whole thing up the ass," – he lowered his head a little – "with this ridiculous vendetta of yours."

Sands didn't reply. But she rolled her head a little, trying to relieve the pressure.

"Oh – does that hurt?" Sterling noticed, his voice full of mock concern. "I *am* sorry. So very sorry. That you should have to suffer a little for *fucking everything up*." He stopped, looked away and suddenly pushed himself to his feet. He glanced around the room, then grabbed a second chair. He lifted it behind him and then swung it crashing into her side. The shock hit her more than the pain of it, but with no way to stabilise herself she fell sideways, and the hard floor did hurt. Then he did it again, beating her twice more in the side. Sands could do nothing to protect herself, but the way her chair had fallen meant its frame took the brunt. He then put the chair back down next to the dining table, then reached down and lifted her upright again. Her skin crawled where he touched her. He sat back down. Then he laughed.

"Your face!" he chuckled, shaking his head and finally taking a long, deep breath.

"I am sorry, Angel. We all have our weaknesses – I needed to burn off a little rage just then, you probably remember from when you were a girl that sometimes I felt a little *physical learning* was in your best interests? This time I did not wish to draw any blood. It's very hard to clean up. As I'm sure you now know." He dragged the coffee table in front of him and placed a cushion on it to put his feet up. He picked up the coffee mug again.

"As I was saying, I have put a lot of time and money into setting myself up here. A lot of effort on my part. And my intention was to stay here. To build a new life, a quiet life, where I didn't need to look over my shoulder, or slip into the violent ways of my youth. And you, my dear oldest daughter, have completely fucked it. You and that stupid fat-French-fuck of a journalist, but more so you. Because I dealt with him. I *handled* the situation that arose from him needing to die." He stopped suddenly, looking her in the eye.

"You tried to find me yesterday? Do you know where I was? Of course not, you're not a part of the investigation are you? I was speaking with a certain Commissioner Morel. The idiot investigating the awful murder of Pierre Cloarec. And he was eating out of my hands. Like a tame, fucking puppy. He completely buys the cover that I've carefully constructed for myself. He has no doubt that I am a former American diplomat, with no involvement whatsoever in the death of Monsieur Cloarec. He has no doubt that the formidable Barelli twins – who apparently ply their murderous trade in the employment of Vicenzo Mancini – although I'd never heard of any of them – were behind poor Pierre's death. And without you, *sticking your fucking little beak in*, that would have remained the case, and I could have stayed here. I could have drunk my freshly roasted coffee. I could have taken my little fishing boat out on clear days, when the swell is light. I even thought I might write a memoir, presumably to be published after my death, but still..." He stopped again and made a steeple with his hands, pressing them to his mouth.

"Why couldn't you leave me alone? I did everything I could to convince you I was dead. I had everyone else convinced." He paused, waiting for an answer.

Sands, still reeling from everything that had happened, painfully opened her mouth to reply.

"My sergeant knows I'm here. He's expecting my call. If I don't make it he'll send the police here. They're probably on their way right now."

He ignored her and continued.

"It was the body, wasn't it? The fact I didn't leave a body."

He seemed to muse over this for a few moments.

"Well how could I?" Sterling snapped suddenly, angry again. "After all, I kinda needed it!" With his hands he indicated himself, then laughed hard, looking away. Then he turned back.

"I did consider other ways. A plane crashing into the ocean, where enough bodies were never recovered that my own being missing wouldn't seem suspicious." He paused a few seconds, then leaned towards her.

"I could have arranged that, Angel. I could have arranged that very easily, but do you know why I didn't? Have you got it yet?"

Sands blinked at him; she thought about lying, telling him that Golding was on his way right now. But she knew it was pointless. Instead she connected with what he was saying. She offered a careless shrug.

"I don't care," she said. "I have no interest in your pathetic excuses."

"Because I didn't want innocent people to suffer." His eyes were wide, wild. "I didn't want that. I wanted to be different." He shook a fist at her. "And you fucked it. *You* killed the journalist. It's *your* fault." Suddenly he scratched furiously at his head before calming down again as quickly.

"There was another reason I didn't, if I'm being totally honest, and this *is* a time for honesty, this little heart to heart." He laughed again. "Yes, Angel darling. I suppose the truth is I rather liked the idea of leaving you unsatisfied." He held up his hands. "Guilty as charged. And I suppose I should apologise for that. It was mean of me. I've often been a mean father to you." He chuckled to himself at that, then reached down to the floor, where Sands now noticed a long-bladed kitchen knife. Casually he picked it up and inspected the blade as he continued speaking.

"Even the money didn't even convince you..." He glanced up. "I really thought that might do it. It was a nice touch."

Sands stared back at him.

"Hundreds of millions of pounds. I gave you *hundreds of millions*. How can you call me a bad father after that? How did it feel for you? To be so rich?"

Again she simply stared at him.

"It made me feel powerful. I could go anywhere and know that I could buy every single person I saw." He scoffed. "Apart from you, it turns out."

"I don't want your money. I never did."

"Oh but you spent it though – all your life, remember? When they first locked me up and all my assets were handed over to you. You bought that nice flat on the harbour front. That fancy car. So why not spend the millions? After all I can't ever get them back."

"The only thing I was ever going to spend it on was chasing you down. You knew that."

"Yes!" He hissed the word. "But I didn't think you'd succeed. And that's what makes me so *fucking pissed*. Now that you've destroyed all this," – he waved his hand around the room, still holding the knife – "I'm going to need money to set myself up again. And now I don't have it. I won't even have my assets. This house here." He shook his head again, then slowly drew his arm back. He paused a moment, and then threw the knife at her. She had no time to move, but the tip of the blade struck the wooden frame of the chair, where it dug in and vibrated to a halt.

The recklessness of the act seemed to calm him. He laughed.

"Wow. You really do have all the luck, don't you Angel?" Sterling laughed again, deeper this time. "I have been practising a little knife-throwing, but I'm really not good at all."

Sands blinked again, trying to reduce her heart rate, her mind replaying the shock of the knife spinning towards her. A noise, unbidden, emerged from her lips.

"Oh, quit your whinnying, girl. You were always such a whining child." Sterling looked away in disgust. "I'm almost embarrassed for you." He shook his head, looking out of the window again. Then he looked back, right into her eyes.

"You know, before you die, you might as well know what's going to happen next." He stopped, rose to his feet and then turned away, speaking to the window.

"I no longer intend giving up my life of violence. By which I mean I'm not going to fight it. To be honest, it was always quite an ask, a little outside my true nature. And you've given me back my taste for it. So, from here on in, and until someone stops me, I'm going to rage against the world. I'm going to kill whenever and whomever I feel like killing, and there's going to be many – oh, so many – before someone takes me down." He paused, spinning around to face her. "And that's on you, Angel. That's all on you."

He chuckled again, then took a moment to top up his coffee. The French press was nearly empty, but he let the last few drops drip into the cup.

"And you won't be here to see it. But I wanted you to know what your legacy is. *Detective Sands*. The late and failed daughter of Charles Sterling. I want you to know what you're leaving behind." He drank the last of the coffee and turned the empty mug around, showing it to her.

"Looks like my coffee break is over. Time to get back to work."

FIFTY-THREE

Sands could do nothing while he took a trolley – the upright type often used to carry boxes around warehouses – and manoeuvred it behind her chair. Then he tipped it so the chair leaned backwards onto it and practised moving her a little around the room. He seemed dissatisfied, and then crouched by her feet, using silver carpet tape to secure her feet and the chair to the trolley. He grunted as he worked, and she looked down onto his thinning hair, greying at the roots. When he was finished he stepped back, inspecting his work. Then he moved forwards and wrapped tape all the way around her head so that it covered her mouth.

"Stay there," he said, offering a mirthless smile. He seemed to have slipped into a new mood. More serious, focussed.

He left by the back door, and although the rear window of the cottage was partially exposed – he'd drawn the curtains on the front windows – she couldn't see much except for the ria, slowly sliding past with the tide. The rain had stopped now, but the sky was still grey and threatening. At first she tried to prise her hands loose. There was just a little bit of play where her left hand was bound so she kept pulling at it, twisting, working it, trying to increase the movement he'd left her with. After a while she realised there was something else she could do, another sense that she wasn't using, and she stopped moving and worrying at the knots around her hands, this time just to listen.

There had been something, a sound in the very background of her consciousness, and now she focussed upon it, finally isolating it from the silence of the room and the sounds of her own body. It was the throb of an engine. She closed her eyes to understand it better, and pictured it, moving from right to left and then rising in both pitch and volume. Then it shut off completely. She waited in silence to see if it would come back. A few minutes later another noise returned, the whistling Sterling had produced when he was pretending to be Brown. The quiet was suddenly shattered as the rear door flew open.

"You still here?" he asked. "How about we take a boat ride?"

He'd thrown on an orange waterproof jacket, the legs of his trousers tucked into rubber boots, and he kept whistling as he strode over to her and leaned her back onto the trolley. He rolled her towards the door of the cottage and then outside.

"There is a chance someone might see us." He spoke casually but apparently without fear as they proceeded down a path through the cottage's rear garden towards the jetty. "But I rather fancy anyone who does see will just think you're in a wheelchair. And anyway, there are very few people in the village this time of year. The scourge of second-home owners, huh?" The path wound slightly uphill, finishing at the same level as the wooden boards of the jetty. Soon she saw water on either side, and then he spun her round, making it easier for him to move her, and she spotted a small fishing boat moored at the end.

"It's rather lucky that the tide's in," he told her as he pushed her forward. "I can't get the boat in at low tide, but then I suppose I should acknowledge the part luck has played in this whole sorry affair. I'm lucky that Pierre tipped me off about my appearance in his article. And I'm certainly lucky I called by the bar this morning, otherwise Jacques wouldn't have told me that an English detective was sniffing around, and that he'd been stupid enough to tell her where I lived. I wouldn't have had time to prepare, and who knows what might have happened then? Maybe you'd have got the upper hand? Maybe you'd have actually caught me." As he spoke his face changed, as if he were wondering how to load her into the boat.

He shrugged. "Well, this might hurt a little, but never mind." With that he tipped the trolley forwards so that both Sands and the chair fell forwards into the open cockpit of the boat. There was nothing she could do to break her fall, and pain shot through her body. But again the chair took at least some of the impact. Even so, the air was knocked from her lungs again and some time passed before she was fully aware of anything beyond the fear and the pain of every breath. Her face was pressed against the rugged plastic floor, the stink of fish and diesel fuel nearly making her gag.

But instead Sands focussed. While Sterling was moving her he hadn't bothered to remove the kitchen knife he'd thrown at her, and it was still sticking out of the wood of the chair. But now it was gone, presumably knocked free as he'd pushed her into the boat. She felt for it on the floor of the cockpit behind her.

"Bumpity-bump," Sterling said behind her. Then the boat rocked as he jumped in after her. He went into the boat's half-cabin and used a wrench to wake the engine into puttering life. Then, still on her side in the bottom of the cockpit, she saw his boots stepping forward to untie the boat's mooring line. He returned to the cabin and stood at the wheel steering the boat, ignoring her as he revved the motor hard. She felt them moving, picking up speed as they cut out towards the middle of the ria.

He began to whistle again, its higher pitch cutting though the regular strumming of the diesel engine.

"Just sit tight there, Angel," he said as he saw her still trying to move. "We're not going far."

FIFTY-FOUR

At first the water was smooth. Sands was still lashed to the chair, on her side in the bottom of the boat's cockpit, unable to see over the sides. But after some time – she guessed about twenty minutes – the boat began to roll. Gently at first, but indicating they'd left the sheltered waters of the ria and joined the open sea. Sterling widened his stance, his seaboots wedged against the sides of the boat's little cabin.

To begin with, Sands spent her time feeling around for the knife, but soon it was clear that wherever it had fallen it was out of reach. But when the boat started to roll she tried again, and finally – with a sense of disbelief – she located it. It then took a while to spin it round and find a position where the blade pressed against the rope and tape wrapped around her hands. She had to stop a few times when she saw Sterling glancing around to check she was still there, but her body hid what she was doing with the knife.

Pain shot through her wrists as she twisted her hands as far as she could to angle the knife. Twice she dropped it and had to scrabble behind her to find it again. Her whole body cried out in protest, but finally she found a way to hold it, and was able to use the vibrations of the engine to slice at the bindings. She was making progress. She began to consider what she might do if she were able to free her wrists. She worked out she had to free her legs as well. Otherwise it would be easy for him to overpower her again. But it seemed possible. Sterling's attention was mostly on steering the boat. She just needed to fight through the pain, keep working the knife against the rope.

But then they arrived at their destination. Sterling cut the engine.

The noise had been so loud Sands hadn't realised how it had drowned out everything else. But suddenly everything came flooding into her consciousness – the gurgle of water, the rustle of wind around the boat. And then Sterling, a phlegmy coughing and spluttering. Clearing his throat.

"You might be wondering what we're doing here," he told her, breaking his silence for the first time in at least half an hour. He crouched down, readying himself for something. Then he roughly rolled her chair round so that she was on her back. And then with some effort he pushed it up towards the back of the boat, allowing her to see out over the stern. Her hands were still bound but the ropes were nearly cut through. She had to hide the knife up her sleeve. She had no idea how visible it was, or if he was even looking.

"Over there" – he lowered himself a little to her eye level and pointed out over the back of the boat – "is the Raz de Sein. Do you know what that is?"

The boat was rolling in a lumpy, awkward swell, uncomfortable but not dangerous, but it was being visibly pulled backwards by a tidal current towards a very different sea. Two hundred metres away, perhaps less, the sea's surface began to roughen significantly, and beyond that became a maelstrom of white water, some waves standing still and others crashing into them from horrible angles. Here and there black rocks broke the surface, currents swirled around and through them.

"It's one of the most treacherous tidal races in Europe. Twice a day the water here runs through at about ten miles per hour." He had to speak up now against the roar of the water. "That might not sound much, but there's a vicious network of rocks, mostly just below the surface.

"You can sail through it, of course. But you have to pick your moment. Slack tide, when there's less water rushing through. If you tried to take a boat through now, with a flooding tide, it would be like sailing through a cheese grater." He gave a theatrical shudder.

"When I heard you were coming I thought, how do I get rid of you? I thought about cutting off your hands like I did to the Frenchman, but not even Morel would believe that the Mancinis had returned. And disposing of a body is such a precarious process." He sucked in air through his teeth. "But then I realised that I had this, so close. The perfect place to launder a body."

The current was already pulling them towards the race, the boat and the water around them moving as one, little whirlpools already forming.

"I won't even have to go to the trouble – or the risk – of untying you. If that's what you're hoping for. Some dramatic escape." He chuckled. "There's three hours left of tide, it'll drag you through the race. The waves will pummel you against the rocks, and if you're lucky it'll deposit you out to sea. If you're not lucky it'll just leave you far enough outside the race that when the tide turns, it'll pull you right back in." He turned to her again. "Your body. I'm talking about your drowned, battered, dead body." He shrugged.

"Either way, they'll be nothing left of that chair. And if they do ever pull your body out, there won't be enough left for them to even identify it. For a little while you'll be a Jane Doe. And after that you'll be forgotten." He laughed, a little sadly.

"But I won't forget you, Angel. You don't have to worry about that."

He fell silent as he began to spin the chair around, her on it. He leaned her forward to heave the chair up onto the rear bench-seat. It wasn't quite wide enough, but he reached behind him and dragged a heavy wooden box under the chair's front legs, so that Sands found herself facing the stern of the boat, but much higher up. She felt no fear. Now that her back was to him again she withdrew the knife and focussed on finishing the job of cutting the bindings. She was close now, but time was short. She felt the blade nick her fingers, wincing at the sharp pain but not slowing down, working the knife against the hard rope.

"Well," Sterling said, 'any final words?"

Sands said nothing; she barely heard him she was concentrating so hard.

"Nothing to say? I thought better of you. You sister didn't say much either, when I cut her throat." He gave a short laugh again, but still looked sad somehow.

"You know I sometimes wonder if I should have done this a long time ago, put you out of your misery with your mother. You were always so damn miserable; it came across as a little ungrateful, you know that? But maybe I was at fault. I was selfish. I wanted to keep you alive because I liked you. You were like me—"

The knife suddenly caught on the final few threads of rope and, with a gush of surprise, Sands felt her hands come free. But as they did so the handle of the knife slipped from her grasp. They were surrounded by spray and the roar of water now as the boat was pulled towards the narrowing of the sea where the tide was racing through. The knife fell to the floor of the cockpit, rattling loudly against the plastic. Sterling saw it at once. For a second his face fell, but then he smiled again.

"Well, well." He used his boot to pull the knife back towards him, out of her reach.

"You managed to winkle that free, did you? You always were a fighter. But it's not going to do you any good." He bent down to pick the knife up, seeming for a moment transfixed by the blood from Sands' wrists. Then he just watched her. The noise around them had increased; Sands could see with her peripheral vision that they were at the beginnings of the race now. If Sterling didn't start the engine and begin motoring away, they would all be sucked in. He seemed to know it too.

"It's time, Angel," he said. "I wish there was another way."

"There is," Sands began to say, ripping her hands clear of the tape. She lunged for him, her shoulder muscles screaming with pain, but also with the force of her determination. "There's this way."

For a hopeful second it seemed she might make it. She tried to aim her thumbs to connect with the pupils of his eyes, but she'd only been able to release her wrists, not the second binding of rope and tape that he'd wrapped around her upper body. And when her shoulders used up all the freedom they had, her hands swung uselessly in front of her. All he needed to do to avoid her was take a step back.

But it was enough. She saw the expression on his face change. From cool, calm hatred to fear. Surprise and shock, and a moment of panic as he slipped backwards, falling arse-first into the cabin.

Sands recovered first, but she was placed so precariously, high up on the back of the boat, that she had nothing to hold on to. The chair began to rock backwards, the boat rolling and twisting more and more as the water around them chopped up. In front of her, rolling on the floor, Sterling began to laugh as he realised what was happening. Sands knew it too, but there was nothing she could do. The chair kept rocking, rolling back-wards. Her arms flew out to the sides, as far as they could, in an attempt to steady herself, but it was too little too late. Sterling's laugh followed her as her view spun upwards to the sky, and then backwards, down towards the boiling ocean. The roaring water was not enough to mask the sound of her father, his laugh somehow suggesting both surprise that her hands were loose and certain knowledge that it wouldn't make a blind bit of difference. Then she hit the hard water, and at once it closed over her head. First translucent, then green. And finally a bitter, salty black.

For seconds she tried to hold her breath. But then she had no choice but to inhale.

A LETTER FROM THE AUTHOR

Thank you for reading the third book in the Detective Erica Sands series! I know I've left it on a bit of a cliffhanger, but I promise the next (and probably final) book in the series will be out soon, so you won't be left clinging on too long. If you want to join other readers in hearing all about my new releases and bonus content, you can sign up for my newsletter here!

www.stormpublishing.co/gregg-dunnett

I also run a slightly more detailed newsletter, where you can hear about new releases and get a bit of insight into how I came to be a writer, and how publishing has allowed us to move to Spain. You can sign up to this on my website at www.greggdun nett.co.uk

If you liked it and want to leave a review that would be fantastic. If you didn't like it and wouldn't like to leave a review, that would also be good.

I'll admit the series has taken quite a journey too. It started out as a Dorset-based police procedural, and it's ended up travelling through France, Brazil, Vietnam, Switzerland, and the Cayman Islands. I suppose that was all inevitable once Sterling escaped from prison—he was never going to stay put in the same county where he was locked up!

I hope you've enjoyed reading it as much as I enjoyed writing it. I've tended to write this series alongside standalone psychological thriller novels, and they've needed deeper thought, more effort – these books on the other hand have just felt like fun. Which is after all the point of curling up with a good book.

Thank you so much, and onto the next!

Gregg Dunnett

facebook.com/greggwriter

Printed in Great Britain
by Amazon

58351711R00179